Evading Darkness

The Darkness Duet
Book One

K.M. Baker

Copyright © 2024 by K.M. Baker

All rights reserved.

No part of this publication may be reproduced, stored in a retrieval system or transmitted in any from or by any means, without written permission from the publisher, except as permitted by U.S. copyright law. For permissions contact: kmbakerauthor@gmail.com

This novel is entirely a work of fiction. The names, characters, and incidents portrayed in it are the work of the authors imagination. Any resemblance to actual persons, living or dead, events or localities is entirely coincidental. All songs, song tiles and lyrics contained in this book are the property of the respective songwriters and copyright holders. Designations used by companies to distinguish their products are often claimed as trademarks. All brand makes and product names used in this book and on its cover are trade names, service marks, trademarks, and registered trademarks of their respective owners.

Cover design and chapter art: Maree Rose

Editor: Taylor at Deliciously Dark Editing

Content Warning

To the readers who wish to go in blind, please know this is a Dark Romance and is a work of fiction. It does contain explicit 18+ content that I do not condone outside of a fictional world. This is not a fluffy romance, although some may disagree, depending on how dark you like your books. Callie's story is filled with ups and downs and ends on a cliffhanger.

If you are like me and love the shopping list noted below. Have fun and enjoy the ride!

If you have any questions or feel like anything should be added to this list, please do not hesitate to reach out to me via email at KMBakerauthor@gmail.com

Triggers:

Adult Language, Alcohol use, Anal, Arson, BDSM, Bondage, Branding, Breath play, Captivity, Degradation, Drug Use/Abuse, Dub-Con, Edging, Forced Orgasms, Foster Care, Grief, Hitmen, Humiliation, Kidnapping, Knife play, Masturbation, Mental Abuse, Mention of Drug Overdose, Mention of Non-Con, Mention of Sexual Abuse of a Minor (flashback), Mention of Sexual Assault of a Minor (flashback), Mention of

Suicide, Murder, Orgasm Denial, Panic Attacks, Praise, PTSD, Punishment, Sex Toys, Somnophilia, Spitting, Squirting, Stalking, Trauma, Verbal Abuse, Violence, Voyeurism

To all you dirty sluts who like a little pain
and praise with your pleasure. This one's for you.
Beg for it.

Playlist

Chapter 1 - New Medicine - Past the Past

Chapter 2 - Marry Me - Jason Derulo

Chapter 3 - Today was a fairytale - Taylor Swift (Taylor's Version)

Chapter 4 - Right Now - Fire From The Gods

Chapter 5 - Stalker - Stevie Howie

Chapter 6 - Everybody's Fool - Evanescence

Chapter 7 - Love Again - The Kid Laroi

Chapter 8 - Who's Going Home With You Tonight - Trapt

Chapter 9 - Breadcrumbs - Jacob Lee

Chapter 10 - You're Going Down - Sick Puppies

Chapter 11 - Alkaline - Sleep Token

Chapter 12 - Prisoner - Miley Cyrus feat. Dua Lipa

Chapter 13 - Price to Play - Staind

Chapter 14 - Gates of Ivory - Dayseeker

Chapter 15 - Ivy (Doomsday) - The Amity Affliction

Chapter 16 - Blurry - Puddle of Mudd

Chapter 17 - I Knew You Were Trouble (Taylor's Version) - Taylor Swift

Chapter 18 - Breakdown - Breaking Benjamin

Chapter 19 - Stuck In My Head - Blu Eyes

Chapter 20 - Anywhere But Here - Mayday Parade

Chapter 21 - Knife Prty - Deftones

Chapter 22 - Love The Way You Lie - Eminem feat. Rhianna

Chapter 23 - Psycho - Asking Alexandria

Chapter 24 - Talking to Myself - Sleeping With Sirens

Chapter 25 - Comedown - Bush

Chapter 26 - Rise Above It - I prevail

Chapter 27 - I've Got A Plan - Sullivan King

Chapter 28 - Awake and Alive - Skillet

Chapter 29 - Fast Car - Luke Combs

Chapter 30 - I'm Gonna Be (500 Miles) - The Proclaimers

Chapter 31 - I Get Off - Halestorm

Chapter 32 - Rain - Sleep Token

Chapter 33 - Hollow - Wage War

Chapter 34 - Let Me Be Sad - I Prevail

Chapter 35 - The Grey - Bad Omens

Chapter 36 - Work Song - Hozier

Chapter 37 - Darkness Settles In - Five Finger Death Punch

Chapter 38 - Rise Up - Secrets

Chapter 39 - Hivemind - Acacia Ridge

Chapter 40 - Self-Destruction - I Prevail

Chapter 41 - Welcome To Hell - Sum 41

Prologue

Callie - Three months after my 24th birthday

I never planned on being back in this office staring at the same scratched-up floorboards that I used to stare at as a teenager when my father would lecture me about the responsibilities of being an Ashford. Here I am. After years on the run, I let my guard down and gave in to the illusion of living a normal life.

I accepted the possibility of having a family one day. I thought I could move on from my past. I should have known it would catch up with me. I spent so many years I spent bouncing from town to town, keeping as many people as possible at a distance. I always made sure I had a way out, a backup plan if I ever encountered a messed-up situation. All of it was for nothing because here I am, right back in the one place I never wanted to be.

I should have been more prepared. I never should have let myself get complacent. Instead of watching my back, I was living in my fucking fantasy world. A million thoughts race through my mind. I thought I found a man I could confide in. I trusted this son of a bitch, and he brought me right back to everything I've been running from.

Realizing I've zoned out for the speech he's been reciting, he walks toward me and grips my chin, forcing me to look up at him.

"You need to learn your place, Callie. You may be Gabriel's daughter, but I will not tell you again." He gives me a look that would have any other girl instantly submitting.

"Fuck you." I spit.

That was not the response he was looking for because he ripped me out of my chair and slammed me against the wall with so much force that a photo frame fell to the ground, and glass shattered around us.

"Do I need to force you to your knees and shove my cock so far down your throat that you remember exactly who I am to you?" He hisses.

"Don't fucking touch me. You're nothing to me, and I'll never be yours." My lip curls up in disgust.

He leans in so close that I can feel his breath on my neck, making me want to gag, and whispers in my ear.

"You will be mine, and I'll force that attitude of yours right into submission if I must. Now be a good girl, go to your room, and get changed. We have an important dinner to get to. There's someone who's been waiting to see you. I believe you remember the way." His smug smile adds flames to the burning fire inside me.

When he finally leans back to give me the space I desperately need, I bite my tongue and slip out of the old office, walking right up the stairs to what used to be my childhood bedroom.

Chapter 1
Callie - My 24th birthday

It's been a long time since I've celebrated my birthday, but this year everything's different. I finally feel a sense of happiness for the first time since I turned 18. My life has evolved so much since landing in Braxton Falls. This small town drew me in like a moth to a flame. I fell in love, and it feels like home in a way I can't explain.

Most days, I try not to allow myself to focus on my father or my fucked-up upbringing, but today, the memories keep finding ways to draw me back in. My birthday. It's always the worst on my birthday. I want to be focused on my bubble of bliss, but I'm continually drawn back into thoughts of the life I used to live and how I got here.

I've spent the past few years moving from town to town every few months. It was the easiest way to ensure my father and his secret society never found me. I never planned to stay in Braxton Falls, but when I met Julian and Avery, I couldn't leave.

Julian and I met at the grocery store close to where I lived at the time. Living life always on the move makes things a constant struggle financially, so when the cashier told me my total was $8.16 more than what I had in my pocket, I was trying to figure out which items I could live without for the next week. Just as I was grabbing the ground meat to have her take it off my bill, he swooped in like Prince Charming and handed the cashier a ten-dollar bill to cover it.

I smiled and tried to tell him it wasn't necessary, but he looked at me with the kindest expression and said, "A beautiful girl like you should always have everything she needs."

Normally, a line like that would make me cringe, but the way he said it seemed so trusting. He was genuinely giving me a compliment. I accepted his gesture, thanked him, and made my way out of the store to head back home. As I was walking out, I heard him running up behind me.

"Excuse me, Miss. If this is too forward, please forgive me, but something about you makes me think I'd regret not asking you out. You wouldn't, by chance, want to go grab a cup of coffee with me, would you?"

I've always passed on these kinds of advances. The idea of dating felt like a betrayal to Maxton's memory. I had a few one-night flings here and there when I felt the urge to be dicked down, but I never allowed myself to get close to another man since his death. Julian had just been so kind that I couldn't say no to him. Part of me knew it was time to try and move on if I wanted any chance at a normal life.

It was just coffee. I figured it would be harmless. There was no way he would be interested in me with my dull brown hair and hazel eyes. I'm petite, but to most people, I'm invisible. There's nothing about me that would stand out in a crowd, and I like it that way. It makes it easier to blend in. If that's not enough of a deterrent, after he found out about my boring life, he would move on and forget all about me. I told myself to just go on the date. I might as well get a nice cup of coffee and banana nut muffin out of this whole ordeal. That's not what happened, though. He found a way to stick around.

Julian is the typical tall, dark, and handsome type that all the girls swoon over. He's a few years older than me and has the most stunning almond-shaped green eyes, black hair that is always gelled to perfection, and a jawline that you could crack a tooth on. He has the perfect shade of sun-kissed skin and more muscles than I think he knows what to do with.

While being good to look at is definitely a plus, it's always been his selflessness that drew me in and gave me the courage to trust him. He would give someone the shirt off his back if it meant they were more comfortable. In my world, people like him don't exist. Somebody always wants something from you. My own family planned on using me for their benefit, so finding Julian has always felt like a rare anomaly. He is my blessing in disguise, and here we are today, about to reach our 1-year anniversary, celebrating my birthday at my favorite restaurant in town.

He snags a tortilla chip from the tray in front of us, dipping it into the spinach artichoke dip. This dip is one of the best things on the menu. They make it extra creamy, and every bite feels like heaven is melting in your mouth.

"I have a business meeting on Tuesday in Atlanta with some of the senior members of my company," he casually tells me, and my face drops with disappointment. "I'll be heading out of town Tuesday morning, but it'll be a quick trip this time. I should be back home with you by Friday evening. We can spend the whole weekend together snuggling up and watching movies."

"You're leaving again? I wish you would've waited until tomorrow to tell me." I grab another chip and shake my head at him.

"I wanted to give you as much notice as possible. I know it's been a bit frustrating." He pulls up one side of his mouth to give me a comforting smile.

"Julian, they keep pulling you in for more and more of these meetings lately. I feel like I've barely seen you over the last month." I furrow my brow and glare up at him. He needs to know how annoyed I am.

He reaches across the table to grab my hand reassuringly. "I know, sweet girl, but I'm so close to getting the promotion I've been waiting for. Once I finally have it, things will slow back down again. It's just been a very unusual transitional period for the company."

"Well, the company seems to forget its employees have personal lives, too," I throw back.

This is the fourth meeting he's had over the last three weeks. Something about a big acquisition or merger that's happening soon. I don't know. We don't go into detail about his work because it stresses him out. I know he's a business manager for a worldwide company, but that's about it.

There are a lot of things he doesn't like to talk about, including his past. Usually, that would be a red flag for me, but with how kind and trusting he is, I don't mind him keeping some things to himself. I have plenty of secrets of my own. We're happy, and I trust him. That's all that matters. If I ever find out he's lied to me about anything, I'd have a completely different mindset, but he would never lie to me. He's too good.

"It'll all be over soon, and you won't even remember all this stress a few months from now." He lets go of my hand to grab his water and take a sip.

"You're probably right, and I'm sure I'm overreacting about the whole thing, but I just miss all the time we used to spend together."

"Sweet girl, we have the rest of our lives to spend together." His eyes narrow slightly at the remark.

I roll my eyes at him. Obviously, we have all the time in the world unless my past catches up with me. My mind drifted from our dinner to a time in my life when everything was different.

Rogue, my dad's perfect little society, wasn't always a bad place to be. I remember the grand balls my family would host at the compound, with tons of singing and dancing. All the members came together to celebrate whatever big event was happening within the community. It felt like a fun little fairytale, but my sweet, innocent mind hadn't been let in on the darkness just yet. Slowly, my father changed my perception of everything. The older

I got, the more cruel he became, finding creative ways to ensure I never made him look weak. My father, the great Gabriel Ashford, was the leader of our society, just like his father and his father before him.

Our family line is as close to royalty as you can get in our world. To most people, my life looks perfect, but being the so-called princess of a century-old society comes with a mess of duties to live up to. My father insisted he was going to have a son after I was born, but my mother was never able to have more children. I was always his disappointing consolation prize. He made sure to remind me as often as possible.

There are four founding families of Rogue and ten council seats. The council members hold all the power, voting on all the society's decisions. These members all live in houses spread out around the compound.

The council seats are composed of five citizen representatives elected from the guard, my father, his second in command Barry Michaels, Steve Johnson, and Austin Roberts. The latter two are the last descendants of their founding family lines.

Each of the founding families was entitled to a seat on the council that would pass down to their heir upon death. Steve and Austin have no children, so when they die, their seats will sit empty, just as the 10th seat currently sits.

Not long after my father took over as leader, one of the founding families opted to leave the main living quarters of the society's compound and move to a small town across the country. They wanted to raise their child outside the confines of Rogue's walls, and it ended up being a fatal mistake. The family didn't have the security they needed to protect themselves when someone burned their house down. Both the parents and their newborn died in the tragic fire just days after their move.

The whole event was a major upset for our community. My father refuses to talk about it. Afterward, he and the council ruled that in the event any founding family line was eliminated, their seat on the council would remain vacant as a reminder of that loss to society. Thus, the empty 10th seat.

The server stops at our table, snapping me out of my thoughts and back to the present as she sets our meals in front of us. I am here at dinner with Julian. My father can't find me. I remind myself. I take a few sips of my water to try and keep my mind at ease before looking around at our food.

Julian ordered his usual medium-rare steak, asparagus, and mashed potatoes. Without saying a word, he grabs his knife and dives right in. Typically, I order the chicken parmesan, but being that it's a special occasion, I decided to switch things up a bit, so I went with the blackened salmon instead. I'm a real risk-taker.

"This looks amazing." My eyes go wide with the amount of food on the plate. There's no way I'll finish all of this. "I don't know why I never ordered this before. It smells so good!"

He chuckled. "You're a creature of habit, sweet girl."

No, I'm not. I think to myself.

"Eat up. We have a busy night planned," he says with a wink.

"What sort of big night do you have planned?" I raise an eyebrow at him.

"You wouldn't want me to ruin the surprise now, would you?" He takes another bite of his steak.

"Are we going dancing?" I've been telling him about how I wanted to try taking one of those salsa classes for a while now. We could make it like dirty dancing by getting all sweaty by dancing and then go home to bang it out.

"No, we aren't going dancing. At least not today." He looks up at me with a look of warning, obviously wanting me to drop it.

"Come on, you know I'm terrible with surprises. Just tell me." It's true. I really hate surprises.

"Callie, I'm not telling you, so drop it." His tone is a little more fierce than usual, which causes me to make a face at him.

"Chill out, Julian. You don't have to be so serious."

"I'm sorry, sweet girl. I just put a lot of effort into making sure today was a good day for you. I don't want to spoil anything."

He wants to make sure today is a good day. I don't think today will ever be a good day for me. The flashbacks pull me back in.

I was one day shy of 18 when I ran from Rogue. My only belongings were some clothes and a few mementos that were stuffed in a backpack and placed on the escape route Maxton, my boyfriend, and I planned on taking. We wanted to start our lives together, free from the politics of the secret society we grew up in. We never got the chance.

When my 18th birthday drew closer, my father began having conversations with me about the duties that would be required of me. He told me when I turned 18, I was to marry Damien Michaels. Some 28-year-old man whom I don't have any memory of ever meeting. He is the firstborn son of my father's second-in-command, Barry Michaels, and has been living with one of our international chapters for the last 10 years. When I asked around about him, nobody who knew of him had any kind words to say. Apparently, he caused a lot of trouble in his late teens with members of the guard and was sent away, unofficially, of course.

One of the guards I asked said that he beat his brother to near death when he told Damien he couldn't bring some random girl onto the compound with him. Another guard claimed he broke his nose because Damien decided he looked at him funny.

I'll never understand why my father agreed to marry me off to someone as barbaric as Damien sounded, but then, my father was no stranger to cruelty. I spent a good portion of my late teens being told how worthless I was and that I would never be prepared to rule his people. He would say, "Women have too many emotions. A real leader should know how to be cold and calculated." No wonder he wanted me to marry Damien. That man sounded perfect for the job.

Historically, within Rogue's bylaws, there was nothing stating a female couldn't hold a position of power in our society. They just never considered it would actually happen. A typical man's way of thinking. Men rule men, and women play the role of doting wives who get the privilege of wearing fancy dresses and holding dinner parties. When it became apparent there would be no male successors from any of the founding families, the council had no choice but to accept me as their next leader. Of course, they added stipulations to my leadership because why the fuck would a woman be held to the same standard as a man?

Together, with my father's influence, they decided I needed a husband. I would marry the son of my father's second-in-command to ensure I could adequately uphold the needs of Rogue. Upon taking leadership, my husband would become my second-in-command. From there, if the council ever deemed that I put my own needs over the good of the society, I would be forced to step down, and my husband would step in my place until our child was old enough to take over his rule.

They also assumed I wanted children because that's what every woman wants, right? In their minds, it was a perfect solution. Being married to Damien would reassure the community that a female leader would not change anything, and the needs of Rogue would continue to be placed first and foremost. I was making a sacrifice by getting married, and they would respect me more for it. Everyone wins. Everyone except me.

At the time, I was hopelessly in love with my boyfriend, Maxton, and my father was well aware of this. I always thought there would be some way to change his mind and prove to him and the council that I didn't need to marry Damien to put the needs of the society first. I should've known better. My father doesn't have an ounce of kindness in his heart. Why would he give a fuck about my feelings?

One night, my father commanded me to his office, and I begged him to call off the wedding. He told me, "Callie, I know things don't seem fair, but you will marry Damien. Your little infatuation with the Maxton boy ends now. As it currently stands, you are betrothed, and it's a shameless act for someone who is to be married to be fucking around on her fiancé. You don't want your future husband to think you are a whore, do you?"

The fact that he could completely disregard my feelings, force me into a marriage, and then belittle me was the determining factor in my decision to leave.

"Callie?" I hear someone say my name, but I'm so lost in this memory that I can't focus on it. "Callie? Are you okay?" Julian's voice pulls me back to reality as a tear slides down my cheek. I quickly wipe it away.

"Sorry, I got a little stuck in my head. You know birthdays are hard for me. What were you saying?" I smile, reassuring him.

Julian doesn't know the details of my fucked-up childhood or the society I'm hiding from. He doesn't know that I was almost forced to marry. He definitely doesn't know that my mother and boyfriend died on the same day, right in front of me, or that my father was the one to pull the trigger. How the hell would I even explain that to someone? Talk about baggage.

Julian doesn't know any of it. He is such a kind-hearted man. How can I drag him down with the mass of problems that are associated with me? When he asked me about why I struggled with the day, I told him I went through something traumatic, and because he is who he is, he never pushed for more details.

"I was just saying, I think we should go for a walk to the waterfall after dinner," he says, "I know you love it there."

I clap my hands in front of me, and a huge smile crosses my face. "Is that my surprise?"

"Part of it, yes." He chuckles.

Braxton Falls Park is one of my favorite places. If anyone ever questioned what the town was named after, it wasn't hard to figure out. The park's waterfall was one of the things that drew me here when searching for a place to relocate. I always tried to find towns with waterfalls when I moved. Something about sitting at the edge of the rocks on the river shore and listening to the roar of thousands of gallons of water rushing over the edge of a cliff at one time brings me so much peace. It's the one place I always go whenever I need to clear my head to think or just try to calm my nerves.

"I love that waterfall! Of course I want to go," I tell him, grinning from ear to ear.

"Good. I don't like seeing you so sad on a day that should be celebrated. My sweet girl should always be smiling." He reaches over and grabs my hand to comfort me. "I plan on making it my personal goal to change your mindset on your birthday! We should be doing all of your favorite things." He winks.

"Oh, there is still plenty of time for us to do all my favorite things tonight." I give him an alluring smile and bite my lip while raising my eyebrows at him a few times. He just laughs.

"Come on, let's finish up and head over to the park." He flags the server over to grab our check, and a few minutes later, we are in the car and driving down the road.

Chapter 2
Callie

Julian turns into Braxton Falls Park and pulls the car into the parking lot. There's a short walk down a paved path, and it's still early enough in the evening that the sun is still up. We should get to the falls just before sunset. The view we're about to see is going to be insanely beautiful. Showing up here right now was all timed impeccably. It's the perfect ending to what is normally a hard day for me. If only I could get my mind to stop wandering back to the past.

As if he could feel my brain starting to shift into overdrive again, Julian grabbed my hand, intertwining his fingers with mine to ground me and bring me back to the moment. We walk down the small path and with every step, I hear the roaring water getting closer and closer. As we crest the hill, the falls come into view, and he grabs me by the waist to pull me into him, kissing my forehead and resting his chin on top of my head for a few minutes. I'm the perfect height for him, with my face snuggled right into his chest. I wrap my arms around him to let us share in this moment.

The sound of the gushing water drowns out all the noise in my head. I love this man. After a few minutes, Julian pulls back, looks down at me, grabs my hand again, and nods over to the picnic area to our left. I glance over to the table, which is usually barren of anything besides insects and maybe a few leaves from the adjacent trees. How the hell did I not notice this when we walked up here?

Tonight, the table is covered with a white satin tablecloth and a sign with words I can't quite make out, although I have a pretty good guess based on the vibe of everything else. A row of candles and rose petals lined the walkway to the table, making it so much more beautiful than it already was with the sun beginning to set. I look over at the man walking beside me, and understanding begins to set in. My gaze drops to the ground. He wants me forever. Am I ready for this? Maxton wanted to be my forever, too.

I met Maxton at 16. We bonded over our birthdays, only a few days apart. He was the first person I chose to love and everything I could ever dream of. He was tall, with eyes as blue as the ocean on a summer day and short brown hair that he liked to keep buzzed. He was a little lanky, but I knew that as we got older, he would grow into himself and be the kind of man every girl wants. The best part about him was that he was mine, was being the keyword.

We spent most nights together since his family also lived on the compound. His father was a member of the guard and an elected council member.

I used to sneak out to meet him in the field behind our houses after my father locked himself in his office to work. We would stay up all night talking and daydreaming about what our lives would be like together.

He was my first everything. My first kiss, boyfriend, partner. I lost my virginity to him, and I always thought he would be my forever. We planned on going to college, traveling, getting married, and having the sweetest little family, topped off with a big fluffy dog named Ralph. We made so many plans that we never got to live out because my father took him from me.

We planned on leaving to start our forever the day before I turned 18. I was supposed to marry Damien the next day, and we thought everyone would be too busy with the wedding plans to notice us running about. My mom was going to help us sneak past the guard. She understood what my father was taking away from me and always wanted me to be happy, no matter what path of life I chose. I'm not sure I would have known what real love was if it hadn't been for her. Somebody must have overheard us making our plans.

After we made it through the back gate and to the path next to the road where Maxton's car was parked, my father stepped out from behind the trees, aiming a gun at Maxton's head. I tried to tell him not to hurt him. I begged him and told him over and over that I was so sorry. I told him I would come back and marry Damien if he let Maxton go. Nobody would ever know we tried to leave. The sick fucker looked at me, grinned, and said, "I don't need your apologies or promises because you will do what I say regardless of what happens to your little boyfriend."

My mother stepped between Maxton and the gun to try to reason with my father, but it only took a moment for him to lose control and pull the trigger. The loud bang made my ears ring, and when I looked at her, I saw blood pouring from her chest as she dropped to the ground in front of me.

Something flashed in my father's eyes when he realized he let his anger take over him, and his wife was lying there unmoving in front of him. I took advantage of the brief moment of weakness and tried to pull Maxton out of the way toward his car. We only made it a few steps before I heard another ear-piercing shot and felt his hand leave mine. I knew I had just lost my entire world in a matter of minutes.

I looked over my shoulder and saw him lying there. I wanted to fall down and pull him into me to hold him and reassure him that he wasn't alone, but I had to keep moving. He would've wanted me to get away. After everything, I couldn't let my father drag me back and force me to marry Damien.

My mother's kindness was gone. I would've been left with those two evil men. There was no way I would survive them, so I ran. I ran as fast as I could to the car, ripped the door open, shoved the backpack off my back, and floored it.

Thankfully, Maxton was smart enough to leave the keys in the ignition in case we needed a quick getaway. My father took another three shots at the car as I sped away, but they didn't hit anything important. I stayed up driving all night until I ran out of gas and ditched the car because I knew they would be looking for it. The next day, I spent my birthday curled up in an alley in some random city by myself, mourning the deaths of both my mother and boyfriend. Birthdays have never been the same since.

I shake the memory of the worst day of my life from my mind and glance back over at Julian. He wants to make my birthday memorable. I won't allow myself to be upset. He worked so hard to make tonight perfect, and I refuse to allow my haunting past to ruin this for us.

"Julian, what is all this?" I ask him. He doesn't answer me. We wander closer to the setup, and I am able to make out the words on the sign: Marry Me? I freeze. My legs begin to feel heavy, and I bring my right hand to my mouth in an attempt to cover my shocked expression. Julian steps in front of me, and I bring my gaze up to his eyes.

"Callie, you are the most important person in the world to me. You know that, right?" I slowly nod. He reaches out his hand, prompting me to place mine in his, and as if we're in the scene of a movie, he drops to one knee and looks up at me with the most adoring eyes.

"Spending the last 11 months with you has been a dream. The way you make me feel, I've never felt about anyone in my life. I know there are still some things that you aren't ready to talk about, and that is okay. I will be here for you with open arms when you're ready to share that part of your life with me."

"Julian, I.."

"No, please let me finish," he tells me, so I nod, and he continues.

"I want you to be the first person I see when I wake up and the last person I see before I go to sleep. I want your good days and your bad days and for us to have a family and grow old together. I never want to spend a day thinking about what life would be like without you because I am so in love with you, my sweet girl."

I gasp as he pulls a small box out of his pocket, opening it up to reveal the most beautiful white gold ring. The band has a row of small stones stretching across one large round stone in the middle. It has to be the most beautiful ring I have ever seen.

"Callie, would you do me the honor of becoming my wife?"

"Yes!" I squeal, jumping up and down. He stands up, and I jump right into his arms, wrapping my legs around his waist and peppering him with kisses all over his face. After a few minutes, he pulls away from me long enough to speak.

"We can do this here if you want, but I would prefer if you let me take you home so I can show my new fiancé just how much I love her," he says with a wink.

"Oh, now you're talking." I grin as I slide off of him and slap his backside before taking off in an almost sprint to get to the car. The faster we get there, the faster I get my hands on this man.

Chapter 3
Callie

The drive back to the house feels like an eternity. Who knew a 10-minute drive could feel like 10 years? Fiancée?! Are you kidding me? I look over at him and just take him in. The moonlight makes his eyes shimmer a perfect shade of green, and don't even get me started on his lips. His usually defined jaw is currently covered in stubble, which he lets grow out because he knows how much I love the feel of it between my legs.

He catches me staring at him, and his mouth curves up in a mischievous grin. "Like what you see?"

Before I can answer, he brings his hand over and places it on my thigh. I glance down to see his firm grip just above my knee. One touch from him right now is enough to ignite my entire body. I feel my cheeks flush as I recall exactly what that hand is capable of doing. My heart begins to race in my chest with a frantic need for him. I pull my legs together to try to ease some of the ache pulsing down to my core, and it doesn't go unnoticed.

Julian keeps his eyes on the road as he slowly inches his hand further up my thigh until he reaches the hem of my dress and slides under it. My breathing changes to small, quick, shallow breaths as his hand reaches the spot I've been yearning for him to touch. He swipes across the front of me, finding my panties soaked through with arousal.

"Someone has been having some dirty thoughts," he says.

The only response I can articulate is a cross between a low hum and a soft moan. He grabs the front of my panties, pulls them to the side, and runs a finger through the wetness. Then he slowly drags his finger up to my clit, rubbing small circles that send shocks of electricity through my body.

My head falls back on the seat as I moan his name, "Julian." My hips raise, craving more, as he dips back down to my entrance to gather more wetness and continue to tease me. "I need more," I tell him, and he chuckles before pulling away from me and placing my panties back in place. Letting out a frustrated grunt, I look over at him to glare and watch as he brings the finger he was just teasing me with up to his mouth to suck it clean. "Fuckkk!" I groan.

"We're almost home, sweet girl. I plan on doing way more than a quick finger fuck in the car." He pats my leg and focuses back on the road.

Will it actually be more, though? One thing about Julian is that I've always felt like he's holding back in some way. The sex we have isn't always bad. Sometimes, I'm satisfied, but not every time. I wish he would do more. I want him to be possessive and demanding and take what he wants. I want him to tie me up and use me until I beg for him to stop because I am so blissed out from pleasure that I physically can't take anymore. Everything in my life is always so controlled. The bedroom is the one place where I wouldn't mind my man taking that control from me.

We pull up to our house and into the driveway a few minutes later. The place isn't grand by any means. It's a cute little 3-bedroom, 2-bath home with an open concept and an attached garage. We are a bit outside of town, so the closest neighbors are roughly a half-mile away.

We moved in together a few months after we started dating. The apartment building I lived in at the time was being condemned by the city. I told Julian I would likely have to move out of town because there weren't any apartments in the area I could afford, and he insisted I move in with him. He kept saying how he planned to ask me soon anyway, that it was all perfect timing.

Shutting off the car, Julian steps out and walks over to my door, opening it for me. I place my hand in his, and that familiar heat returns as I look up at him, smiling. We walk toward the house, and he puts his hand on the small of my back. Once inside, I throw him a flirty look over my shoulder in an effort for him to get the hint and ravage me already.

He slowly removes his shoes, placing them neatly on the shoe rack, before walking into me. His hand comes up to caress my cheek, and he leans down to kiss me. My lips part, and his tongue slips between them. He kisses me with a passionate need, moving his hand to the back of my head and weaving his fingers through my hair.

We make our way to the bedroom, tangled in our lust. He rubs up and down my body, grazing my nipples and tweaking them just enough to send sparks right down to my core. Grabbing my left hand, he brings it up to his lips and kisses my ring finger. "This looks good on you."

I grin and reach for the button on his pants before stripping him bare from the waist down. He doesn't protest so I sink to my knees in front of him to show my gratitude for such an amazing day. My head lands perfectly at eye level with his cock, and I peer up to look him in the eyes from my vulnerable position. I see a slight tic in his jaw and take that as my cue. I grab his cock and run my tongue from base to tip, licking the small bead of cum that has gathered on the top. I swirl my tongue around his tip before opening my mouth to take him to the hilt, bouncing my head up and down as he grunts in pleasure.

"Yes, sweet girl, that feels so good."

I continued bobbing my head, picking up speed before beginning to feel his balls tighten. In one swift motion, he pulls back from me, lifts me up, and tosses me onto the bed on my back. As if acting on instinct, I flip myself over so that I am on all fours with my ass in the air and my chest pushed down toward the mattress, holding myself up with my elbows while he rips open the condom and slides it onto himself.

"Yes, you always know exactly how I want you," he praises me.

The mattress dips behind me as his hand runs along my back and up to my ass in front of him. He gives it a light smack, and I moan out in pleasure. His cock slides along my entrance, gathering wetness before he slams into me all at once, causing me to scream. "Fuck, Julian!"

Reaching down, his hand grips the back of my neck, pinning my face to the mattress. My back arches further in response as he continues to pound into me from behind. In and out, over and over again, I feel that familiar heat begin to build at my core as he fucks me with everything he has. Tingles start moving around my body in all the right places.

"Yes, please don't stop," I beg, and he picks up his pace.

I'm right there, right on the precipice of falling apart, and I feel him shudder behind me. He lets out a small, satisfied grunt and slows his thrusts. My heat cools right back down, and disappointment sets in. So close... so fucking close.

This isn't the first time he's brought me right to the edge, only for it to end with me being let down. The first few times this happened, we talked about it. One time, he spent 20 minutes trying to work me back up to what I needed, but I was never able to get back there. Something about the pressure of needing to perform had me so far in my head that I couldn't let go. He pumps into me a few more times while I let out a few moans and clench myself around him enough for him to think I am having an orgasm. I suppose if we are going to spend the rest of our lives together, this is definitely something he and I need to talk about again.

I roll over to lay on my back, feeling frustrated as he walks into the bathroom to toss the condom and do his post-sex routine. After a few minutes of staring up at the ceiling, he comes back in and lies down next to me, completely oblivious to the fact that I didn't actually finish.

"What a perfect ending to the most perfect night. I still can't believe you said yes." He leans in, giving me a quick, chaste kiss.

"Of course, why wouldn't I say yes?" He hums with approval, and I notice his eyes looking heavy. "Get some sleep, handsome. I'm going to read a bit before coming to bed."

I slide out of bed, grab his shirt off the floor, and throw it over my body. Then I pull open my nightstand and grab the latest smutty book I've been reading before heading to the spare bedroom. There's no way I will be able to go to sleep this wound up, so I might as well read. Before I read, there's something I need to take care of. I keep a small vibrator in this room for this exact reason.

Locking the door behind me, just for good measure, I walk over, toss my book on the bed, and grab the stashed vibe. This will have to be quick. I'm already turned on, so I won't need much time anyway. I prop myself up in the bed with my back to the headboard and knees bent, letting my legs fall to the side in front of me. I click on the vibrator to the highest setting and begin rubbing it up and down from my clit to my pussy, then gently push it into me. Yes, this is exactly what I need.

I work myself up to where I can begin to feel those familiar sparks warming from within and bring my other hand down to my clit. I focus here with slight pressure, moving around in circles while pushing and pulling with my other hand. Everything builds, and the tingling feeling is back. It moves from my center down my legs and arms and works its way through my body. I find my release and explode, letting out a low moan of pleasure as I shudder through my orgasm.

It's not as satisfying as it should be, but at least I'll be able to relax now. I give myself a few moments to catch my breath before going to the bathroom across the hall to clean up and quickly pee. Afterward, I grab a glass of water from the kitchen and head to bed.

When I walked into our room, I noticed Julian fast asleep on his side, snoring like he couldn't have a care in the world. Setting my glass on the nightstand, I climb into bed beside him and roll over to plug in my phone. Before putting it down to go to sleep, I decided to send a quick text to Avery.

> Me: Brunch tomorrow? I have big news.

Avery: How far along are you?

> Me: HA HA BITCH.. I'm not pregnant... Don't put that kind of energy on me right now.

> Me: So brunch?

Avery: You're seriously going to make me wait until tomorrow?

> Avery: What is it?! Just tell me now!

> Me: Sorry, it's late, and I'm going to bed.. so sleepy..

> Avery: Fine. Maria's at 11! We can get drunk on those good-ass mimosas, and you can spill whatever this big news is that you're torturing me with by making me wait to hear.

> Avery: Fyi, if you're taking me to brunch to tell me you're leaving town, I'm going to kick your ass.

> Me: If I were leaving, I would already be gone. Besides, who said I would even tell you?

She responded with six middle finger emojis because, obviously, one wasn't enough.

Avery knows a little more about my life over the last few years than Julian does because I was feeling vulnerable when we met. I had just moved to Braxton Falls a few days before and was in the alley outside the restaurant she worked at, bawling my eyes out. It was another miserable birthday, thinking about the past.

We were strangers, but she waltzed right over to me, scooped me into a big hug, and asked if I was okay. Something about her just felt so safe and comfortable that the words flowed right out of me. I told her that I spent the last few birthdays grieving the deaths of my mother and Maxton, and now I was hiding from the man who killed them.

She doesn't know that man is my father or that there is also an entire secret society I am hiding from. This was all before I met Julian, and my plans to leave this town changed. It was also before she became one of the most important people in my life, my best friend.

It was like our souls recognized each other and knew we were meant to meet each other. We joke now about how maybe in a past life, we were sisters or something. We have since made a pact that we will never leave each other dry unless it's a life-or-death situation. Even then, we promised to always find a way to check-in.

I send her a few heart emojis and place my phone on the nightstand. I want to be the big spoon tonight, so I roll over to Julian, wrap my arm around his waist, and snuggle my face right into his back until I fall asleep.

Chapter 4
Callie

I wake up alone and feel slightly disappointed when I run my hand over Julian's side of the bed. It feels cold. Where did he manage to run off to this early in the morning? He doesn't usually wake up before nine on Sundays because we like to spend that time together. I roll over to grab my phone off the nightstand and catch a glimpse of the ring on my finger. Extending my hand in front of my face, I turn it from side to side so that the diamonds can catch the light, admiring its beauty. The man really picked a beautiful ring. I cannot believe that actually happened last night. It all just feels surreal.

After losing Maxton, I never thought something like this could ever happen. This whole year has been a strange series of positivity and luck for me. Finding Avery, Julian, and now the possibility of really settling down. I could have a real family, one that chooses me, unlike my father. Thoughts continue to race through my mind, and I'm hit with the harsh reminder that it's only a matter of time before Rogue catches up with me.

They have people from all over the world, which is one of the many reasons I have never stayed in one place longer than a few months. I always made sure my job was under the table, either waitressing or bartending, and never made any connections deeper than surface-level friendships with coworkers.

A few times, I caught a glimpse of a raven, and it was enough to scare me into immediately packing up and leaving. All Rogue members have a raven brand somewhere on their body. The stupid society has it as its symbol. It's supposed to represent all the changes they are going to make in the world. Mine is on my ankle.

Normally, you aren't branded until you're 18, and it's a choice. My father thought it would be a fun exercise when I defied him once as a teenager. He wanted me to feel the pain and remember what my future was. I don't even recall what I did that made him so mad. Reaching down, I run my finger along the raised skin, remembering the day he gave it to me.

He pulled me down to the basement by my hair and shoved me in a seat similar to a dentist's chair. I was so confused with what was happening that I didn't fight him when he leaned it back and strapped me in.

"I told you there would be consequences if you embarrassed me." He always had hatred in his eyes for me. I was so scared, but I couldn't show that. If I showed fear, that would make the punishment worse. I lay there, not saying a word. I just watched as he grabbed a metal stick from the corner of the room and made his way to the table sitting next to it. My eyes widened when he picked up a torch gun and started heating the metal.

"Let me remind you of your future."

I tried to wiggle in the chair, but the straps were too tight. After a few minutes, he held the bright orange metal in front of me, and I could feel the heat radiating off it.

"Please, Father. I didn't mean to. I will be better, I promise."

"You are always making promises you don't keep, Callie. Always a disappointment. Let this be a reminder of that. You have duties. You have no choice but to be better."

Before I could say anything else to him, the metal was pushed onto my ankle, and I let out a gut-wrenching scream. He didn't numb the area or give me any warning. I could smell my burning flesh and started to get dizzy from the pain. He pushed it harder into me, and tears streamed down my face.

"Tears are weakness, Callie." Those are the only words he said to me before pulling back the metal and tossing it over his shoulder.

He left me lying there for hours. By the time he allowed my mother to come down and unstrap me, I had fallen asleep, unable to handle the throbbing pain any longer. She pulled me in and held me while I sobbed. My sweet mother was the only other person who understood what living in that household was like.

I shake my head and try to clear my thoughts of the painful memories. I have to tell Julian about my father and Rogue soon. He needs to know what our future could potentially look like. For all I know, he may not want to marry me after he finds out.

Whether or not I want it, I am the future leader of the society. My father will not live forever. When he passes, it will be my birthright. They have to be looking for me. The man I grew up with would stop at nothing to get me back and use me for his own gain.

My phone pings, and I see a text from Julian telling me that he woke up early to go workout. It seems a bit odd. He never goes to the gym this early. Typically, he goes in the evenings. Maybe he went early today so we could have the entire evening together since he's leaving for his trip soon. He should be home by the time I get back from brunch, so we can cuddle up on the couch.

It's time to pull myself out of bed and get the coffee going so I can get my day started. On my way to the kitchen, I grab my book from the spare room to read a few chapters this morning. As I continue down the hallway, I spot Julian's home office, and an idea pops into my head. I'm still only wearing his t-shirt that I threw on after sex last night. It is not very often that I feel brave like this, so why not send my new fiancé a nice picture to look at while he showers after his workout? It'll be another special thank you to him for wanting to be with me forever. I'll sprawl myself right over his desk so he can think of me every time he goes in there to work.

When I went to open the door, I realized it was locked, which was unusual. I've never noticed it being locked, so I'm unsure why it would be now. I'll have to ask him about it later.

I decided to head back into the bedroom instead and arrange myself on our bed, laying down with the covers off and his shirt trailing just above my center. I snap a picture of the hem of the shirt and my exposed thighs and send it to him, letting him know what he is missing out on this morning.

Smiling to myself, I realize that being a tease is kind of fun. I might have to do it more often. The rest of the morning flies by as I finish my coffee, make myself a snack, and shower to make myself presentable for brunch.

Pulling up to Maria's, I see Avery standing out front waiting for me. She's wearing her short blonde hair in half-up, half-down space buns today. Her shirt is a vibrant mixture of colors that match her blue eyes. I trail my gaze down to her pants, the signature bell bottoms she likes to wear, and smile. Avery has always been a little eccentric with everything about herself. She is a free spirit who loves to go along with whatever life throws at her.

Maria's has been our go-to brunch spot since we met. Early on, we decided we needed dedicated girl time each week to update each other on everything we didn't want to say via text. Sometimes, I think it's all just an excuse to indulge in the bottomless mimosas, but I don't mind because I love spending this quality time with her.

After exiting the car, I ran over and wrapped my arm around Avery's.

"I'm so excited we can finally catch up," I say, and she rolls her eyes at me.

"Cals, we wouldn't need to catch up if you just told me what was going on when you texted me last night."

I try to resist the urge to smile at her smart remark. Walking up to the hostess stand, I noticed Emma was working today. She instantly recognizes us and tells us she will make sure we get our favorite table. It's the little one in the back corner, away from everyone and next to the emergency exit.

I catch Avery giving Emma a look that I can't explain, but a moment later, the look is gone, and she is back to herself again. Emma went to school with Avery, and there has always been some sort of weird vibe between them that I could never put my finger on. Oh well, it's not my business. If Avery wants to tell me about it, she will. Maybe after the few mimosas I plan on having today, I'll ask her about it.

A few minutes later, Emma lets us know our table is ready, and we can head over to it. Maria's is not a fine dining establishment if we compare it to places in big cities, but for our small town, it perfectly fits the vibe.

The rustic decor is lined with windows on one entire wall and a bar with bench seating stretching across the other. The wall with windows has a row of tables and chairs, each seating four people that can be pushed together, if need be, for larger groups. There are two booths at the back of the building with the emergency exit placed between them, which can each seat four people if you squeeze in, but sitting with two people is more comfortable. We made the one by the window our go-to spot.

We sit down in our usual chairs, mine being the one that has a full view of everyone and everything happening in the room. It's a habit I can't seem to break. I'm never able to let myself feel comfortable if I can't see what's going on around me at all times. Another reason I like the table next to the emergency exit is if

Rogue were ever to find me, I have my escape route. The server walked over to give us our menus before taking our drink order and walked away to give us a few minutes before ordering our food.

"So..." I start to say.

Before I get the chance to tell her the news, Avery grabs my hand and wrenches it up between our faces. Eyes almost bulging out of her head, and she says, "Um, excuse me, what the hell is this?!"

I giggle. "Well, that's why I wanted to meet you for brunch." Shrugging, I lift my hands up and say, "Surprise, Julian and I are engaged."

Her face shifts to concern. "Callie, I don't want you to get the wrong idea here. I'm really happy for you IF this is what you want, but I'm not going to lie. I'm a little worried. Things between you two have been moving so fast, and there are parts about you he doesn't even know yet. Are you sure this is what you want?"

"Honestly, I'm a little overwhelmed, and I don't know how to feel about it. I love Julian, really, and I'm happy and excited, but you're right. There are things he and I haven't talked about. I'm just terrified once he finds out, he won't want anything to do with me."

"Babe, if he really loves you for you, then that shouldn't be a concern at all. I still get weird vibes from him, though, full disclosure. I know we've talked about this before, but some of the things he does just don't feel right to me."

"I hear you, and I will be careful, but I haven't seen that side of him. He's never been anything but kind around me. It's actually a little disturbing how much of a perfect gentleman he has been."

"Okay, if you're happy, then I'm happy. I just don't want anyone hurting you. You've been through too much already."

"That's another thing, Avery. I really want to talk to you about some stuff. I think telling you may be a nice trial run before telling Julian," I say nervously.

"You know you can tell me anything." The look of concern on her face assures me that she's telling the truth.

"I want you to be safe, and I can't guarantee your safety if I tell you what I'm about to tell you."

"Jeez, Callie, are you being hunted by some freak government group that plans to use your organs on the black market or something?"

"You know, I really worry about where your mind goes sometimes, but no, I am not being hunted to be harvested for my organs. It's serious, though, and I need you to tell me you really want to know because if the wrong person finds out you know the truth, you could end up living your life on the run just like I've been for all these years."

"Listen bitch, I thought we already established that if you have to run again, I'm going with you. You're my ride-or-die, and there's nothing you can tell me that will scare me away at this point. Spill it."

Looking up at her, I see the expression on her face. She's serious. Avery is the closest thing to family that I have left in this world because I'll be fucking damned if I ever consider my father "family" ever again. I take a few deep breaths and give myself a moment to really consider if this is something I'm ready to do. These secrets have been a weight on my shoulders for six years now.

"Okay, promise you won't freak out and commit me or report me to the police or anything crazy?" I want her to know the severity of all of this.

She narrows her eyes. "Enough with the theatrics Callie, spit it the fuck out already."

I look down at my hands sitting on my lap and twiddle my thumbs. I can't bring myself to look at her, so I keep looking down at my hands as I tell her my darkest secret.

"The person I've been on the run from for the past six years is my father. He murdered my boyfriend and mother right in front of me the night I tried to escape the secret society that he is the leader of. Oh, and I'm the next in line to take over when he dies."

"Well, fuck," she says with a sigh.

I look up at her, and her gaze is nothing but comfort and support. Not a single part of her expression appears judgmental at all. She reaches her hand across the table and holds it out, waiting for me to place mine in hers, so I do, and she smiles and says, "Did you think a murdery father and secret society was going to freak me out? I do have questions, though."

Relief rushes through me, and I flag over the server to make sure she orders us another round of mimosas before deep diving into the inner workings of the society and the night Maxton and I tried to get away.

"Avery, I need you to promise me you won't tell anyone what we talk about today. It's against society's code of ethics to expose it to non-members. If they ever find out you know about them, they will kill you." She gives me a slight nod.

She and I spend the next hour continuing to drown ourselves in mimosas as I give her a full crash course on Rogue for dummies. I explained the council to her and what my role would be if I ever went back. I tell her about how I've managed to stay hidden from them for so long and how my father wanted me to marry Damien. It feels like a huge burden lifted off my chest to finally be able to talk to someone about all this. The entire time, she listened, encouraging me to tell her more.

"Now, do you understand why I'm so leery about telling Julian? He's such a nice guy. How can I willingly bring him into my fucked up world?"

She eyes me for a moment. "I stick by what I said earlier. If he really loves you, then he won't care. It might take him some time to adjust to the whole secret society bit, but if you plan on marrying him, you have to tell him first. I love you, but you can't commit to forever with someone who doesn't know about such a huge part of your life. Have you even told him about Maxton and your mom?"

"No, he knows that something bad happened, but that's the extent of it. I never went into detail, and he never pushed me to. I'm pretty sure he thinks I'm some orphan nomad angel who he just happened to stumble upon."

I look up at her to see her laughing.

"You are anything but an angel. If he thinks that he truly is delusional."

"Hey, shut it." I giggle and down the rest of my third or fourth mimosa. I've lost count at this point, but I am feeling a bit tipsy, so I should probably cut myself off. I convince myself one more won't hurt.

"One more drink, and then we have to get out of here."

"Fine, now that we have gone over your dark and sinister past, tell me more about this engagement. I need all the details because I know that must have been an eventful day." She winks at me, and I roll my eyes. "I mean it, Cals! I want every single detail."

I go on to tell her about dinner, the waterfall, and sexy time. I don't tell her that it ended with me finishing myself off. That feels a little personal, but she seems satisfied with what I tell her. The server came back one last time for us to pay our bill before leaving. I have to get home to my man. He hasn't texted me back since I sent him that picture earlier, and I'm dying to know what he thought.

Walking out of Maria's, I head over to my car so I can lock it up before hopping into the Uber that should be here in three minutes. I am way too tipsy to drive home today. I should have prepared for this by giving Julian a heads up so he could Uber here and drive my car back, but it'll just have to sit here until later when we can come back to grab it. As I make my way to my car, I notice a piece of paper that someone slid under one of my wiper blades.

I stop dead in my tracks and look around the parking lot for anything that may seem out of place. Nothing stands out, so I grab the paper, and as I read it, I feel the color drain from my face, my body instantly becoming rigid.

"We are watching."

Three simple words, we are watching, are enough for me to want to throw up everything I just ingested. I turn away from my car and dry heave a few times before I manage to regain my composure. Snapping my body back up, I frantically searched the parking lot for any clues as to who may have put this here. There are only a few cars sitting around, and they are all vacant.

Across the street, I catch a glimpse of a black sedan with dark-tinted windows driving away. Is that who put this here? I honestly have no clue, and I feel the panic beginning to set in. My heart is racing. They fucking found me. I need to get out of here. They have been watching me. It has to be a sick ploy from my father to let me know that he knows where I am. I am right on the edge of completely spiraling out when the Honda Accord I have been waiting on pulls up.

The driver rolls down the window, "Callie?" he says. "Umm, yes," I reply, slipping into the backseat, trying to keep myself calm with some small talk on the way home but silently panicking.

Chapter 5
Barrett

I watch as she gets out of her car and walks over to the little blonde girl with the septum piercing. Outside of the boyfriend, she spends the majority of her time with this girl. She seems to be the only other fixture in her life. They link arms and walk into Maria's.

They come here quite frequently. This is one of her few regular spots outside of home and the sporadic shifts at the bar where she works. The visits here at Maria's are not always on the same day, but Saturdays or Sundays seem to be the preferred days for the two of them. I'm guessing it is so they can take advantage of the bottomless mimosas. Sometimes, they have to call a ride home when they leave here. The blonde usually drinks more than the one we're watching, though.

Originally, I thought this would be the best spot to carry out our plan. We could pretend to be the ride coming to pick her up. It would be easy. She would walk right up to the car and climb in willingly without any struggle or fight. The only issue with taking her here is that we never know when she plans to drink enough to need a ride home. Most of the time, she's responsible about it and drives herself back. That friend of hers, though, is definitely more reckless. We wouldn't have a problem picking her up as a fake driver if we needed to as a last resort.

We have been watching Callie for a few weeks now. Ever since that son of a bitch Gabriel went back on his word and now refuses to give me and my brothers what we're owed. He hired us for a job and asked us to take out someone who was no longer of use to him. Apparently, he was on some timeline and needed the job completed as quickly as possible. He had some kind of position he wanted to fill that had yet to be vacated. We were to take out some sorry soul named Barry Michaels.

I didn't ask too many questions. It's not my job to ask, and if I'm honest, the less we have to know, the better. He gave us a name and a basic outline of his schedule. The man was such a creature of habit it was almost too easy. Most people always have the same sort of daily patterns they stick to. Seb had him pegged from the alleyway after one of his late-night meetings with his lady friend. We checked her background to make sure she wasn't anyone important that might ask questions if he stopped coming around, but she was just another run-of-the-mill whore who he was paying to fuck. If he stopped coming around, she would just assume he'd had his fill and went back home to his boring life.

One quick shot between the eyes was all it took, and he dropped like a fly. The police are calling it a botched burglary, and they have no leads on who their suspect may be. They won't have any, either. I'm too good for them to have any kind of leads. I made sure all the cameras within a 20-mile radius were wiped. What a strange coincidence that there was a freak electrical surge that took out all video feeds in the town for 28 seconds during the time of the murder. Most people wouldn't think to wipe cameras from surrounding areas. They always go for the quick, obvious feeds, but I am thorough and don't like to leave anything up to chance.

We get random requests like this from people pretty often. Sometimes, they're more detailed, and we're brought in on why someone wants their enemy killed, and sometimes, we only have a name and an envelope of cash.

We've managed to make a name for ourselves in the criminal underground. We get the job done. The Monroe Brothers. We are discreet but efficient. We only ask questions that we need answers to in order to complete the job as quickly as possible, get paid, and move on to the next. Sometimes, people pay us with money; other times, we are paid with information, that is, if the information interests us. Gabriel has a very large chunk of information we're interested in. It's something Sebastian's been trying to track down with no success.

It's been a long time since someone failed to fulfill their end of our bargain when hiring us, but here we are. It didn't take long to figure out Gabriel had a precious little girl. Pictures of their family were easily accessible online.

I found it odd that the photos changed to only him five or six years ago. His wife and daughter were no longer included. Maybe they had some sort of falling out, who knows. I really don't give a fuck. It's not my problem to try and figure out their family dynamic. My job was to find her, and I did.

It took some digging to find her. She managed to be pretty good at staying off the grid and keeping her head low. It was pretty impressive. Eventually, I got a hit through her boyfriend, and that led me right to her. That guy is a fucking dumbass.

When we realized she was only one town over from us, it was all like a perfect little gift of fate. Outside of Maria's and work, she doesn't do much. There's one grocery store she frequents usually once a week, but most of the time, he is with her. We can't get to her with him there. This will need to be handled without him knowing. The easiest way to take her without suspicion is to make it look like she left him, so he won't even bother looking for her.

When she's home, she spends most of her time sitting on the couch or reading in her room. She thinks nobody can see her, but we are always watching. I'm always watching. I had cameras installed in every room pretty early on when her boyfriend was away because it made things easier. Watching her on the screen isn't the same, though. Kyler and I still prefer to stalk her in person. Sebastian fills in when he can, but he prefers the two of us to handle it. I don't mind. I like to watch.

I hoped Gabriel would learn the error of his ways and just give us what we were promised, but here we are. He made a mistake when he double-crossed us. He may think we're just a group of dumb kids, but in my 25 years, I've never been dumb. Quite the opposite, actually.

Callie and her friend spend a long time inside Maria's this time. I peer into the window that gives me a clear view of her corner table and see her order another round of drinks. This is the perfect opportunity to have a little fun. Usually, we don't like to play with our prey before pouncing on them, but she intrigues me.

I grab my notebook off the back seat and a pen from the glove box and scribble down a little note for her on the corner of the page. I make it just big enough that she will see the paper but small enough that she will need to grab it off the windshield before reading.

Grinning, I write, "We are watching," then stroll over to her car and place it under her wiper blade before walking back to my car. Now, I watch and wait.

They say their final goodbyes as her friend gets into her Uber, and I see Callie walk over to her car. Her entire body tenses up the minute she notices the paper. She glances around but has no clue what she is looking for.

When she grabs the paper, her usual blush-colored cheeks become a porcelain white. She whips her body around and heaves a few times before lifting her head up and scanning the parking lot, hoping to find out who left the note for her. The fear in her eyes makes my cock stir. Her driver has to be close, so I start the car and drive down the road before it pulls up. Once I am a good distance away, I pull off into a Park and Ride and give myself a moment to bask in the scene I just witnessed.

This girl does dangerous things to me. We haven't even spoken yet, but I want to pin her up against a wall and fuck her mercilessly until she is screaming my name with my knife at her throat. Thinking about that and reminiscing on the fear in her eyes just moments ago has my dick so hard it's painful. I pull it out and begin to stroke it as I think about the fucked up things I would do to her tight little body.

I can picture myself wrapping my fingers around her ponytail and forcing her face up so I can devour her lips. I would whip her around, grab her by the throat, and pound into her from behind with her tits pressed firmly against the brick wall as she took all of me. I can almost hear her wince from the pain of the brick rubbing her exposed skin raw. In my mind, she comes apart on my cock, her pussy spasming and squeezing me as I tighten my grip and give myself a few more strokes before letting loose into my hand.

Fuck, I wish it was her pussy I was blowing my load into instead of my hand. Jerking off on the side of the road isn't something I make a habit of, but there was no way I would've been able to drive home comfortably with how hard my cock was after seeing the fear on her face from that note.

I use my other hand to reach over to the passenger seat and grab a shirt from my gym bag to clean myself off. This girl is a means to get what we want from Gabriel, and that's all. I need to remind myself of that. Seb has made it perfectly clear we need to keep our distance from her until we get what we are owed.

Getting close could complicate things because there's a chance, we may have to send pieces of her to her father to prove a point and get him to cave into our demands. Kyler already went and got himself attached. He was always quick to obsess over things. I need to make sure I don't follow suit.

Chapter 6
Callie

I've been pacing back and forth in the hallway of our house for the last six hours, trying to wrap my mind around what I should do. My thoughts are racing at every possibility. Julian texted me a few minutes ago to tell me he was hung up on something and wouldn't be home until late tonight. I don't think I can be here alone while waiting for him to get home. We were supposed to spend the night together and then all day tomorrow before he leaves for his business trip.

The fact that we just got engaged yesterday, and he has more important things to do today, makes me slightly annoyed. It's most likely because I'm on edge from that note. Usually, things like this wouldn't bother me as much. I'm not the kind of girl who needs to have her man around her 24/7 or know where he is at all times. Right now, I just don't want to be alone.

I know Avery and I were just at brunch earlier, but it's all too much for me, so I pick up the phone, scroll to her name, and press the call button. I hate talking to people on the phone, so when she sees it's me calling, she immediately knows something is wrong.

"Cals, is everything okay?"

"Avery, I need you to come over NOW. I'm freaking the fuck out." My breathing begins to quicken, and I feel the panic rise. I take a deep breath to try and calm myself as she tells me she is hopping in her car now and heading my way.

She was smart and got a ride to Maria's earlier because she knew we would end up drinking more than our fill. My car not being here at the house is the only reason I haven't bolted from town yet.

"Babe, listen to me. I will be there in 10 minutes. I need you to just keep breathing, ok?" I keep her on the line, but it goes silent while she drives, as if she knows I need her comfort but don't want to talk about it over the phone.

"I'm pulling in the driveway now." I click off the call and run over to the door, ripping it open. As soon as she walks up the doorway, I pull her in for a giant hug and try my best to center myself. She squeezes back until I let go enough for us to take a few steps back into the house and shut the door.

"Okay, spill," she says. "What's happening? Did Julian do something?"

"Remember what we talked about earlier?" I blurt out. My voice is full of very apparent panic.

She nods. "Yeah, what about it?"

"I think they know I'm here." I pull the note from my pocket and hand it to her, and her eyes widen when she reads it. "I found this on my car after we left Maria's. What if they know I told you, Avery? God, how could I be so fucking stupid? I should've never gotten you into this mess."

"You don't know this is from them." She shakes her head and touches my arm to reassure me.

I shake her off of me and begin to pace around the room. "Who the hell else would it be from? Why would anyone else have a desire to tell me they're watching me?"

"You said if they found you, they would make you go back, right?

I nod and give her a few minutes to explain her train of thought.

"If this was them, wouldn't they have just come and grabbed you instead of leaving you weird notes saying they were watching?"

She has a point, but I'm not fully convinced yet. "Maybe my father just wants to play mind games with me before he does. You don't know how cruel he's capable of being."

Avery throws her hands up in the air, clearly frustrated with how I'm acting at the moment. "I won't let them take you, Cal. You really need to talk to Julian, though, because if this is them and they're watching, who's to say what they would do to him. You said your father killed your boyfriend and mother, right?"

"Oh my god! He's been so weird all day. What if they got to him? What if they know he proposed last night, and my father hauled him away somewhere and is sending me messages from his phone to keep me thinking everything is okay before they come and take me back?"

"Give me your phone," she says, and I hand it over to her. She scrolls through the contact list until she finds Julian and hits the call button, placing it on speaker. He picks up on the fourth ring. Instantly, I feel myself calm down, at least a little bit.

"Hey, sweet girl. I can't really talk right now. I had some work stuff come up today after the gym and am about to go into a meeting. I'm so sorry. I promise I'll be home as soon as I can. Is everything okay?"

"Julian, this is Avery. I just wanted to let you know I stopped over to hang with our girl for a little longer, and I plan on having her completely inebriated by the time you get home so I can celebrate the big news with her. Congratulations, by the way."

"Oh, hi Avery, um yeah, that's fine. You could have just texted me, though. I thought something was wrong. Just make sure she drinks water while you have her drinking whatever else. I really have to hop off here if there's nothing else. My meeting is about to start."

"Actually, yeah. Callie's car is still at Maria's."

"No worries. I'll have a co-worker drop it off after our meeting. I really have to go though."

"Sure thing. Bye," she says as she clicks the end button on the phone before looking at me. "See, he's fine. You're overreacting."

"I don't think I am reacting enough in this situation. There are too many unknowns right now, and my first instinct is to run from all of this so that if they're watching me, I can get away in time."

"Callie, look at me. You're done running. You built something for yourself here, and I have your back. Go sit your ass on the couch. I'll make us something to drink so we can talk through all this shit calmly and figure out the next steps. I know I've already said this, but if you really think this is your father, you have to tell Julian. He should be involved in whatever decision you make going forward."

"I know." I sigh, flopping down on the couch.

Avery wanders over to my kitchen to mix us up a classic gin and tonic. Gin isn't a go-to liquor choice for most people, but it's my absolute favorite. It tastes like pine trees and happiness, which is exactly what I need right now to drown my thoughts. She saunters to the couch, sits beside me, and hands me my glass.

"Okay. Let's think about this. Is there anyone else that would leave you something like that?" she mumbles while sipping her drink.

"I honestly have no idea. Outside of my father and the society, I never let anyone in until I came here and met you and Julian."

"You said he's going through some business acquisition, right? Maybe he pissed someone off?" She places her glass down on the coffee table.

"It's possible, but again, the most obvious scenario here is that my father has finally tracked me down." My father has to be involved somehow.

"I just don't think it's your father, Cal. My gut is telling me there's something we are missing."

We talk for another two hours, exhausting every possibility, but I'm still convinced this is my father's doing. I'm several drinks in now and tired of talking about it, so I ask her if she wants to catch up on our favorite TV show. It's based on a book series where the lead female travels back in time and is forced to marry a hot Scotsman. What an inconvenience for her. We've been bingeing through the last few seasons, trying to get our fix. The hot Scotsman is my favorite, but Avery is obsessed with his godfather.

I glance at my phone and don't see any new messages from Julian, so I text him to make sure he's still ok. This entire situation has me on edge. It's a little after midnight now. He should be home. I see the three little bubbles pop up, and a few seconds later, he replies that he is finishing up and heading home soon. I'm not sure what he considers soon because we watch two more episodes of our show before I doze off on the couch.

I'm woken up by the smell of black licorice and tobacco-Julian. I snuggle into his arms as he lifts me up to carry me to our bed and tucks me under the covers. He's gone for a few minutes and then comes back and slides into bed with me, wrapping his arm around me possessively. As I drift back to sleep, I hear him whisper something about me being his. I couldn't quite make it out because my dreams pulled me back under, but it seemed a little odd.

The next morning, I wake up to the smell of coffee, throw on a pair of leggings and an oversized tee, and make my way to the kitchen. I barely remember Julian bringing me to bed last night, and I have no idea what time it was. Avery is awake and sitting at our breakfast bar, sipping on a cup of coffee, and having a casual conversation with Julian when I walk into the room.

"Ah, my sleeping beauty," he says as he walks over to me and gives me a chaste kiss on my temple.

"Morning. Please tell me there's enough coffee for me because my head's pounding. Ave, we went a little too hard on the gin last night."

She giggles. "Sounds like someone is getting a little too old to hang with the big dogs."

I turn and glare at her.

"Cal, if you're good, I'm going to head home. I think I should give you and your fiancé some time together."

I walk over to her, give her a big hug, and whisper in her ear, "Thank you. Keep your phone handy in case today goes wonky." She nods, then walks over to slip her shoes on and head out.

After making my way back to Julian, I wrap my arms around his waist and look up at him. "What time did you get in last night? I tried to wait up."

"It wasn't until a little after 3am. I'm sorry, sweet girl. It was one thing after another with work. They needed me to complete one final trial run before we take over our new acquisition."

"Hmmm. I thought you were coming home after the gym. I didn't know you had to work," I say as I trail my hands up and down his back, looking up at him with sultry eyes. "Also, I sent you a picture yesterday that I haven't heard a word about mister."

"Oh, I remember the picture." He smiles and brushes his lips against mine as his hands move down to cup my ass before lifting me up. I wrap my arms around his neck and my legs around his waist. Leaning into him, my lips part, and he slips his tongue in, teasing me before kissing me deeply. Pulling back for a moment, my eyebrows scrunch together.

"How come you had your office locked yesterday? I was going to sprawl myself over your desk so that you would think of me every time you work in there, but I couldn't get in."

His lips turn up in a grin. "Now, that sounds like something we should rectify."

Slowly, he walks us toward his office, completely ignoring my question. I take the opportunity to lick and suck up his neck, nibbling slightly on his ear. He hardens beneath me as he pulls the door open and sits me on his desk. I place my hands behind me and lean back as he says, "Lift."

I obey immediately, and he grabs my leggings and underwear at my waist to pull them down. In seconds, I'm bare from the waist down on his desk. My shirt and bra come off next and are tossed in a pile with the rest of my clothes. He takes a step back to look me up and down, smirking at the view of me fully naked on his desk, so I spread my legs for him.

"You are a vision." He steps back into me, putting his hand on my chest and pushing me gently until I am lying down with my legs hanging over. My stomach is peppered with kisses from him.

"So beautiful." The kisses make their way down lower until I feel his breath blowing just above my pussy. I prop myself up on my elbows, so I have a prime view of him hovering right between my legs.

"Mine," he growls. I let out a breath and nod at him. He's being a little more possessive than usual, but I don't mind.

His head dips down to my center, running his tongue up the length of my slit, and I let out a moan. "Yes." His tongue devours me like I am his last meal. I tangle my fingers in his hair to guide him right where I need him to be. He shoves two thick fingers into me, making me scream in ecstasy, "Julian!"

His pace is relentless as he pumps his fingers in and out of me, curving them ever so slightly to hit that magical spot. I feel myself getting closer and closer to the edge. Suddenly, his lips suction themselves to my clit, and I lose all sense of myself grinding on his face. My body erupts, and my pussy tightens around his fingers as I come with a fiery need. He continues working me until my body relaxes. My fingers fall from his hair, and he looks up at me.

I don't know who this man is today, but I'm loving every fucking minute of it. I lay my body back down on the desk to catch my breath when the paper next to me captures my attention.

"Julian, what is this?" It's his flight confirmation for his trip. "I thought you told me you were going to Atlanta. Why does this paper say Nashville?"

He looks down at the flight confirmation, eyes widening for the briefest of moments before he catches himself and relaxes them. "Atlanta? Why would I tell you I'm going to Atlanta? I've been going back and forth to Nashville for the last month now,

Callie. We've talked about this quite a few times. You must have gotten it confused with something else."

This whole situation is weird. There is no way I would confuse the two cities. They aren't anywhere near each other. Nashville is dangerously close to Rogue. I would have remembered if he mentioned it.

"Julian, I know for a fact you told me Atlanta. Why are you lying to me?" I ask him while looking into his eyes with fierce determination. He needs to know that I won't back down on this until he tells me the truth. I won't allow someone to lie to me and let them stay in my life.

"Callie, I've never been to Atlanta," he states firmly and then chuckles. He chuckles like what I'm saying is the most outrageous thing in the world. He is really going to hold onto this lie. He just told me at dinner the other night he was going to Atlanta. I know it!

I've had enough of this bullshit. I slide my bare ass off his desk and grab my clothes off the floor, forcing them back onto my body. "I'M DONE JULIAN! I won't be with a liar," I yell at him.

"Callie," he calls out, but I ignore him. Once all my clothes are in place, I storm out of the room, my shoulder bumping into his arm on the way out. This mother fucker is seriously going to try to gaslight me right now. Absolutely fucking not.

Chapter 7
Callie

I need time to think, so without saying another word, I storm into the kitchen, take off the ring he gave me, place it on the counter, and grab my keys to run to my car. Again, my first instinct is to pack a bag and get the fuck out of town. It would be so easy to start over like I've done so many times in the past. Avery would never let me go alone, so I would have her by my side if that's what I chose.

In the madness of rushing out of the house, I realized I didn't grab my phone. Whatever, the only person other than Julian I even talked to is Avery, and I'm not ready to tell her about this yet. I sure as fuck have no desire to talk to Julian. I don't want to talk to anyone.

Avery told me countless times that she didn't like Julian because she always felt like he was being dishonest. She genuinely believes the person he is putting out to the world is someone completely different from his true self. We just had this conversation again yesterday. Have her instincts been right all along? I can't tell her about this mess until I have time to decide what I want to do.

He's never lied to me that I know of, but they always say that people closest to you, who are on the outside looking in, have a clearer representation of your relationship dynamics. They aren't clouded by emotions and heartstrings. People from the outside can see through the bullshit sometimes. Maybe I should have taken her opinion more seriously.

I just don't understand why he would feel like he needs to lie now. I've always told him from the start that I'd rather he be upfront with me than dishonest and let me find out about it down the line. Lying has always been a hard line that I drew in the sand. If people are capable of that, then they're capable of worse. I don't have the space for that kind of person in my life, not with Rogue and my father still out there. This whole situation is a major red flag. What else could he be lying about? Fuck, our whole relationship could be a farce for all I know.

As if that wasn't bad enough, the fact that he tried to gaslight me just blows my mind. I know that he told me several times he was going to Atlanta, not Nashville. Every time someone mentions that city, I'm ravaged by all of the terrible memories that surround it.

Nashville is the closest major city to Rogue. It was where my mother would take me as a kid when we had our days off the compound. It's where Maxton and I planned on catching the bus to get out of town and start our new lives together. I've spent countless days in that city, discovering its history. One of my favorite memories was a day out with Maxton and our mothers at the Opry House. The performances we saw were a once-in-a-lifetime kind of thing for me. I would definitely remember if he told me about Nashville.

Was I wrong to let Julian in? I spent so long keeping everyone at a distance to protect myself, and here I am, feeling stupid as fuck for giving him my trust. It takes so much time for me to feel comfortable enough to open up to someone, and I did that for him.

One lie is enough for an immediate shut-down response from me. Where do I even go from here? How do I process this information? Most people would be able to take some time, come together to find a solution, and maybe work things out and be stronger for it in the end, but I don't know if I want that now. I should just let things be over.

Before I realize where my absent mind has taken me, my car is pulling into the parking lot of Braxton Falls Park. I need a break, my own personal off switch, and this is the only place outside of Avery's where I feel safe right now. There are only two other cars here, thankfully. With any luck, whoever was in those cars would be walking the other trails, and I could have the waterfall to myself.

I park in the spot closest to the trail and take the short, familiar walk back to the falls. Just a few days ago, I was leaving here the happiest girl in the world, full of hope. Julian had proposed. I thought everything was falling into place, that we would live out our lives together. I knew things were too good to be true.

I walk over to the picnic table by the falls and flop down on the bench to stare out at the roaring water. The water seems lower today, causing more white caps to form on the flowing river. I watch as the water whooshes in circles around the rocks, crashing up against them and then splashing back down, mesmerizing me. Glancing back up at the waterfall, I take a deep breath, letting the smell of the water and earth float around and ground me.

I think back to the engagement just a few days ago. The last time I saw the bench I was sitting on, it was covered in white cloth and candles. Julian was kneeling right next to the spot, giving me the promise of forever. That day feels a bit like a lie now, too. My thoughts aren't my own at this moment. They belong to my insecurities and the disappointment I've faced in the past.

Did he cheat on me? Does he have a whole other family out there somewhere that he was keeping from me? Maybe his hypothetical girlfriend or wife or whatever is sick or pregnant or something that involves going back and forth to doctors' visits, so he has to keep flying out to be there to support her. She probably thinks he is on some business trip when he's here with me.

I laugh to myself. I have a pretty amazing ability to go from zero to one hundred when I encounter the slightest problem. Am I even allowed to be upset with him about this? I've been lying about such a huge part of my life. A lie by omission is still a lie, and this one involves my entire childhood and potential future adulthood.

I close my eyes and take a few more deep breaths, refocusing on the rushing sound of the falls to let it clear my thoughts. I don't know how long I sit like this, but the anger in me begins to recede.

This all has to be some sort of misunderstanding. I'll just go home, talk to Julian, and we can figure it out from there. We can get back together. If his lie proves to be fact, I'm gone so fast. Avery will get an immediate phone call to fill her in on all the details, and we can book our bus ticket out of here to move on to the next stop of our lives. Tonight, I will end all doubts.

I hear a rustling noise in the tree line to my left and look over my shoulder. It's the middle of the day, so it's not unusual for there to be someone else in this area of the park. When I don't see anyone right away, I'm not alarmed.

I glance back at the falls again and stand up to walk over to the edge of the water. I hear another loud shuffle behind me, and this time, when I turn around, a man is standing near the table I was just sitting at. He's tall and has most of his face covered up by the hoodie-hat combo he is currently wearing. I watch him for a moment to see what he's going to do next as he takes a seat on the bench. Okay, what the fuck, weirdo.

Turning back to the falls, I feel the hairs on the back of my neck stand up. My body is uncomfortable with this man being so close to me, so I decide it's a good time to leave. I've done what I needed to do here anyway. A few moments after I started walking back to my car, I peered over my shoulder and found that the man had stood up and was looking right in my direction. I'm not close enough to make out any details of his face.

My body's alarm bells start to ring. There's something off about him. He's just standing there, staring at me. Could he be with Rogue? I'm not taking the chance. I move quickly to my car, looking behind me every few seconds to see if he's advanced. He's keeping a steady pace behind me at a respectable distance. A normal person would not see an issue with this. We're in a public park in the middle of the day, but my instincts are telling me to proceed with caution. My heart is racing. Keep your shit together, Callie, and get to the car. You're so close.

I see my car and hope springs in my chest. The man is still a good distance behind me, and by the time he catches up, I'll already be on my way out of the parking lot. I'm safe, and I can go home.

I pull the driver's side door open and slide into the front seat as fast as possible, clicking the locks for good measure. Something shuffles behind me, and I bring my eyes up to the rearview mirror to check it out. Out of nowhere, a body sits up in the backseat. My eyes go wide. Someone else is locked in the car with me. Fuck, you know better than this! Always check the back seat. I stumble around a bit, and just as I am about to make my move for the knife in my center console, the person leans forward, wrapping one arm around my chest. I pull up my arm and grab at their hand to pull the leather glove off of me just as they swing their other arm around the other side of my seat and jab something into my arm. Looking down, I realize they injected me with something.

Panic really begins to set in as the world around me starts to fade away. I try to fight it, but the darkness surrounds my vision as I attempt to push their arms off of me. My body feels heavy. My mind is telling my arms to move, but they don't respond. Finally, the drug wins, and everything goes black.

Chapter 8
Kyler

I see her speed out of the driveway, almost like she's running from something. I don't know what went down in the house because I don't like watching the feeds when she's intimate with him. The last thing I saw was the two of them in the kitchen before I shut them off. Everything was fine.

What set you off, little wanderer? I see the furrow in her brow as she whips the car onto the street, driving away from the house. She's clearly upset. This does something to me. For some reason, I don't like the idea of her being upset. I want to pull her into my arms and hold her until she smiles.

I follow behind her car at a safe distance as she takes a few turns. I already know where we are headed. She's upset, and there's one place I know she loves going to when she needs to decompress. After our latest chat with Gabriel, Seb told us to move forward with any opportunity to take her. It looks like today might be the day. She hasn't been doing much outside the house on her own lately. She only works maybe one shift a week at the bar now. When she leaves the house, she's with the blonde girl or her boyfriend. I can't stand him. He smiles at her, but his face falls into a scowl as soon as she turns away. There is clearly some sort of front he doesn't want her to see.

After watching her over the last few weeks, I feel strangely protective of my little wanderer. Realizing this may be the opportunity we've been waiting for, I pick up my phone and call Sebastian. He answers almost immediately.

"Hey man, is everything ok? I'm just finishing up my meeting in town," he says into the phone.

Seb is the one who fields the requests for our services. Most of the time, Barrett is able to compile enough information about them with his hacking skills, but on occasion, we receive a request from someone who keeps a lower profile. Seb meets these clients face-to-face so that he can get a feel for their vibe. He goes into these meetings masked, dressed in black jeans, a long black-sleeved shirt, and leather gloves to keep himself unidentifiable. Seb is careful and calculated and will always ensure he's doing everything he can to protect his family. Family is everything to us. Once we found each other, we clung on and never let go.

"I'm fairly certain the girl is heading to the falls. We're ready for her, right?" The excitement is seeping through me. I can't wait to have her closer.

"Did something happen? This isn't her normal behavior," he asks. Here he goes with his questions.

"She ran out of the house, all upset. I think she and her boyfriend got into a fight. He most likely won't be looking for her right away. I'm tailing her now. She just pulled into the park."

Seb takes a minute to think before saying, "Him being upset with her could definitely work to our advantage. We can get her secured in the room before anyone even realizes she's gone."

I smirk at his mention of that. Soon I'll be able to watch her while she's sleeping.

"I can meet you in the parking lot at the park. I'm only a few minutes away. Do you have everything we need?"

"Of course, I have it. I haven't left the house without it since you told me it was fair game to take her." I look over to the passenger seat and see the mask, leather gloves, and drug-filled syringe sitting next to my black hoodie.

"Good. I'll call Barrett and let him know we are moving forward so that he can disable any cameras in the area and wipe the last hour off of them," he tells me, like any of it makes a difference to me.

"See you in a few," I say, hanging up and tightening my hands on the steering wheel as I pull into the parking spot next to her car. His priority is the cameras; mine is the girl.

She is already out of view by the time I pull in. She must have really needed to get up there to clear her head. Soon enough, whatever she's trying to process won't even matter. She will be locked in a room under our pool house until we decide the best way to use her against her father. Gabriel really fucked up when he decided to go back on his word with us.

I grab my gloves and slip them on while waiting for Seb. A few minutes later, he pulled in and met me at my passenger side door.

"How do you think we should do this?" he asks as I toss him the hoodie and grab the syringe.

"I will slip into the backseat of her car and wait for her to leave. The element of surprise might work best for us. That way, she doesn't have a chance to fight."

He nods. "True. We don't know how she will react when her survival instincts kick in. I'll head to the falls and try to be as creepy as possible. Maybe we can speed up this process, so we don't have to wait so long." A mischievous grin spreads across his face.

"Got somewhere to be?" I ask him curiously.

"I just want this shit done so we can get our payment. If word gets out that we let someone go back on their deal, bad things could happen."

"If you say so," I tell him.

"Barrett said her phone's location is showing it's still at her house, so we don't need to worry about making sure it's off," Seb says while putting the hoodie on.

"Even better." I smile.

"Let's get this over with," he mutters before walking off.

He's always in a bad mood anytime she's involved. I tried to keep most of the watch duties between Barrett and me, but we can't do it all. I shrug and move to take my place in the back seat of her car, being careful to take the top off of the syringe so I was ready for her to make her grand appearance. Who the hell doesn't lock their car doors? You are just asking for trouble, little wanderer.

I placed myself behind her driver's seat and laid down on my right side. It's not the most comfortable, but I won't have to shift my body as much when I lean up to surprise her. Some time passed, and I heard footsteps leading up to the car. Whoever it is, it sounds like they are breathing heavily. It's showtime.

The door to the car whips open, and she rushes to lock the door behind her. As soon as the locks engage, I slide my body into a sitting position. Her eyes flick to the rearview mirror after she hears me move, and they almost bulge out of her head. Before she has time to react, I lean forward and shove my left arm between the seat and the door, wrapping it around her chest. She feels so warm, and her body distracts me for a brief moment. This is the first time I've been able to touch her after watching for so long.

She tries to rip at my arm, bringing me back to the task at hand. I raise my right hand up and plunge the needle right into the upper part of her arm, making sure to inject her with the entirety of the drug. It won't hurt her, but it will put her under for quite some time. She might wake up with a raging headache, too, who knows. She continues fighting it for a few minutes, which surprises me, but eventually, she succumbs to the drug and goes limp. Her head begins to fall forward, and I catch it with my hand, bringing it gently to the side so she doesn't hurt her neck.

After securing the lid back on the syringe's needle, I put it in my pocket and hopped out of her back seat. I open her door and wrap my arm around her to lift her bridal style. Her head flops onto my shoulder as I move her from one vehicle to the other, sending a rush to my heart. Her body naturally wants to lean on me. She looks so good in my arms with her head tucked into my chest. I don't want to put her down, but unfortunately, I do.

I slide in with her once she is secured in the back seat. Seb makes his way around to my front seat and nods in my direction before starting the engine to drive us back to our place. We can come back and pick up his car later. We don't know how long she will be out, and the last thing we need is for her to wake up while driving.

I watch as she lies there, sleeping, with her head nestled in my lap. She looks so peaceful. I know that as soon as she wakes up and realizes she's not where she's supposed to be, her peace will be replaced with fear. I wonder what kind of reaction she will have upon waking. Will she immediately go into victim mode, yelling and screaming for help, or will she take it all in and internalize being strategic?

The way people respond to a crisis says a lot about them. She doesn't strike me as the kind of person to be weak. Personally, I'm hoping she's the strong and strategic type. There are too many weak women out there in the world. It would be nice to be in the company of a strong one. I know Barrett would likely enjoy the fear, though. The sick bastard gets off on the fear and pain.

Growing up with a father like Gabriel, I can assume he prepared her for a situation like this, whether she realizes it or not. After he went back on his deal with us, the guys and I did some research on Gabe. There isn't a lot of information out there that Barrett doesn't have access to, no matter how discreet it's supposed to be. He's good at what he does.

Gabriel leads his own little community. We didn't dig too much into the specifics of what their stupid society represents because, quite frankly, it doesn't matter. These communities always think there's nobody else out there like them, like they're something special. The truth is, there are more of them than they realize. The whole "Secret Society" bit is actually pretty common. We've worked with several people who are part of them and have hired us for various jobs. Usually, they need someone to take out the competition for them because it's against their rules to murder within. The solution is always to hire outside help. That's where we come in.

Pulling up to the house, we stop at the gate, waiting for Barrett to buzz us in. Nobody gets through this gate without one of us allowing it. The house is surrounded by a twelve-foot-tall iron fence equipped with both motion and heat sensors. Any slight difference in the normal ecosystem surrounding the place sends an alert directly to our phones. Seb and I don't know much about the ins and outs of it all, but we have been trained enough to know when it's a real threat versus a squirrel running along the fence line. The gate has a biometric scanner that can only be overridden through a program on Barrett's phone. We never have to worry unless, by chance, we encounter a better hacker than our guy. The odds of that happening, though, are very slim.

The gate creaks open, and we pull the car through, waiting in front of it to ensure it fully closes behind us. We always wait. We don't want to let any unexpected guests sneak in. Our ruthless reputation wasn't earned by letting someone sneak up on us when our backs were turned. Once the gate closes, Seb drives up the long driveway, pulling my car right in front of the door. I slide out, lifting her bridal style again so she is back where I want her, against my chest. She smells nice. It's the perfect mixture of grapefruit and roses. It reminds me of my childhood.

The guys and I all grew up in foster homes. It's how we all found each other. None of us really enjoy talking about that part of our lives. We got lucky when we were placed with Ms. Monroe. She brought us together. She ran the only group home where I didn't experience any kind of abuse. Seb and Barrett were already there when I was dropped off. Initially, she put us all in a room together because we were the same age. Seb is the oldest, but only three months separate his birthday and mine. Barrett's birthday falls right in between ours. We formed an instant connection.

Letting yourself get close to people is dangerous when you grow up in the system because you never know when that will be taken from you. You can be moved in the blink of an eye, and the harsh reality is that when you're moved around so much, it is almost impossible to keep in contact.

Somehow, we stayed with Ms. Monroe until we all aged out. We got a place together and built a life for ourselves. A few years later, when she passed away, we decided to take her last name to honor her memory. It felt like the right thing to do to solidify ourselves as a family.

I was in the system the longest. I have very few memories of my birth mother before she was killed and none of my father. My memories of my mother are all a little blurred at this point, but I remember her smell. It's so similar to how this girl smells. Having another female so close to me with this similar scent has me feeling more protective than usual. I want to hide her from the darkness of the world.

Fuck, I can't be thinking like this. Seb keeps reminding me she's a job and nothing more. We need to make sure we keep our sights set on the prize. Apparently, once we figure out how to best use her to get Gabriel to give us the information we need, she will be out of our lives for good. I'm not completely sold on the idea, but there's no way she will even want to be anywhere near all of us once she wakes up and realizes we've taken her.

Seb walks ahead of me as I carry her back to the smaller building behind our house. From the outside, it appears to be a regular pool house. We designed it that way on purpose. The top floor is your run-of-the-mill pool house, equipped with a bathroom, outdoor shower, bar, and lounge area. Behind the bar is a small storage room filled with miscellaneous supplies. Hidden along one of the shelving walls is a door leading down a set of stairs.

We walk through the pool house and make our way down the staircase. There are two floors below the main building. The first level is an underground surveillance room filled with computer screens and images from various cameras around the property. This is Barrett's sanctuary. Lately, the only feeds he's pulled up are the ones from the girl's house. Now that we have her, we don't need to watch them anymore.

The bottom level houses our own personal prison cell. Seb places his hand on the scanner, which opens the door to the lowest level. If someone ever managed to find their way down here, they would never be able to access this room without one of us.

This room is smaller because it was split. Half of the space down here is an entrance area filled with a few chairs. The other half is a sealed room similar to an interrogation room but fully furnished with everything one might need for a long-term stay. The door to the room can only be opened from the outside. There is two-way glass, so we're able to sit down here and watch our prisoners if needed. The glass appears to be a mirror from the inside, but anyone who's watched a crime show or two in their lifetime can figure out this is not the case.

I step into the room and carefully place her down on the bed, wiping the hair from her face. She has a small button nose and light freckles that can only be seen up close, as if she spent a little too much time in the sun. She is fucking gorgeous and doesn't even realize it.

We leave the room and shut the door, sealing the locking mechanism on our way out. Seb walks over to the chair closest to him and takes a seat, so I follow. Now we wait and see what kind of reaction she will have to waking up somewhere strange. We don't want her to hurt herself, so staying close is the only option for the time being. We need to be around if we have to go in and sedate her again. If that happens, we may need to tie her to the bed to calm her down. My cock instantly hardens at that thought.

Chapter 9
Callie

*E*verything is exactly as I remember it in my head. My picture frames, the stuffed elephant, my closet filled with clothes from years ago, the pile of clothes on the floor lying there as if I had just worn them yesterday.

I walk around the room, and it hurts to be here. I hear my mom call for me. "Callie, come down for dinner, sweetie." That's not right, my mother is dead. My father killed her in front of me.

I walk out of my room and down the stairs, turning into the dining room, but the scene changes, and suddenly I'm walking into Julian's office. He looks up at me, "It's about time you came back. I was about to send out a search party to look for you.

"Come back?" I don't remember going back home. He gets up from behind his desk and walks over to me. His hand reaches out, and he wraps his fingers around my neck, squeezing tightly.

"Julian, I can't breathe." My hands come up to his wrists, clawing at them to try and get him to release his grip. My airflow constricts, and panic flows through my entire body.

This isn't right.

He pushes me back against the wall of his office, never letting up on his grip. It's so tight. Everything around me goes black, and I *feel my body go limp. When I open my eyes, my head is resting on the table at Maria's.*

"Cals, I'm sorry, but I have to go. I love him." Avery is telling me about how she met someone, and they are moving across the country. The fuck? She never wanted to leave me before. Who the hell is this guy? I've never met him, but she's willing to change her entire life for him. She's going to leave me behind like I mean nothing. Everything starts spinning, and all my nightmares blur together.

I hear my mother, feel Julian's grasp around my neck, and watch my best friend get in her car and drive away from me. I'm frantic. I don't know what to do. Everything feels like it's crashing around me. I jolt awake, my body bolting upright to a sitting position.

That was one of the craziest dreams I've had in a long time. I take a second to bring my heart rate down before my eyes scan the room around me. Am I still asleep? I don't recognize this place. I feel a dull headache similar to a hangover, and things begin to come back to me in pieces.

My first thought is that they found me. My father found me and brought me back to Rogue. I take a few deep breaths to try and center myself as I peer around the room to figure out where they put me. This doesn't look like any of the rooms I remember. I grew up at the compound. I know every space there is to know, and this one doesn't fit. Did they have something remodeled for when they found me? A special prison for my father to throw me in. I don't think my father would get approval from the council for that. They never changed what the founding fathers built unless they had to.

If my father didn't take me, then who did? I take inventory of the room. It's small with white walls, a twin-size bed, a metal framed door with no handle on the inside, and a large mirror that I am 99% certain is two-way glass. Why else would there be a mirror the length of the wall? Is somebody watching me? Below the glass, there is a two-by-two-foot piece of metal with hinges flush to the wall. It seems like something that can be opened from the outside to place things in and out of the room. To the left of the bed is a small table with one chair, a couple of blankets piled beside the bed, some notebooks with crayons, a stack of old romance novels, and a small hamper filled with clothes. On the other side of the table, I see a small toilet, a sink, and a shower with a floor drain. The floor is slightly angled in that corner so that the water will drain down. The whole area is completely open to the rest of the room. This is my own personal jail cell.

I throw my legs off the side of the bed, feeling a little bit wobbly, and the room spins a little, likely a side effect of whatever they used to get me here. Everything went black, and I lost consciousness so fast.

After a few moments, I regain my composure and walk to the hamper to peer inside. The clothes all seem baggy and nothing fancy. Comfort seems to be the goal. How kind. There is a pair of yellow slippers with smiley faces on them. Sure, because anyone would be happy to be here. Everything looks like my size. Wherever I am, they plan on keeping me here for a while.

The thought of being trapped in here and not knowing anything at all has my anxiety through the roof. My hands feel clammy when I remind myself to breathe. *Stay calm, Callie; now is not the time to freak out.* I close my eyes and bring myself back to the present. I've been mentally preparing for something like this to happen my whole life.

Without a strong mental presence, I would have died. That was one of the few lessons my father taught me growing up that I now appreciate. He used to lock me in a cold, dark room by myself for hours on end and only let me out after he felt confident my emotions were under control. He always said emotions are weakness. I let myself grow weak over the last year being in Braxton Falls with Julian and Avery. There's no room for that shit right now.

I sit down at the table and train my gaze on myself in the mirror. I've seen better days. My hair is messier than usual. There are big black circles under my eyes that also happen to be puffy and red from crying at the waterfall.

I regret that whoever took me gets to see me in such a vulnerable state. I need to harden myself and let my survival instincts kick in. They must be watching me from somewhere. Either through the mirror I'm currently staring at or some sort of hidden camera. It may even be both. I will not be the girl to beg them to let me out or scream for help. I'll bide my time and keep my shit together until I find out exactly who or what I am dealing with.

The first thing I need to do is work through what I know so far. There were at least two men. They had to be men based on what I can pinpoint about each of them. The one following me at the falls was tall, somewhere around six feet. I am just over five feet, and from the distance he was at, it seemed like the top of my head would reach his shoulders. The one in the back seat of my car smelled so good. There were hints of iris and cedarwood. It has to be some kind of special cologne. The clothes on both men were loose fitting, but they seemed strong. They were patient. This had to be a planned attack. They were far too prepared for it to be random. Regular people don't carry drugs that can make you pass out.

The splitting headache and nausea I'm feeling currently are almost enough to make me want to crawl back into bed and sleep, but right now, I need to focus on remembering as much as possible while it's still fresh. Every detail is a potential item I can use to my advantage. That's when I realize I was in such a hurry to get to the falls to clear my head that I didn't do my usual checks. I'm always so good at watching my surroundings, but I let my emotions cloud my rationality. I checked the parking lot, but I wasn't watching to see if I was being followed, and I didn't lock my car. I gave them the perfect opportunity to carry out their kidnapping with ease. How fucking stupid. My father was right. Emotions are weakness.

Normally, people in my situation would not be calm. Freaking out would be useless. It would only show them I'm weak. I'm already here, and by the looks of the room, there's nothing

I'll be able to do to get out unless they want me to, so I'll play the smart game. I'll wait until they come in and tell me what the fuck they want with me. When they finally reveal themselves, I'll flip on my charm and be the poor, sweet, innocent girl who is only a victim of circumstance. Hopefully, my captors really are men. They'll be so quick to fall for that shit. It'll be the perfect opportunity to give myself time to discover what makes them weak and get myself out of here. That's the plan. I will do it by any means necessary.

Avery's going to freak out when she realizes I'm missing. Julian, I don't even know. He may not even realize I am gone for a few days. Due to our fight, he probably thinks I went to Avery's house for some space. He leaves for his trip tomorrow or today, depending on what day it is. Avery has to realize something isn't right. I have to trust that she will. I wish she was here to help me out of this mess, but I am so thankful she isn't. I'll find a way out of here one way or another. Once I do, whoever put me here will pay. For now, I'll continue to sit and stare at my reflection in the fucking mirror until my captors decide to move the next chess piece of this little game we are playing.

Time continues to tick by, and nothing happens. I have no idea how long I sit in this rickety chair, but my eyes are getting heavy, so I walk over to the bed, pull up the covers, and slide in. The lights are still on, and I don't know how or if they even turn off, so I pull the blanket over my head and doze off.

I stir when I feel a slight pressure on the corner of the bed. My whole body goes rigid, and I wait for what happens next.

Nothing. The lights are out now, and the blanket has been pulled down a little past my shoulders from what I can feel. I just lay there unmoving, trying my best to keep my breathing as even as possible.

"I know you're awake. I can hear the change in your breathing," a strange voice says. "Go back to sleep. You look so beautiful when you sleep."

The pressure from the bed disappears, and the door pulls shut. What was that all about? I don't like how nice he was. He could have done whatever he wanted to me while I was lying here vulnerable, but he just sat there and watched me sleep. Who does that? I can handle straightforward criminals who want to use me for their benefit for whatever reason, but his motives seemed different; they were softer, and it made me uneasy. I'm not sure how to take advantage of kindness and softness. Being agreeable at this moment is the best option, so I listen like a good girl and go back to sleep.

Chapter 10
Sebastian

This wasn't the reaction I expected from her. She's oddly calm. Most people in her situation would be banging on the door, screaming at the top of their lungs for someone to help them, or at the very least walking around to see if they could find a way out. She didn't even attempt to open the door or the drop box. It's almost as if she knows we're sitting out here. She's just sitting there, staring at her own reflection.

If I didn't have plans for her, I would allow myself to be impressed by her strength. I need to keep my head on my shoulders. My brothers already let themselves get attached to her, and we just got her in our grasp. Barrett will never admit he feels things, but I can tell she intrigues him. Kyler is not even trying to hide his affection. He has a strange fantasy about being able to watch her as much as possible.

Before we took her, I watched her here and there but mostly tried to keep my distance. One night, I allowed myself to get close enough to strike up a small conversation, but it didn't result in much. She was working at the bar, and I needed a drink. I think about the night I strolled right in and sat on the bar stool.

The place was run-down and full of your typical drunk regulars. When she walked over, I instantly smelled her. She had a distinct smell of grapefruit. Fucking delicious. I told her I wanted their best whiskey on the rocks, and she reached over to the top shelf, grabbed a bottle, and poured it into the glass. I really didn't care what kind of whiskey it was; that wasn't the purpose of being here. I was curious about her. I wanted to have an anonymous opportunity to get into her mind before having the pleasure of her company at the house, day in and day out.

I watched her for a moment. It was as if she was working on autopilot. She could probably do it with her eyes closed. I thought it was the perfect opportunity to strike up a conversation.

"You work here long?" I asked.

She smiled. "Sort of. I've only been in town for about a year, but I've spent the last few years being a bit of a nomad. I've worked at a ton of bars along the way. It's how I prefer it. Not having anything to tie me down." She walked back down the bar to grab another man's beer and set it down for him.

I thought maybe her being on the move would explain why Barrett wasn't able to find any recent pictures of her and Gabriel. She picked up a few glasses to clean.

"Your family doesn't mind your lifestyle?" I casually asked. Her eyes went hard and blank, as if family was a completely off-limits topic for her.

"Don't have any family. Sorry, but I really have to get back to work. There are a few things that need to be done before we close. Let me know if you need another drink." She walked away.

I bring my mind back to the present as I walk back into the kitchen and spot Barrett by the refrigerator and Kyler eating at the breakfast bar. This is perfect timing to have a nice little chat about what we are going to do with the girl in the pool house, considering we can't keep her there forever.

"You guys have a few minutes to talk about what we're going to do with the girl?" I ask them.

There are a few pieces of bacon left on the stove that I snag as Barrett speaks up first. "Sure."

Kyler takes a bite of his toast and then proceeds to talk with his mouth full like a fucking animal. "Yeah, we need to figure that out. It's been almost a week, and she hasn't tried anything. She's just lying in there like she's waiting for something."

"I think it's time for us to let her out of her little cage and see how she handles it." The two of them nod in agreement.

"What's the play here, Seb? Are we going to reach out to Gabriel and dangle his little fruit so we can get paid, or what?" Barrett asks.

Kyler interrupts, "We don't know if that's the right move yet. What if Callie is able to give us more valuable information?"

That thought did cross my mind. "Kyler's right. She may know exactly what we're trying to force out of Gabriel and then some."

"You think she knows about Maxton?" Barrett questions.

"I think it's worth asking her. She's his daughter. Surely, she had access to some type of information. We just need to get it out of her. I don't really care about how we do it. I guarantee she knows something," I tell them.

Kyler tilts his head like he's deep in thought before he blurts out, "I like her. Would it be wrong to say I want to keep her?"

"Ky, she's not ours to keep. We need to tread lightly. If she doesn't know anything, we'll still need to use her to get Gabriel to cooperate," I tell him.

He pushes his plate across the counter in frustration. "We've been waiting for the last six weeks for him to fucking cooperate. If he was going to tell us what we want to know, he would have already."

All of this for some random girl he's never even had a conversation with. She's already coming between us, and she's only been here a week.

"At least give me the go-ahead to play with her while she's here. I don't know how much longer I will be able to keep my hands off of her." Kyler says while looking at me with his damn puppy-dog eyes.

My eyebrows shoot up with concern. "Do you really think it's a good idea to get involved with her?"

"Why the fuck not? I can have some fun. Maybe she'll catch feelings and feel compelled to tell us everything. Besides, even if she says she doesn't know anything, we can't trust that she's telling the truth. Everyone wins this way, Seb. Just let me entertain myself," Kyler pleads.

Barrett's gone completely silent, leaving me to hash this out with Ky. "Fine. If you think flirting your way into her pants is going to make her talk, then have at it. Just remember who your family is at the end of the day. If we have to use her to our advantage, you need to be willing to let that happen. I won't let a piece of ass come between us."

"That's fine." Ky smirks.

"Great, well, good luck then," I tell him, completely annoyed at the direction this conversation went.

"So, we agree? I'll start my pursuit tonight." Ky looks way too excited to be able to get to spend more time with her. This is going to bite us all in the ass.

Barrett doesn't give any kind of opinion on her at all. He just shrugs like this conversation is beneath him. Usually, he has more input to add, but he's being oddly quiet. I'm sure it has something to do with the girl. He also wants to play with her, but he'll never openly admit it like Ky does.

I look over at Kyler to humor him and say, "Tomorrow, you can even bring her up from the cell and take her to the pool. Make it a fun swim day for all I fucking care." Excitement fills his eyes.

I turn my gaze to Barrett. "Barrett, I want you watching the cameras while she's at the pool just in case she tries something funny or manages to take advantage of the lovesick puppy over here." Kyler glances my way and narrows his eyes at my remark, but I'm not wrong. "I'm going to hang back as long as possible without her catching sight of me, just in case she remembers me from that night at the bar. I don't want it fucking up whatever you get going with her." I nod in Kyler's direction.

"Agreed," the two of them say in unison.

"Great, now let's have a drink because things are about to get a whole hell of a lot more complicated starting tomorrow."

We make our way through the house to our lounge room, which comes with a fully stocked bar, couch, 60-inch 4K TV, and pool table. We hang out here most days when the three of us are all together.

Chapter 11
Kyler

I like to watch her sleep. The other guys have been down here to drop off meals here and there, but I'm the only one who's come into the room with her. She calls to me in a way I can't explain. She has a calm, relaxed demeanor when she's unconscious. It's been six nights now since we took her. I've snuck into her room at one point in the night for each one of those nights. The first day, it was only for a few minutes because I felt her wake up and didn't want to risk her fighting me to try and escape. To my surprise, she's still calm. She hasn't tried to pound on the door, scream, or make any effort to get out of here. It's like she has accepted her fate, which is a bit nerve-wracking.

Keeping her in this room long-term is not the ideal option, but we don't know how she will react with a little freedom. The human body can only go so long without seeing daylight before it slowly starts to go crazy, and we don't want to hurt her.

I'll let her see me with the lights on for the first time tomorrow and go from there. Who knows if we'll even make it up to the pool. She could go into full attack mode as soon as I'm standing there in front of her. That would be unfortunate. It's time to get her out of here. She is, after all, innocent in this whole mess. Her father is the only reason we even took her.

Sebastian decided to hold off on contacting Gabriel until we see if we can get the information we're searching for directly from her. Barrett and I agree that this is the best route. My reasons are a little selfish. I want her here with us for as long as possible. Tomorrow will change it all and set a tone for how we proceed. I can't wait until tomorrow. I want to see her tonight and test the waters a little bit.

I slip back into the room to see her sleeping on her back. The blanket has fallen to her knees, and her erect nipples are visible under the white shirt. My whole body freezes when I glance further down and notice she has no pants on. She chose to only wear a shirt and panties to bed tonight.

Oh, you naughty little minx. I want to rip off her shirt, pull those panties to the side, and give myself a nice taste. Would she fight me? Fuck, I'm sure she tastes delicious. Sweet like the grapefruit and roses she always smells like.

My hand runs along the bed as I walk toward where her hair is splayed across the pillow. She's so beautiful. Listening to the steady sound of her breathing has a calming effect. Carefully, my knuckles graze across her cheek, and she stirs but doesn't wake. I trail my thumb along her bottom lip. These plump red lips that would look amazing wrapped around my cock. My finger slowly slides down her neck and across her collarbone. A trail of goosebumps forms, and a light moan escapes her. Even in her sleep, she craves my touch.

I move lower to her nipples, lightly circling around each one before going back and forth between them. The rise and fall of her chest increases. I want to slam into her until she screams my name and comes around my cock. I want to tell her what a good girl she is as she takes all of me. She's not ready for that yet. For now, I'll settle for these small touches. My hand cups her breast, squeezing until she hums in approval. The way her body reacts to me is beyond my expectations. I roll her peaks between my fingers, and her hips raise slightly. Her lips part, but no sound escapes.

I didn't plan for her to allow me to touch her like this in her sleep. I slip just under the top of her panties and run my hand along the edge, waiting to see whether or not she will wake up. Her hips continue to lift subconsciously, a silent invitation that I am happy to accept.

I slide my hand up and down her entrance, and she moans again, spreading her legs for me to have better access. Gradually, I push a finger into her warm pussy before gently moving in and out. She's so wet for me already. I pull out of her after a few minutes and lick her wetness from my finger. I was right. She tastes absolutely amazing.

A small whimper leaves her lips at the loss of my touch. I'll give you whatever you want, wanderer. My other hand comes down to caress the side of her face and she leans into the touch. I trace my thumb along her bottom lip again, smirking to myself when her eyes finally peek open.

"Open," I tell her. She parts her lips obediently for me, and my thumb slides right in. The feel of her wet mouth has me wanting her on her knees. "Suck." Those luscious lips close around my thumb. "Good girl."

Focusing back on her soaking pussy, I gather her moisture and bring it up to her clit before pressing down on it. She moans louder, her hands fisting the sheets next to her. I rub small circles, watching her writhe under my control, her eyes never leaving me the entire time.

Little by little, I glide my fingers back down to her entrance and shove two deep inside her. She whines and arches her back off the bed. My other hand leaves her mouth, and I use it to focus on her clit while I pump two fingers in and out of her, the sound of her wetness filling the air. Her breathing quickens, and I feel her walls tighten around me. I know she's close, so I curve the tips of my fingers inside her, hitting that perfect spot. She lets out a scream as her pussy clenches and spasms around my fingers. "That's a good fucking girl," I tell her.

After adjusting my cock, I bring my fingers back up to my lips and suck them clean. I want her to know what she does to me. "You come apart so beautifully, wanderer," I murmur, and she closes her eyes for the briefest moment, like those words were exactly what she needed to hear from me.

She looks down at my bulge, and I know she wants to return the favor. I'm tempted, but this isn't about me tonight. Tonight was to help her feel safe with me.

"Not tonight," I tell her, and she simply nods.

The blanket is still bunched down past her knees, so I pull it up, walk over to the table we have set up for her, and sit in the chair so I can watch her for a bit. "Go to sleep, Callie. You've been so good for us the last few days that we're going to reward you. I'll come back to take you up to our pool for a bit tomorrow if that's something you think you'd like."

"Ye- Yes, I would love that. Thank you," she stutters. Her voice was barely a whisper. It's the first words she has spoken to me since I've come down here, and I want to hear more.

"I'll be back to get you tomorrow then. Rest up, beautiful." She closes her eyes and does just what she is told, like the good girl I know she wants to be for me.

Chapter 12
Callie

What the hell got into me last night? I just let him do whatever he wanted to me and lay there, not saying a word. I'm not that girl, but being here and not knowing who they are or what they want has me so confused. Part of me thinks the right move is to be pliant, while the other part says to stop being such a weak bitch, show them you're strong, and don't blindly accept things from them.

I find it strange how comfortable I feel around him, the one that visits my room at night. He seems gentle. I'm not naive enough to believe he's a saint. He's one of the reasons I'm locked in this damn room. It was dark, so I couldn't make out much of his features, but the way he looked down at me when I woke up to him touching me made me feel protected. Thinking about his hands running over my body has me biting my lip and wishing he would come back.

I've always craved a dominating touch from someone. Julian was gentle with me. He got me off sometimes but never fully gave me what I needed in the bedroom.

This is all a prime example of exactly how messed up my mind is right now. I'm comparing sex with my fiancé, ex-fiancé, fuck I don't even know what he is at this point, to a stranger who kidnapped me. Way to go, Callie, you're one bad bitch. A random man touches you, and you melt like butter. I really need to get myself together if I'm going to find a way out of here.

He told me he's taking me to a pool today. I didn't say no because seeing something besides the same white walls is something I desperately crave. All morning I've been sitting at this stupid fucking table, about to lose my mind from boredom. I can't say for certain how long I've been down here. My guess would put me at a few days, but there's no concept of time without windows, and I'm not sure how long I was passed out when they first brought me here. The drug could have had me unconscious for a few hours or a few days, depending on how my body handled it or if they kept injecting me.

Meals have all been brought at random times. One day, they brought a ton of food all at once, and another time, I waited a long time in between each meal drop. Before last night, there was no interaction with them outside of the little slot under the mirror opening and closing.

I learned to tell the difference between who brought the supplies based on how they smelled. The one who likes to watch me sleep smells like irises. One of them smells like leather, and another smells like vetiver. I've noticed three distinct smells so far. There may be more who haven't been put on delivery duty, but right now, I know there are at least three of them.

In the time I've been here, I've read six books from the stack on the floor and made good use of the notebook. The crayons have been a bitch to try and use to journal with, but I wanted to write down everything that I could remember since the day at the falls. I realize there is a 99% chance there's at least one camera in here, and they can see everything I write, but I don't care. The reminders are for me to keep my mind sharp. I still don't know what they want with me. If they found out the connection between me and my father, I might actually be fucked, and not in a good way. My father would lay the world at their feet to get me back.

A strange scraping sound emits from the other side of the room, and I look over to see the door has opened. A man with bright blue eyes is staring at me. I get a whiff of a familiar scent: iris. This is my nighttime visitor. Seeing him in the light for the first time causes my stomach to flutter.

He's tall with strong arms that have tattoos covering the length of one of them. His hair is a dusty blonde cut short on the sides but longer on the top with a length that has it sweeping over to the side in the most casual way. My eyes trail down his body glancing at the tattoos down his arms and landing on his hands in his pockets.

Memories of what those hands did to me last night flash in my mind. Immediately, I shoot my eyes back up to his, and he grins like he knows exactly what I was thinking. Are you fucking kidding me? Even his smile is gorgeous. He reaches out a hand in my direction, wanting me to take it, and I look at him with caution.

"If you're done eye fucking me, we can get you out of this room for a bit. Unless you prefer to stay here and find another way to occupy our time, I am more than willing to oblige." Cheesing from ear to ear, he wiggles his eyebrows at that last comment.

I shake my head and walk over, placing my hand in his to placate him. He interlocks our fingers and leads me to my first glimpse of sunlight since being taken. It's weird holding hands with him. Warmth spreads through my entire body, but it's also chilling at the same time. I'm pulled to him in a way I don't understand.

We walked through a small room outside my cell with a few chairs. Glancing back at the other side of the mirror, my suspicions are confirmed: two-way glass. These creepy fuckers were down here watching me. We go through another doorway that leads to a set of stairs and climb up to some kind of storage room. I look around, but nothing really stands out.

As we emerge, my free hand comes up to cover my eyes. The brightness from the sun is blinding. When my eyes adjust, I take in my surroundings. The room is your typical pool house. Full windows run the entire length with views of the pool and a house behind it. Some furniture is scattered through the space, and a full-length bar is next to the doorway we walked out of. The man who brought me up here has taken a seat in one of the chairs and is watching me closely.

Feeling brave, I make myself right at home by walking over to the bar and grabbing the first bottle of top-shelf whiskey I see. I need something quick to calm my nerves. I pop the top off and bring the bottle right to my lips, downing a few swigs. The man's eyebrows raise, and he laughs. Gesturing the bottle toward him, I ask, "Want a drink?"

"No, but please continue to help yourself." His eyes never leave me with every move I make.

I grab a glass and pour myself a hefty amount before sauntering over to the chair across from him and sitting down.

Wasting no time, I jump right into what I want to know. "Who are you?"

"There it is. I'm surprised it took you this long to ask with how calm you've been over the last week."

A week. I've been here a whole fucking week in that room. Sipping on my drink, I try my best to continue the conversation and hopefully steer it in the right direction. "I wasn't in the mood to talk."

"Clearly," he says. He knows I'm up to no good. "I'm Kyler, and while I'm sure you have a bunch of questions to throw at me, we aren't going into specifics today. We're here to swim and unwind since you've been cooped up in that dark room for so long. If today goes well, we can fully discuss everything you want to know." I open my mouth, but he interrupts me. "I grabbed a few swimsuits for you to choose from unless you don't want to wear one. The choice is entirely up to you, but you're getting in that pool today one way or another." With a wink, he sets the shopping bag in my lap.

Pulling the first swimsuit out of the bag, I see that it has a black thong bottom and immediately dismiss that option, tossing it to the side.

"Damn, I was really pulling for that one," he says while chuckling.

The next suit is red with white polka dots. The top is your standard halter top, and the bottoms are just classic bikini bottoms, though they still appear to be a bit cheeky. The last one in the bag is the one that ends up being my winning choice. It's a navy-blue suit with high-waisted bottoms and a spaghetti-strap top. It's the least revealing of the bunch, and even though my tits will be fully on display, I don't mind. Part of me thinks I should reconsider the thong suit strictly because I might be able to lull him in with my body, but my D cups will have to be good enough for the job. With the way he's been acting around me, I doubt I even need to try. I can tell this one will be wrapped around my finger in no time.

"Where can I change?" As soon as the words leave my mouth, I realize it's a stupid question. There's no way he's letting me out of his sight, even if it's just to go into a bathroom. My question goes unanswered. He just leans back in the seat, lifts his leg to place his ankle over his knee, and puts a hand behind his head, grinning like a damn fool.

Take a breath, Callie. Don't let this man rattle you. I decide to go for the bottoms first since the shirt I am wearing hangs down a little over my ass. I drop my leggings and underwear and go to slide my suit bottoms up over my leg, but I'm feeling a little wobbly. Apparently, I drank too much whiskey to calm my nerves because I manage to fall right onto my ass, exposing everything to him that I was trying not to. Quickly, I rush back to my feet and finish pulling them up before turning around to rip off my shirt and put the top on as fast as possible. I glance over at Kyler and see his gaze transfixed on me.

He stands and pulls off his shirt, revealing his tattooed chest and abs that I could wash clothing on. Intricate designs swirl around one another, weaving a story that I am so curious to unravel. He grabs his belt and pulls it free from his jeans in one swoop, sending a jolt of electricity right to my core.

"Should I set this aside for later?" he asks while eyeing me curiously. Before I can answer, he chucks the belt to the side and strips down to only a pair of dark grey boxer briefs. My eyes roam to the bulge between his legs. "If you keep looking at me like I'm a snack, I may have to give you something to eat."

Fuck, he did not just say that to me. I avert my eyes and stare out the window, so he walks up to me and grabs my hand again. "Come on, little wanderer. Let's go swim."

The pool is a long rectangular-shaped inground pool with stairs on one end and a hot tub area on the other. I slowly walk in until the water rises above my shoulders. There is a small ledge around the entirety of the pool that allows you to sit inside the water, so after a few minutes, I prop my ass on it and take a moment to enjoy the warmth of the sun on my skin. Water is my safe space, and even though it's not the same as the falls, being here allows me some time to forget my reality.

My thoughts drift to Julian and Avery. Are they looking for me? I'm still unsure of how I feel about Julian and his lies, but I miss Avery so much. She must think I ran off even though I promised her I wouldn't.

Kyler cannonballs into the pool, splashing water all over me, and I scowl at him. "I thought the whole point of you bringing me up here was so that I could enjoy myself outside of the cage you have me in," I shout out.

"Oh, that's what you thought?" He swims over in my direction. "What if I told you the real reason, I brought you up here was so that I could see you in that." A finger points to my swimsuit.

"If that's the reason, then I would tell you it's a waste of time because we both know there are cameras in that room, and if you really wanted to, you could see me any way you want." He positions himself in front of me between my legs that are dangling off the ledge.

"That's true, but it's not the same. I wouldn't get to be this close to you." His fingers trace along the infinity symbol on my wrist that I got in memory of Maxton. I knew there were cameras. At least he confirmed my suspicions on that. He lightly grips my jaw and turns my head until our eyes meet. "You like it when I'm close to you, don't you?"

I swallow hard. Do I like it? My mind is telling me no, but my body is telling me a whole different story. Thinking about what this man could potentially do to me has my body on fire. He slowly trails his finger down my neck, across my collarbone, and into my cleavage. I take a breath as he pulls his hand away and slowly leans down, using his tongue to trace up the same path his finger just took. My eyes close, and my head tilts to the side to give him better access to my neck. When his lips finally meet mine, I allow them to part and let him in. What starts out slow becomes more passionate. His hand weaves itself into my hair, pulling my head back and leaving me gasping for air.

"I think you like it when you don't have control. You like the idea of being held here against your will by a strange man. You're so willing to give yourself to me. Tell me, Callie, if I wanted to take you right here, right now, would you fight me? Would you let me fuck that sweet pussy?"

Would I? The honest answer is yes, even though I don't think he would take it that far. He pulls me back into him for another devouring kiss, his tongue sliding inside of my mouth, causing me to moan in approval.

"Yeah, that's what I thought," he says before swimming away. My body feels colder at the loss of him. What the hell is this man doing to me? Am I developing some sort of Stockholm syndrome?

We swim for a few more hours before I notice a second man appear from the house. He is a little taller than Kyler, with sleeves of tattoos going down both his arms and along his hands. I can't quite make out what they are. His hair is dark brown and clipped short on the top with a fade along the sides. I don't have time to pick up many more of his features because as fast as he appeared, he disappeared.

"Who was that?" I ask, but again, my question gets ignored.

"Come on, let's go eat," Kyler mutters in my direction.

I hesitate as he pulls himself out of the pool and reaches down to lend me his hand. We walk to a nearby chair to pick up the towels before making our way to the sandwiches in the pool house. I quickly grab mine to eat it, not even looking to see what it is. Letting myself starve won't accomplish anything.

Kyler sighs and looks up at me. "I really hate to do this, but I have some things I need to handle this evening, so when you're finished, I have to take you back downstairs."

"Will you come visit me again tonight?" The words slip out before I even have a chance to realize what I just confessed.

"If you want me there, I'm sure I can make some time for a visit."

"I don't like being alone so much. I miss having someone to talk to." My eyes cast down at the floor. I don't want to see his face. I'm struggling to figure out if I'm telling him this as part of my plan or as an admission.

"Hopefully soon we can bring you up to the main house, so you have better access to me and the others." I gaze up at him and see his eyes grow wide for a brief second. He immediately gets up and starts cleaning up our mess as if he realized he had let something slip out that he shouldn't have. The others? How many of them are there?

Chapter 13
Julian

I came home from my trip, and she's still not home. The trip ended up being longer than I planned, but something about this isn't right. I should've heard from her by now. Fights like that never happen between the two of us, but she kept asking me all those questions about Nashville. Just more stress I don't need.

This whole acquisition has been one thing after another, and the weight of it all just keeps piling on top of me. I need to make sure everything is perfect. We only have a short time left before the last few pieces fall into place and life calms down again. I don't know why I didn't just tell her from the start that I've been going to Nashville for the trips. That was an oversight I now regret.

I overheard her talking with Avery once about how that city brings up bad memories for her, so I thought it would be easier on her if I didn't mention it. I wanted to spare her from having any negative thoughts because I know there are things she hasn't felt comfortable opening up to me about yet.

Sure, I lied, but I lied to protect her. I thought she would at least give me the opportunity to explain myself. I need her to be happy. I need her to want to be with me. I know I can convince her what I did was the right decision if she just talked to me. When everything was happening, and she stormed out of the room, I expected her to go in the other room to cool off, maybe take a few hours to herself, and then come back out to talk things through, but she went straight to her car and left. This reaction is definitely not like her.

I suppose it was only a matter of time before a fight like this happened. You can't have a perfect relationship all the time. We will grow from this. I know we will. She is mistaken if she thinks that one little lie will be enough for her to end things between the two of us. I won't let her go that easily. I'll fight for her. She's everything I want, everything I need. My future with her is bright and strong. She told me she was done, but I won't let it end like this.

I tried to call her a few hours after she left, but her phone rang in the other room. It's a bit odd that she didn't come back for it while I was away. I'm going to find her. I need to find her, or the last year will have been completely pointless. I put so much time and dedication into building trust with her, and I know she was so close to opening up to me. She was going to finally tell me about her past and why she is so reluctant to get close to anyone.

Today, I decided enough is enough. It's time for me to call Avery and tell her to come home. Her friend isn't my biggest fan. She's most likely telling her to cut ties with me completely and move on, that I'm some kind of evil person. She's always treated me like the bad guy, even though I have never done anything to her. My response to her standoffishness has always been to keep my distance from her.

I don't have Avery's number saved in my phone, so I use Callie's to call her. The phone only rings once before she answers with a raging ball of fury. I click the speaker button just in time for her to start yelling.

"It's about damn time bitch. I was about to send out a search party for your ass. I thought you left me despite our clear conversations about this," she yells through the phone.

"Uh, hello?" I retort.

"Julian? Put Callie on the phone now!"

"What do you mean put her on? She's not with you?"

"If she was with me, why would I tell you to put her on the phone? For fucks sake. Let me talk to her."

"Avery, this is serious. If she's not with you, I don't know where she is. When's the last time you saw her?"

"When I left your house last week."

"Have you spoken to her since then?" I ask her.

"No, I haven't talked to her. Where the hell is she?" she yells.

"That's what I am trying to figure out. I just assumed she was staying with you." My tone is shorter than usual.

"Why would she be staying with me? How long has it been since you've seen her?" she asks.

"Maybe a few hours after you did. We got into a big fight, and she stormed out," I say.

"She stormed out, and you didn't immediately chase after her? Yeah, that tracks."

"Look, I'm aware you don't like me, but can you keep the sarcasm to yourself while we figure this out? I thought she would take a breather at your house for a few days and come right back."

"Julian, it's been a week, and you're JUST NOW calling me to see if she is here!! What kind of person goes a whole week without seeing or hearing from their fiancé before checking on them?"

I'm not going to tell her that she said we're done. I know she didn't mean it. Fuck, she's right. I should've checked sooner. Frustrated, I run my fingers through my hair as I pace around the room.

"I thought she was ok. I honestly thought she was with you and that she would come home when she was ready so we could talk," I admit.

Avery sighs. "Well, she's not here. I have no idea where else she could be because my best friend's shitty fiancé just told me she's been missing for a week. You know, unlike you, I actually care about her safety. What if she's hurt or something. We literally would have no way of knowing because you waited a fucking week to check on her."

"Her phone is here, but I have an idea. There is a tracker in her car. I should be able to log in to the app and see where it is," I say.

"You put a tracker on her car? Again, you wonder why I don't like you. You're literally a psycho. I'm going to go out on a limb here and say she didn't agree to this tracker being placed. You're really out there being a creep and watching everywhere she goes. What the fuck asshole!"

"Look, I know there are things she hasn't told me about her childhood. I'm sure you know everything since you apparently know her better than me, but I wasn't sure what sort of demons were in her past. I did it as a precaution. If something ever happened to her, like right now, I would have a way to find her. I'm not watching her location all the time." I walk into my office to grab my phone and pull up the app. "It says she's at the supermarket. The one downtown."

I'm a little confused as to why she would go there and who she's actually staying with, considering her best friend is on the phone with me, and she isn't with her.

"Come pick me up before you go to her. If she's pissed at you, she most likely won't want to see your face. I can check on her and find out what's going on," Avery tells me.

"I'll come get you, but I'm not letting her out of my sight until she talks to me. It was one stupid fight. Be ready and waiting outside your house. I'm leaving now and will be there shortly."

I pocket Callie's phone along with mine and grab my keys to head out the door. The sooner I get a chance to talk with her, the better. I haven't been able to calm my nerves since Avery told me she's not with her. What the hell am I going to do if she is actually missing? I need her by my side.

My drive is quick, and Avery slides into my passenger seat without a word as we make our way to the supermarket. I pull in and drive around until I find her car parked in the midst of all the others. We wait a few minutes for her to come out of the store after noticing her car is empty, but after about 20 minutes, she still hasn't come out. I find myself getting impatient. This cheap tracking app only gives the vehicle's location, so I have no way of knowing how long she has been inside.

"I'm going inside to find her," I say and throw my door open to head into the store. The passenger door slams behind me, and I turn back to see Avery walking a few steps behind me.

"You didn't think I was going to let you go in alone, did you? If Callie doesn't want to be around you, I won't allow you to force her to stay."

We walk up and down the aisles, all while watching the tracker on the phone to make sure it doesn't move.

"I don't think she's in here," Avery says, and then I catch her saying something under her breath that I don't think she wanted me to hear. "She left without me."

I spin around, placing myself right in front of her. "What did you say? Left without you?"

She sighs and starts walking around me, out of the store. "Fuck, look, it's not my place to give specific details, but before coming here, Callie never stayed in a town longer than a few months. If her car's here, then she most likely jumped on a bus and left town. She's not stupid, and we won't find her unless she wants us to."

"The Callie I know would never leave me without talking to me first." The frustration in my tone is evident.

"You didn't know everything about her, Julian. You know the Callie she WANTED you to know. That doesn't make it the real her."

Is it possible that I don't know my girl? There's no way. I drop Avery off back at her house and head home to try and formulate some sort of next step to figure out where she is. She has no money, no phone, no car, and no job. There has to be something I'm missing here. I refuse to believe she just up and left me over one silly fight.

Chapter 14
Callie

I'm back in this little cell, sitting on the bed, staring off into space. He kissed me. I can still feel his lips on me, trying to devour a piece of my soul. I bring my finger up to my lip and gently rub it as I get lost in thoughts of the kiss. Not long ago, I would have never wanted anyone to kiss me besides Julian. He hurt me, and that set off a string of events that led me here to this very moment.

I should feel bad about kissing someone else. What kind of person does it make me to admit that I enjoyed another man kissing me when there is a man who is probably frantically searching for me at this moment in time?

My fingers continue tracing over my lips as I think about the moment he grabbed my hair. Nobody's ever touched me like that. It was gentle yet demanding, like no matter what I tried to say, he was going to take what he wanted from me. He had complete control, and I was all too willing to surrender it to him.

Kyler seems like a nice guy, similar to Julian, but he has a dark side to him to balance out that sweet side. That's how my brain is internalizing this whole situation. I see the two of them with so many similarities that I make excuses that it's all ok. Julian turned out to be a liar. Is Kyler also a liar? I don't want to stick around long enough to find out. My priorities are getting myself out of here, finding a way to contact Avery, and moving on to the next part of my life.

I need to figure out exactly where I am, considering I have no idea. We could have driven 10 miles down the road or 10 hours when they took me. I have no way of knowing. I noticed from being up at the pool that there don't seem to be any other houses nearby. They likely don't have close neighbors, so that option is out. Why would they take that risk just to have someone call the police?

My thoughts drift back to Kyler telling me he thinks I want to be seduced by my captor. He's not wrong. There's something about him that I'm drawn to. I find myself hoping he stops to visit me in this hell hole tonight. I'm telling myself it's so I can keep trying to sway him into catching feelings for me. Even as I think that I realize the lines have started to blur on my end. He's been a constant thought since the first night here.

There's nothing to do in this damn place. My mind is too fucked up right now to read or write, so I have resigned myself to my own personal workout plan. It involves walking in circles in this small ass room, and well, nothing, that's it, I'm just walking in circles. I'm pretty sure I've done close to 200 laps at this point when I hear someone speak through the room. "If you keep walking in circles, you'll get dizzy."

"Kyler?" I question.

"Not Kyler, princess, but I'll be sure to let him know you're staying active."

"Who are you?" I yell out, but I don't get any additional responses. Maybe the voices were actually in my head, and I imagined it. I keep walking, occasionally changing directions, trying to pass the time.

Kyler taking me up to the pool was one of the worst things he could have done. I was fine living down here, not knowing how much time has passed or thinking about the outside world. Ever since being up there and coming back down here, the darkness in this room feels so much darker. These walls feel like they're closing in on me. I miss human interaction. It's all feeling eerily familiar to the darkness of my father. I don't like the person I am becoming due to this seclusion. I pride myself on always being strong and capable of handling anything, but right now, I have doubts. This is the first time I've had to prove that strength, and here I am, starting to crumble under the pressure after only one week.

The lights click off, and my thoughts drift to Kyler as I walk over to the bed and lie down. He makes me feel more alive than I have in a long time. The last time I felt a pull this strong was when I was with Maxton.

My dreams take me back to one of the nights Maxton and I snuck out to look at the stars. He showed up with a whole picnic basket filled with different fruits and cheeses, then told me that since we couldn't go on a real date, he was bringing the date to me. We laid on a blanket in the field behind our houses, and I closed my eyes as he fed me. We made it into this cute game where I had to guess the fruit he was feeding me. It was so sweet and sensual that we reached second base before we both got too nervous to continue. My heart feels so full and happy here in this memory of him. I allow my mind to fill itself with the sound of his laughter and the feeling of his arms around me in a warm embrace. I wish I could stay here in this memory forever. Even after all these years, my heart still aches for him.

I feel the bed sink beside me, and I jolt awake, eyes snapping open. Kyler is sitting next to me with a look that I can only describe as a mixture of happiness and pain. Is he struggling with seeing me? Was I wrong to ask him to visit tonight?

"Is everything okay?" I ask.

"Everything's fine, wanderer," Kyler says.

I glance at his hand and see him holding a big bundle of flowers. It's dark, so I can't quite make them out, but the gesture alone is enough to pull at my heart. "What are those for?"

"They're for you, wanderer."

"For me?" I ask with confusion.

"Well, yeah, they're not for me, and my brothers wouldn't really care about pink flowers."

Tears well up in my eyes. "Nobody's ever bought me flowers before," I tell him, slightly ashamed at my admission.

"Well, that's a damn shame. You deserve beautiful things all the time."

He reaches toward my face and rubs his thumb along my bottom lip.

"I was wondering if it would be ok if I stayed with you tonight." I wasn't expecting him to ask that. Usually, he pops in and out while I'm sleeping but is never around by morning. The scent of him always lingers as a small reminder that he was there. Admitting I want him near me would show weakness, so I find a way to use this small bit of vulnerability in him to learn a little about him.

"I'll consider it, but only if you tell me something about you. I barely know you," I tell him.

He considers my request for a moment, then nods. "My mother was killed when I was five, and I spent almost my entire life in and out of foster homes.."

Well, fuck, I guess we are just jumping right into the deep end. I was expecting him to tell me his favorite color or food. I shift myself on the bed to focus on his words as he continues.

"One day, she was on her way to pick me up from kindergarten, and the next day, we were burying her. She was a victim of some botched drug deal and was unlucky enough to walk past a group of men at the same time someone decided to shoot at them. If you can't put the pieces together, she ended up in the crossfire and was killed immediately. A few years after I aged out of the system, the guys and I tracked down the guy who fired the gun that took her life. I had my own special little party with him and made sure he felt every ounce of pain I felt after losing her. He got to experience every hit, burn, and kick that I experienced over the years in the system. It was a pretty therapeutic moment for me, actually."

He looks over at me to see my reaction to his story, and my heart hurts for him. The man just told me that he brutally murdered at least one person, but all I heard was his struggle. I'm happy he got his revenge on the man who changed his life. I hope one day I'll have that same kind of therapeutic moment between me and my father. When he realizes his confession doesn't scare me, he continues.

"Anyway, after I got my revenge on the son of a bitch, I was finally able to focus on moving forward with my life. The guys and I built up a name for ourselves, and we've been working jobs and stacking up money to eventually retire and live a life with zero needs."

He has a whole plan for his life, but he can't be much older than me. This admission has me swooning a little. I'm a whole ass mess who can barely make ends meet because I spend my life running from my problems. He took a different route and faced his head-on. If I took that approach all those years ago, I wonder how different my life would be?

"You can stay," I say, scooting myself over as far as I can to make room for him. The mood is too heavy, so I try to lighten it with a joke. "Sorry for the tight accommodations. I requested a queen, but those rooms must've been booked before arriving."

He chuckles and stands up briefly to undress. For the second time now, he is next to me in only a pair of boxer briefs, and a jolt of anxiety shoots through me. What did I agree to? I keep telling myself that I am being cooperative because I want him to fall for me, but that's not entirely true. I said yes to him staying because I want to feel him next to me. He slides under the covers and lays down practically on top of me, turning into me so that our noses almost touch. His arm wraps around my waist, and he pulls me even closer to him. I can feel the warmth of his breath on my cheek.

"If you continue being so good for me, I might have to upgrade you to that queen-size room you requested," he whispers.

My breath hitches as his hand slides down my body until it's firmly cupping my ass. I find myself pushing my hips into the most intimate part of him. My body comes alive when he touches me. I have no control, and it's a real fucking problem. He hardens against me and lets out a growl as I clench my thighs to relieve the tension building up inside me. My body wants him. If he wants to take me right now, I won't have it in me to fight him. Submitting sounds so much more fun.

"So beautiful," he whispers to me. His hand slides from my ass to under my thigh, and in one swift motion, he pulls up on my leg and hitches it over his hip. I am so thankful I decided to sleep in a shirt and panties. I can feel every part of our skin that is pressed against each other. There's a flaming heat building between the two of us.

"Tell me, Callie. If I were to slide inside you right now, would you take it all for me like a good girl?"

"Yes," I whisper. His words send a chill through every nerve in my body. More than anything, I want to be a good girl for him.

He brings his mouth to my neck and licks up the length of it, stopping to bite the sensitive spot right under my ear. A hiss escapes me as my nails dig into his bicep, small crescent moons taking shape on his skin. His hand slides between my legs to tease me. I push my hips forward to nudge him in the direction I want him to go, and he grins against my neck. His fingers slide into my panties and rub against me. The feeling sends an electrical current through my entire body, and I bask in it.

Out of nowhere, I'm rolled onto my back with him hovering over me. He leans down to kiss me, and I can taste the lingering whiskey on his breath. His body slides lower, grabbing my panties and gliding them down to my ankles. I manage to pull each foot out before the bed shifts, and I feel him between my legs. My body tenses at the thought of him being so close, and I know he senses my hesitation.

He glances up as I prop myself up on my elbows to watch his every move. Slowly, my legs are pushed apart as wide as they will go, and kisses are peppered along the length of them. His eyes meet mine when he gets close to my center. A warm breath blows onto my clit, and my whole body shivers in response. I bring my pussy to his face as my personal invitation for him to feast on me, and he fully accepts. He uses both hands to spread me wide and runs his tongue up the length of me before flicking it lightly over my clit.

"Yes, just like that." I gasp before throwing my head back and running my fingers through his hair. Shamelessly, I grind myself on his face, begging for more.

He comes up for a breath, and two fingers slam into me, thrusting in and out. I scream in response when his mouth latches onto my clit, and my pussy spasms around him. My orgasm begins to build, but he pulls his fingers out of me and brings them up to my mouth. "See how sweet you taste." I wrap my tongue around his fingers, licking myself off of him, a groan of approval oozing from his lips.

"I brought a condom, but I would prefer to feel you bare," he tells me as his fingers pull from my mouth, and he stands to shrug off his boxers. I've never let a man fuck me bare before, but I don't want a barrier between us.

"I have an implant, and I'm clean," I confess. When I ran from Rogue, getting an implant was one of the first things I did. I wasn't going to risk accidentally getting knocked up while living a life on the run, and if my father ever found me, he would never know I had it.

"I'm clean. We all are," he tells me. The words *we all* stand out to me. I feel his eyes on me, waiting for me to make my decision.

"I want to feel you," I whisper.

He doesn't hesitate to grab my legs and drag me closer to him. I wrap myself around his hips, and he slowly pushes into me. Fuck, he's big, so much bigger than I'm used to. I feel the way his cock stretches me, and I let out a satisfying moan. He pushes himself into me, one inch at a time, until he bottoms out. I close my eyes and bask in the sensation of him inside me.

"Yes, that's it, take all of me," he tells me as he moves in and out slowly, at first, letting my body become accustomed to his size. He reaches down to tear my shirt down the center, and I wrap my arms around his neck to bring him closer to me. As his pace picks up, our bodies begin bouncing off one another, and the feel of his warm skin on mine is amazing. "Fuck, it's like you were made for me, Callie."

He leans in to kiss up the length of my neck, nibbling, and sucking along the way. I know there will be a trail of bruises there in the morning, but I don't care. All I am focused on at this moment is him, and the way our bodies are melded together. He slowly drags himself out of me before pushing back in, repeatedly, thrusting harder and harder each time. I moan, gripping onto his shoulders while I thrust my hips up to meet his. He pushes into me harder this time, and I cry out.

"Tell me to stop if it's too much," he whispers in my ear.

"Don't you dare stop," I say.

Our bodies move together in a steady rhythm, climbing up this imaginary mountain we've created for ourselves, every part of me heating up along the way. I shouldn't be enjoying this. I shouldn't want this, but I can't help myself. I take a deep breath, and the smell of iris consumes me. He slams into me, hard, again. My pussy clenches, and I moan with pleasure. Fuck, he feels so good.

His mouth meets mine in an all-consuming kiss. Our tongues tangle together in a war of dominance, while our bodies continue to move in sync with one another. Every action has my body burning hotter for him. The fire in me continuing to build to the point of near combustion while he thrusts into me. He leans in to grope and massage my breasts, and I hum in approval.

"Please," I whine, unsure of what I'm even asking for. I want everything he is willing to give me at this moment.

"I can't get enough of you," he groans.

His fingers meet my nipples, and he twists them gently, sending shots of electricity through my body. My breathing picks up, and I can feel myself on the precipice of an orgasm. He slams into me harder, keeping up with his quickening pace. The sound of my wetness fills the air as each thrust becomes more powerful than the last.

"Be a good girl for me, and come on my cock."

My pussy clenches at his command, and everything around me explodes. I clamp down on him hard while riding out the high. He doesn't let up. My body doesn't even have a chance to cool itself down before I find my core heating back up. Nobody has ever made me feel like this before during sex.

He pulls out of me, and I protest at the momentary loss. He lies down on the bed and pulls me on top of him, gliding my hips up and down his length. My body instantly reacts to the feeling of him back inside me. I feel so full. It feels right and wrong at the same time. His arms reach out, and he grabs my hips tightly, moving them back and forth. I grind down on him, chasing another round of pleasure. I tilt my head back and cry out when his cock rubs the perfect spot inside of me.

"Eyes on me, Callie."

"Kyler?" I question him.

"You look like a fucking queen riding my cock like that, wanderer."

I've never been with someone so focused on meeting my needs first.

"You take me so well. Now, give me another one."

His words echo in my thoughts as my body takes what it needs from him. I place my hands on his chest, grinding my hips down as tingles spread through me. His thumb finds my clit, and shock waves consume my entire body. The growing flames erupt, and my pussy clenches around him as I find my release. There's no way to stop it. I come so hard around him, clenching and spasming while he continues pumping into me.

"Good fucking girl."

I slump down on his chest, and he thrusts himself into me. His hips lift off the bed, thrusting at a renewed pace while he chases his own release. When warm liquid fills me, I look up at him. He pauses for a moment, tilting his head to the side, "Where have you been hiding?"

"I like to be invisible," I reply.

He pulls out, and I can feel him dripping from me. Reality sets in with what I just did, and I feel ashamed. I grab my panties, pull them back onto me, and drag the covers up over my body to hide myself. My fists ball at my sides as he sits up on the bed. I can't believe I just let him fuck me.

"Do you still want me to stay, or did this change things?" he cautiously asks.

"I don't know," I confess. My mind is split down the middle, a full internal struggle. One part is saying that I made a mistake by letting him have this piece of me, and the other part is begging to give him more.

"Let me just lay here with you for a bit, and if you start to feel like you don't want me around, you can kick me out. How's that sound?"

"I guess that would be fine. Like I said, though, my bed is a little small."

"That just means I get to snuggle up closer to you, wanderer."

"Why do you call me that? Wanderer?" I inquire.

"I watched you before we brought you here. You have an energy surrounding you. The best way to describe it is you aren't lost, but you also haven't found your place in the world yet. A wandering soul. It was one of the things that drew me to you. It's like you are looking for a place to belong, but nothing quite fits."

"You don't know anything about me," I hissed, irritated by how right he might actually be. I shove out of the bed and walk to the makeshift bathroom to clean the remnants of him off of me.

"I know enough," he spits back. "Where you work, your best friend, your fucking loser of an ex, who, by the way, waited an entire week before he started looking for you, the grocery store you shop at every week, the takeout order from the Chinese place in town that you love so much, chicken and beef with mushrooms and white rice. I thought it was weird at first, but

I tried it and fucking loved it. It's my go-to order now." I wish I could keep the shock off my face as he continues. "Watching you and learning about you has become my favorite pastime. You consume all of my thoughts."

His words are like a knife to my heart. "He waited a week before looking for me?" Tears well up in my eyes.

"Yes, he doesn't deserve you, Callie. He never did. That man was always pretending around you every time we watched him. I don't know exactly what he's hiding, but something is there."

I really mattered that little to him that he waited an entire week before looking for me. Resentment sets in, and I'm almost grateful that I was taken from him. I would have most likely made my way back to him and accepted whatever line of bullshit he used to get me to fall back in line and get back together. If he really loved me, there's no way he would have waited that long to try to find me. My anger at Kyler dissipates, and I make my way back over to the bed with him. He runs a hand along my cheek.

"There's something I wanted to ask you, wanderer."

"At this point, you can ask me anything," I admit.

"How do you feel about moving to the house instead of staying here?"

"Would I have to stay in the basement or another cage?" My tone is a little more nervous than usual.

"No, but we don't have a room prepared for you, so you would be staying with me or my brother, Barrett. We would have to sit down together for you to meet him. He has been wanting to talk to you as well. You'll still be closely watched and won't be permitted to leave the house without one of us accompanying you, but it will give you more free reign than you have in here. We have a pretty impressive home gym with punching bags if you ever want something to pound on besides me." My eyes instantly roll at his last remark.

"If you're giving me a choice, then I think I want to stay with you. I don't want to be here by myself anymore."

He nods. "Tomorrow, I'll take you up to the house to meet my brother, and we can get you situated in my room. Now go to sleep." One arm wraps around my waist to pull me closer, while the other traces the tattoo on my wrist. It's a soothing gesture that I'm starting to love. I find myself snuggling in, and before I know it, my eyelids feel heavy, and sleep takes me under.

Chapter 15
Barrett

Today's the day we move Callie to the house. The guys and I had lengthy discussions about this, and we all agreed it was time. Leaving her alone below the pool house any longer might mess with her head, and that's not our intention. She's just a tool to get to our bigger goal: answers from Gabriel or her if she has them. Hurting her, at this point in time, won't solve anything; in fact, it would likely make matters worse.

Seb still believes the girl might know something, and for now, we play nice. I think that's a risky move, considering Kyler is already hooked on her. I see the allure and enjoy watching her from a distance, but allowing him to continue playing with her could complicate things further. If she doesn't know anything and we have to use her as bait for her father, I don't know how Ky would handle that. He would, of course, do anything for Seb and me, but he likes this girl, so it would hurt him in the process.

I'll keep watching her through the feeds I have set up in the room we put her in. I admit she's beautiful, and I'd love to see how she handles a little pain. Would she crave it like I do?

I've been scrolling through my camera feeds for the last hour, seeing what I can pick up on her friend, Avery. We entertained the possibility of taking her friend to convince Callie to be more willing to talk to us. That would be a worst-case scenario, of course. Getting more people involved would further complicate our situation. If we go that route, we'll have to kill her friend, and we try our best not to kill innocents. She seems to be a regular civilian, but we don't need people like that knowing of our existence.

Avery isn't as easy to track as Callie was. Her movements are less predictable. She's more of a go-with-the-flow kind of person, waking up at all different hours of the day and working completely different shifts at the restaurant. I plan to spend a few hours watching her over the next few days to see if I can pick up on some type of routine that we can count on if we need to take her. The only constant she had was the recurring meetup with Callie at Maria's each week. We took that option out of the equation, so I'll have to find another fixture to pinpoint.

I close out of those cameras and pull up the feeds from the cell. She's still sleeping. I understand why Kyler likes to watch her sleep. She seems so peaceful when she's unconscious. When she's awake, I can see the darkness that she tries to hide from the world, and I know the others see it, too.

She's been too passive since we brought her here, caving to Kyler's wants and needs. We know how she grew up, and her manipulation tactics won't work on us. I'm sure she thinks she can use Ky to get the upper hand. He may seem like a lovestruck puppy when it comes to her, but he knows where his loyalties lie. Contrary to what she believes, some piece of ass will never come between the three of us.

Seb plans to keep as much distance from her as possible until we're ready to sit down with her and talk about Maxton. He's also the only one out of the three of us who talked to her before we took her, so there's always the chance she might recognize him.

Fucker told us we had to keep our distance, but he let it slide that one night he got curious and fucked up. He usually has the most self-control, but getting this information from Gabriel by any means possible has begun to cloud his judgment. It's consumed him lately.

When we decided to bring her to the main house, we collectively agreed she would be with one of us at all times, including at night. There's plenty of room for her to have her own room, but for now, she'll sleep with one of us. If she doesn't like it, she can always stay under the pool house again.

I'm all for this arrangement. I don't mind getting the chance to sleep next to an ass like hers. If I play my cards right, I might even have a chance at making it red and hearing her whine for me. I've seen the feeds of her and Ky. She likes it when he takes control of her. I jerked off to last night's feeds as soon as I watched them this morning. Even thinking about it now has my cock hardening in my pants. The face she makes when she comes apart is like a work of fucking art.

The guys should be down here soon for one final chat before we move her to the house. Ky will give her the grand tour before bringing her to dinner for introductions. Seb opens the door to my security room, and Ky walks in behind him.

"What's our plan here?" I ask them, getting right to the point.

Seb walks over to stand in front of the screens. "She's going to cling to Ky at first. He's become her anchor. I think we should let that happen until we find out if she knows anything worthwhile about Maxton."

"Are we doing the dinner meetup tonight, then?" I'm eager to find out when I get to formally introduce myself to her and get my turn to play with her.

"Do you think we should wait a day? Let her settle in?" Kyler says from his corner of the room.

"It's not a fucking hotel stay, Ky. There's no settling in," I tell him, being sure to make air quotes when I say settling in. "The sooner we get this all over with, the sooner we can find out what she knows. If she doesn't like it, she can go back to the cell."

"Barrett's right," Seb says with a sigh. "We do the dinner tonight, get the introductions out of the way, and find out if she knows anything. If she doesn't, we use her to get Gabriel talking."

"Sounds good to me," I chirp in before Seb continues.

"Kyler, bring her up to the house, give her the grand tour, and then leave her in your room to freshen up. While she does that, we can have the dining room set up for a formal meal, and she can meet all of us."

"Isn't the whole meet-over-dinner thing a bit cliche?" Kyler asks us.

"And what exactly do you suggest? Do you want us to just pop down into the cell now, hold out our hands, and introduce ourselves? Oh, hi, I'm Barrett, one of your stalkers/kidnappers, and we plan to use you to get back at your father for being a piece of shit. Come on, Ky. At least with food, it can be a somewhat neutral playing field."

"You don't have to be a smart ass," Kyler throws back at me.

"Well, don't ask dumbass questions," I tell him.

"Enough, you two. You're acting like children. Get your shit together and stop letting the girl get between you. I'm going to go get started on dinner. Barrett, watch the feeds or do whatever you want. I don't really care. Ky, go grab the girl and give her a tour of the house. Make sure she knows the rules and have her ready for dinner." Seb turns and walks out of the room, leaving Kyler and me down here to glare at each other.

"Better go get your girlfriend," I say with a bit more attitude than I mean to, but to be honest, I'm a little jealous he gets to spend so much time with her. I spin around in my chair and enlarge the camera focused on her. She's wearing one of the shirts I picked out today, and I chuckle. I never thought she'd actually wear that one, but it looks good on her. Before too long, the door behind me slams, and I see Kyler appear in front of her on my screen.

"Let the show begin," I whisper to myself.

Chapter 16
Callie

I wake up alone, but I can still smell him on me. He said today I'm moving up to the main house, so I've been sitting here waiting for him to show up. I'm meeting someone new today, his brother, based on what he's told me so far. I decided to take this extra time to make myself look as presentable as possible. If keeping Kyler on my side becomes too hard, I can always try again with whoever he's introducing me to. Who knows, seeing me being friendly toward them may induce some sort of jealousy in him.

I make my way over to the less-than-impressive pile of clothes on the floor. My options are severely limited, but I finally settle on a pair of black leggings and a dark brown t-shirt with a smiling taco with arms and legs and the words "Taco 'bout fun" above it.

Who the hell even went shopping for these clothes? It's not the sexiest shirt in the pile, but maybe whoever sees me will find it amusing, and I can use that as a way to make conversation. Break the ice a little.

I've been sitting at this damn table for what seems like hours now, and my legs are starting to go numb. I look over to the mirror to take in my reflection while tapping my fingers on the table. I look tired. There are bags under my eyes that could have their own zip code, and the air in here has my skin so dry and flaky. They better have some lotion at this house of theirs.

Just as I'm starting to lose hope of getting out of this room today, the door swings open, and the man I've been waiting for strolls in. He looks me up and down, lifting his eyebrows a little while a smirk forms.

"Nice shirt, wanderer."

"You think so? I've just been having so much fun during my stay here, so I thought it fit perfectly," I say playfully.

"Come on, unless you'd rather stay here." He reaches out his hand, expecting me to grab it, and just like yesterday, he interlocks his fingers in mine to lead me up and out of my cage. It appears to be later in the day. I take in the sun's shadow beginning to set as we make our way toward the house.

"Figured I'd give you the full tour from the front instead of going in through the back. Consider it your official welcome to your new home party." He grins at me, and I roll my eyes. This will never be my home. This is just a bigger cage and one step closer to getting the hell out of whatever mess this is.

We walk in the front door to an open entryway with rooms to the left and right and a hallway straight ahead. To the right is a dining area with a table big enough to seat six. To the left is a small lounge-like area with a TV and a pool table, where I'm guessing they spend most of their time. It looks more used than some of the other rooms. We walk down the hallway beside the stairs that has two rooms off of it. One small bathroom with a shower stall and another locked door that I am not given entrance to. The kitchen has direct access to the dining room, so we walk through both and end up at the main entrance by the door.

He leads me up the stairs to the second floor that's equipped with four bedrooms, each one of them having their own. They claim the fourth bedroom is an occupied office, but I'm pretty sure the locked room downstairs was their office. I think they just don't want me having my own room. Maybe after I convince them that I'm not a flight risk, they'll let me have more privacy and set it up for me. Actually, scratch that, I don't need my own room in their house.

We finish the tour in his bedroom. It's a modest-sized room with a queen-sized bed straight ahead. This would be the upgraded queen-sized room he was talking about the other night. There are two nice-sized windows with a view right to the pool house and two nightstands on either side of the bed with simple lamps that look like they came straight from your average home improvement store. The bedding and decor of the room is black. Everything seems simple.

I catch a glimpse of a photo with three teenage boys on one of his dressers and wander over to pick it up. I study the picture taking in the three figures standing in front of a lake holding fishing poles. They look like they lived a tough life, but they're happy. I wonder who the other two kids are in the photo. One of them has to be Kyler. I should ask him, but not right now. I walk over and flop my ass on the bed, dangling my legs over the side, looking over at him in the doorway.

"So, what now?" I ask.

His eyes darken, and without saying a word, he walks over to me, stepping between my legs. His hand reaches between my chest, and he gently pushes me backward until my back hits the mattress. I feel the warmth of his skin running up the insides of both of my thighs until they get dangerously close to my center. He has a domineering look in his eyes, making my heart pound in my chest.

My leggings and underwear are pulled down my legs, and I lift my hips to aid the process, eyes locked on his every movement. He sinks down to his knees in front of me, tossing a leg over each one of his shoulders, and smiles up at me. "Now, I get my appetizer before we get ready for dinner."

He wastes no time leaning in and licking me from top to bottom, devouring me like I'm his last meal. Instinctively, my hips buck forward, and he pulls back.

"Wanderer, be a good girl and lay still for me." He spreads me open and dives back in, his tongue sliding in and out of me. I moan and reach for his head, but he brings a hand up to shrug me away. "I told you to be good." He nips at my clit, and I let out a yelp as shocks of electricity shoot through my body.

Fuck, I might have to ignore his requests more often. Just as I feel things building inside me, I see a shadow out of the corner of my eye and look up at the doorway to find a man leaning against the frame with his hands in his pockets. How long has he been there?

"What the hell!" I try to sit up, but Kyler holds me in place and picks up his pace with a renewed intensity.

The stranger in the doorway speaks up, his voice sounding fierce but soothing. "I believe he told you to be a good girl. If you don't listen, I assume it's because you want to be punished." A mischievous smile formed on his face. "Do you like being punished? I can help with that."

My body feels hot all over as Kyler slips a finger inside of me and curls it to that perfect spot. I continue moaning and panting as he shoves a second finger into me and starts pumping faster, all while continuing to circle my clit with his tongue.

The man walks over to us, bringing his hand up to my chest and pinching my nipple. Everything feels like I am on fire as my body is thrown into the most intense orgasm of my life. I come all over Kyler's face while keeping my eyes locked on the strange man. Kyler keeps up the pace until he feels my body start to wind down.

"That was quite a show. Dinner is in 40 minutes. Don't be late," the stranger tells us before turning and walking right out of sight without saying another word.

"I think you made a good impression on my brother," Kyler says. "Up, little wanderer. We have to get you cleaned up for dinner. The bathroom's this way."

"Your what?" I ask with confusion. What the hell is wrong with me that I think what just took place was hot as fuck? He leads me across the hall to the bathroom and starts the shower.

"Hop in and wash up. I'll bring you something to wear," he says as I step under the shower, letting the feeling consume me. The water feels like a hug, enveloping me in its warmth. I forget where I am for a few moments until I hear the door open again and peek out of the shower to see Kyler place some clothes on the sink. A simple black dress and flats. No bra and no underwear. You have got to be fucking kidding me!

Chapter 17
Callie

When we walk down the steps and into the dining room, the first thing I notice is that there are four place settings. I thought I was only meeting one other person tonight, but apparently, it's two. A thought crosses my mind: the three different scents.

I take a seat nervously, twiddling my fingers in my lap while wondering if the other two boys from the picture in Kyler's room are who I'm meeting tonight. I have to make a good impression, taking in as much information as possible since this first meeting is crucial in finding the best way out of here.

A few minutes pass before I hear light chatting that sounds like it is coming our way. Out of nowhere, two men appear in the room, and I have to stop my jaw from dropping.

The first man to walk in is the one I saw earlier while Kyler and I were, well, indisposed. I'm pretty sure he is the one who brought food down to the pool as well. He's tall with green eyes and brown hair that's shorter than Kyler's. He has more of a crew cut with a fade look to it. He looks strong, and his upper body appears solid. He has the kind of arms that could pick me up and toss me over his shoulder like I weighed nothing. I briefly picture him doing that and feel my cheeks flush.

There are tattoos down the length of his arms and onto his hands. Now that I have a closer view, I can make out a giant tree that starts on the top of one hand with a root system working its way down each finger. The line work is mesmerizing. I stare at it for a few seconds longer than I should. He catches me and flashes me a grin that could bring the strongest woman to her knees. Fuck, it should be illegal to have dimples like that.

Behind him, another man walks in. I've not seen this man since I've been here, but something about him looks vaguely familiar. I can't place where, but I swear I've seen him before. His dark brown hair is short but long enough that I could run my fingers through the slightly wavy curls. My heart beats a little faster at the idea of touching him. Striking brown eyes meet mine, and he sits at the table across from me. I gaze down at the scruff on his face and think about how it would feel brushing against my skin.

My head is all twisted around, but my body is the best tool I have to get myself out of this mess at this point. If they want to get close to me, I'm going to let them. All of them. It may seem fast after everything that went down with Julian, but part of me wants to hurt him like he hurt me with his lies.

I'm not sure if they know about Kyler and I having sex or if he is even the type to share, but if it gives me even the tiniest bit of leverage to get out of this fucking house, I'll take it.

"Callie, I want to introduce you to my brothers. You may remember Barrett from earlier." The green-eyed one winks at me. He fucking winks, so I roll my eyes, making sure he knows that I like to be a bit disobedient. Kyler clears his throat and then gestures his hand across the table. "This is Sebastian. He won't be around much. You can come to me or Barrett with anything you need." I smile politely at both men across the table who are staring at me.

"Oh, you are more than welcome to come for me... I mean to me anytime," Barrett replies. I should have expected some stupid comment like this after earlier.

Deciding I want answers, I get right to the point. "Why am I here?"

The green-eyed one, Barrett, laughs so hard he almost spits out his drink. "Don't you think that's a bit rude, princess? We haven't even had dinner yet."

"I've been here long enough without answers, don't you think?" I spit out, raising an eyebrow at them.

The guys all share a look, and the one they call Sebastian stands up and asks me, "How do you like your steak?"

"Umm, medium, but can you just answer my question? Why am I here? If you're going to kill me, do me a favor and just get it over with already. I'd rather not wait around for it to happen."

"We aren't going to kill you," Barrett tells me as Sebastian walks into the kitchen. "Let's get through some introductions and maybe get to know each other a bit before we dive into the specifics of why you're here."

I look over at Kyler to see if he will say anything different, but he only brings his hand over and places it on top of my knee in a gesture to calm me down. Fuck their stupid dinner party. I want answers, and I'm tired of playing nice.

Kyler's hand moves slightly up my leg, and I glare at him before shoving it off. He brings it back down with enough force that I know I'll have bruises from the imprint of his fingers tomorrow. Fine, apparently, his hand stays.

After a few minutes of the most uncomfortable silence ever, the door whips open, and plates of food are placed in front of me and Kyler. Sebastian walks back into the kitchen and grabs two more plates, placing one in front of Barrett and the other in his spot.

He sits down, looking at me as I eye up the plate in front of me, and he firmly says, "Eat. We'll talk after you finish."

"Fine. Tell me something, though. Who are all of you?" I question.

The smartass with green eyes decides to answer my question. "We already told you who we are. I'm Barrett, that is Sebastian, and I'm pretty sure you're well acquainted with Ky by now."

My cheeks instantly redden. My eyes dart over to Kyler. His hands shoot up in defense.

"Don't look at me. Barrett here likes to watch the security feeds," Kyler snickers. "He likes to watch in general if you didn't pick up on that before dinner when he walked in on us."

"I like to participate too." Barrett shrugs and chuckles.

"You're the one who talked to me over the speaker the other day. I tried to find the cameras but was never able to, so props for that, I guess."

He grins at the compliment like that was the nicest thing I could have said to him. "I've been watching you for a while, princess."

We eat through most of our meal, continuing to talk about more pointless things, and I grow increasingly irritated with all the fake conversation.

"Can we skip all of this small talk? Just tell me what I'm doing here," I demand, hoping to get answers this time.

"Are you sure you want to know? There's no going back once it's out in the open," Kyler tells me, like not knowing why I've been kidnapped could be better than what he's about to tell me.

"Spit it out already," I state firmly.

Sebastian clears his throat and begins to say. "You see, your father.."

"I fucking knew it," I interrupt.

"Do you want me to tell you or not?" Sebastian scoffs.

"Yes," I grumble. "I won't interrupt you again. Tell me what mess my fucking father got me into this time."

"Your father owes us payment and decided not to follow through. You are here to encourage him to provide us what we are owed. It's simple. He gives us what we want, and we give him you. An even trade, and you can go on living your fantasy lives," Sebastian states.

Oh no, no, no. I drop the fork on my plate, completely losing my appetite. The contents of the dinner I already ate feel like dead weight in my gut. They're going to give me to him. Did they already tell him I'm here? Is that why they moved me to the house? Have they struck a deal with him? My breathing shallows, and my heart begins to race. I can feel the panic setting in. My vision tunnels, and the words around the room start to blur. My head spins with the fear of my father having me back in his grasp after all these years. Everything crashes around me. Memories of the loss of my mother and Maxton. I feel like I am drowning in emotions, and I can't breathe.

I don't realize what's happening until a warm body surrounds me and pulls me out of my momentary state of paralysis. I inhale, and the familiar scent of iris brings me back to reality. It's Kyler. He has me in a hug and is rubbing my back to try to calm me down. Once I stabilize my breathing, he pulls back and looks at me. "Callie, What the fuck is going on. Are you ok?" I look up at him, feeling smaller than I've felt in a long time.

"You can't tell him I'm here," I whisper, tears welling in my eyes. I feel the emotions bubbling up. I'm about to lose it again. "Please." I knew there was a possibility of them being connected to my father in some way, but hearing it out loud, it's all too much for me. "I can find a way to pay you whatever he owes you." My eyes go to the floor, ashamed at how pathetic and weak I must look right now. "I'll do anything you want me to do; just please don't send me back to him."

"He doesn't owe us money," Sebastian says, completely uncaring about my current emotional state.

I look up at him with questions in my eyes. "If he doesn't owe you money, then what does he owe you?"

"Information," he says plainly.

Information? Well fuck I'm surely screwed then because my father never told me anything. I've been away for years, so I most likely don't have whatever information they are after.

"If it's anything I know, you have my word that I'll tell you. I just don't know how much help I'll be because I've been away for over six years, and he never told me much when I was there."

"I find it really hard to believe that the precious heir is not privy to information about the society she's supposed to rule in the future." I don't even question how they know that. They obviously know more about Rogue than the average person on the streets.

"I may be the next in line, but he never planned on letting me rule." I shake my head. "His plan was always to marry me off so that I could reproduce the next male heir. The whole reason I left was because he tried to force me into a marriage."

"I don't care why you left or what your relationship is with your father. I will get the information I'm owed, and if I don't, we will use you to convince him to speak. One way or another, we'll get what we want."

I look around frantically. My body going completely numb. If my father gets me back at that compound, I'm as good as dead. I'll still be alive, sure, but my entire life will be over. He will lock me up somewhere, and I will never see the outside world again. He's not stupid. After what happened with my mother and Maxton, he won't risk me escaping from him again.

Chapter 18
Sebastian

We knew she would be upset about her father being involved in her being here, but this was nowhere near the reaction we expected. In all the research Barrett did, he didn't find anything about a rift between them. We just assumed the lack of pictures of them together recently was due to her partying it up before she had to fall in line.

It hits me that she was down in the cell by herself all that time and never fell apart the way that she did tonight at just the mere mention of her father. Her reaction to him has me second-guessing our next move.

Initially, we planned to contact Gabriel, tell him she's here, and convince him to pay up. After having her here for a few days, the guys both requested I give her a chance to see if she has the information I need. I was on the fence about taking that route, but after seeing what I saw tonight, I decided to give her a chance. If we don't have to send her back to him, I suppose I can deal with that.

I'm flooded with the realization that I'm close to finally having answers. Like Kyler, I never knew my father and barely knew my mother. I remember bits of her here and there, like her beautiful voice. She used to sing me a song that is constantly stuck in my head, but I've never been able to figure out what it was. I cannot recall the words for the life of me, just the melody. She died in a car accident when I was young. At least, that's what the police report says. I had no other family that they could locate, and it landed me a one-way ticket into the system.

I was one of the lucky few and came out of it all with a family. It's not a family in the traditional sense, but Kyler and Barrett are the closest thing to brothers I've ever known. I have Ms. Monroe to thank for that. Our loyalty to one another will never be broken.

About a year ago, Barrett was digging into our old foster files and managed to find a record of who my father was. He's dead now, but we found out he was married and had another son before dying. His name is Maxton, and he is my half-brother.

The job we completed for Gabriel was supposed to result in him passing along contact information for Maxton so that I could reach out to him to see if he wanted to connect with me. I doubt he knows I exist, but I'd love to get to know him. The problem we ran into is that piece of shit Gabe never followed through with his end of the bargain, and I'm pissed as hell. We don't allow people to go back on their word. That makes us look weak.

I look over at the girl who has gone pale as a ghost since bringing up her father. I suppose the only way to find out if she's useful is to come right out with it. "I am looking for information on how to get in contact with my half-brother. I believe he is a member of your society."

"Okay, what's his name?" she asks curiously.

"His name is Maxton," I state firmly.

Her eyes widen enough that they look like they are about to bulge out of her head. She quickly stands up, eyes welling up with tears as if she's about to lose every morsel of sanity. I see her chest rise and fall rapidly and notice her breathing begins to shorten again. This girl is about to fall right into another panic attack at the mention of my brother's name. What the hell is that about?

Kyler calls out to her to try and calm her down like he did just a few minutes ago, but it doesn't work this time. She backs away from him and becomes more hysterical, clutching her chest at the lack of oxygen. She makes a sound like she's not able to breathe, and Kyler tries again to calm her again. It still doesn't work. The next thing I know, she begins to wobble from side to side before ultimately falling forward right into Kyler's arms, passing out. Well, fuck.

Chapter 19
Callie

I wake up in a bed that doesn't look familiar, and my head is pounding. It's been a long time since I've had an episode that extreme. I almost forgot what the aftereffects feel like. The tightness in my chest lingers, along with the raging headache and nausea.

If I had the energy, I would get up and run as far away from here as possible. My fight or flight response has kicked in something fierce. Thinking about Maxton makes me feel as if I was 18 all over again. I try to make sense of the conversation at dinner, but I'm not sure I can. Sebastian is Maxton's brother.

We had been together for years, and he had never mentioned a brother. Sebastian said that he had just found out about him and that they shared the same father. I met Maxton's father. He never seemed like the kind of guy who would have a child and leave him alone to be raised by their mother.

Maxton's father died from a massive heart attack a few months before Maxton was killed. I helped him through his father's funeral and was there for his mother during her time of grief. I can't even imagine the amount of pain she went through after Maxton was killed and I fled. She had nobody there to help her, and that pang of guilt is enough to consume me. I roll onto my side, grasping at the covers, when I hear the door creek open.

Barrett walks over to the side of the bed and sits next to me. Looking down at me, he pushes a strand of hair behind my ear. "When did you start having panic attacks?"

I sigh and feel the tears well up in my eyes again. Just like with Kyler, I feel a weird sense of safety with him. He makes me feel like I want to open up and expose this part of my life. In the past, this is a feeling I've always run away from.

The way he's looking at me right now, he seems tender, almost like he knows exactly what I am going through. In some ways, these guys already know more about me than the man I was going to marry did.

"I was 18 when I had my first. They don't happen often anymore unless I am reminded of..." I trail off, anger welling up inside me. No, he doesn't deserve to know. These men have done nothing but treat me like disposable trash since I've been here. They planned on using me to barter with my father. Why should I give them what they want? When they find out Maxton's dead, everything's going to change. They're going to send me back to him. I know it. I shake my head. "Why they started isn't important. They happen, and I have no control of them."

He nods in understanding. "I haven't had one in years, but I used to have them a lot while I was in foster care. The toll they take on your body is unbearable sometimes. Is there anything I can get for you?"

I see the humanity in him. One commonality that pulls us together. So many people will never experience the paralyzing control of a panic attack. They're lucky.

"Water," I say firmly.

"I'll be right back," he says and stands to leave.

Before he gets out the door, I stop him. "Where am I?"

"You're in my room. I told Kyler I'm keeping you here tonight. The guys agree that since I have the most experience with episodes like this, this is the right place for you to be right now."

"How nice of them to let the damaged ones spend time together," I say with annoyance. He just laughs and heads out to grab the water.

I take this time to study my surroundings. Everything is meticulously organized and clean. Kyler's room had personal items on the nightstand and dressers, but Barrett's are all bare. I'm sure if I got up to look in the closet, everything would be hung up in their appropriate places and most likely color-coordinated. I'm not able to learn anything about him from the state of his room except that he's a neat freak.

He returns, handing me the water, and I take this opportunity to see if I can learn more about him. "You said you have panic attacks, too. What caused yours?" I see some emotion flash in his eyes, and he sighs like he expected this question.

"It's a side effect of my childhood trauma. My brain decided that it would be fun to freak out every now and then, and those freakouts result in panic attacks. You and I are not so different, it seems."

"You don't have to go into detail," I tell him. Sharing the source of your trauma is something extremely personal, and I don't feel right pressing him on the subject.

"Over the years, I've found other ways to deal with the trauma to ease the effects. The panic attacks are less frequent as I've learned to control my emotions more. Pain has become one of the main sources to satisfy my need, should it arise."

I want to ask him what he means, but my body is so weak from my episode, and a yawn escapes my lips. He pulls me into the bed and slides in next to me before I have a chance to ask him any further questions.

"Get some rest. We can talk about all this another time," he whispers in my ear.

In my vulnerable state, I snuggle myself into his hold and catch a whiff of vanilla and leather as my eyes grow heavy, and I drift into unconsciousness.

Waking up, I look over to see his arm draped across my waist. He looks so peaceful sleeping. I study his face for a few minutes before turning to my side and trying to wiggle free from him. I shimmy myself under his arm, and he grabs my waist, pulling me flush against him.

"You can keep wiggling all you want, princess. Just know, you aren't leaving this bed until I do."

I can feel his hard cock pressing against my backside, likely a product of the wiggling he's complaining about. It shouldn't make me want him, but it does. I move my ass into him a few more times, and he groans, gripping my hip tightly.

He pushes himself into me and leans in to whisper in my ear, "If you're going to be a tease, then I'm going to punish you." My body ignites at the thought of him touching me. "Tell me, princess, are you a filthy girl? Would you like it if I tied you up and smacked your ass until it was red and then took you from behind? What if I forced you to your knees and made you choke so far on my cock that the only way you would be able to breathe is if I let you?"

My heart is racing at his words. They send a piercing electric energy straight to my core. Why is he affecting me like this? I shouldn't be letting him anywhere near me. His hand trails down my stomach and stops just below my belly button.

"What would I find if I slipped my hand a little lower?" His mouth nips my ear.

"Nothing, you wouldn't find anything," I tell him, my body knowing damn well that it's a lie.

He pulls his hand away from me. "Tell yourself whatever you have to, princess, but when I fuck you, it'll be because you're begging for it like the desperate little slut you are."

"Good thing that will never happen then," I say. He laughs at me before getting out of bed and walking out of the room, leaving me in his bed, trying to recover from his touch.

Chapter 20
Callie

The days seem to fly by one after another as I bide my time while still trying to find a way to get out of here. I've been here a little over a month now. I sleep with Kyler most nights, but I've started sleeping with Barrett- just sleep. His scent is soothing on days when my mental health isn't the best.

Sebastian has kept his distance and refuses to have an actual conversation with me. I still have a strange feeling that I've seen him before, but I haven't been able to place it. The only time the four of us have been in a room together was the first night when they brought me up to the house for dinner. Since then, it's been one combination or another of Barrett, Kyler, and I.

After my panic attack, Barrett tried to get me to talk to him about what caused it, but I couldn't. I'm not ready to open up, and I don't know what they'll do when they find out the truth. Maxton died at my father's hand, and I did nothing to stop it. Will they realize it was all my fault and use me as revenge? Will they want to kill me to get back at my father? I'm the reason they will never get to meet him. I let them continue to have hope, and it eats at me every day, but I'm terrified of what will happen once the truth is out.

I know they're getting impatient because it's being brought up in conversation almost every other day. Each time I hear his name, my heart races, the panic takes over, and I'm almost thrown into another attack. It takes everything in me to calm down. I know at some point, they'll get tired of waiting for me to talk and force me to tell them, but this is my story, and I will tell it in my own time. I need to make sure I develop enough of a connection with at least Kyler and Barrett before I do so that when the truth is finally revealed, they are less inclined to want to hurt me.

I've started focusing on getting to know them and spending quality time with them. Barrett spends a lot of time at the gym working out and hitting the bags, so I've made a point of joining him. The first few days, I watched him while I ran on the treadmill. It's never a bad idea to ensure you have enough stamina to run for at least an hour at a time if needed. Since then, he's started teaching me some basic kickboxing moves.

I often find myself getting distracted by him not wearing a shirt, and he takes advantage of that, knocking my ass right to the mat. The way the sweat drips down his torso to the deep V of his pelvis should be illegal. Every time he catches me looking, he grins like he won some kind of award. He's still fully convinced I am going to beg him to fuck me, but I don't need to. Kyler goes above and beyond to handle my needs.

Days with Kyler are usually spent at the pool. He swims like a fish and loves seeing me in a swimsuit. I've started wearing the other suits he bought me because I can't always wear the same one. I want to show off for him.

Sometimes, I forget I'm technically here against my will when I'm with him. He's so different from any man I've ever met. He's sweet and cuddly like a teddy bear, but the kind of teddy bear who gets a kick out of stalking you, watching you sleep, and calling you his good girl. My insides melt every time he tells me I'm his good girl.

I've never had the kind of sexual freedom I feel with Kyler. When I was with Julian, it always felt like something was missing. He would take what he needed from me but never made sure that I was fully satisfied. Kyler is the complete opposite. He makes sure I find release at least once before he does. It's like he knows how to read my body like music and plays it like his own personal instrument.

How am I supposed to return to my normal life after all this? I told myself that sleeping with him was my way of trying to draw him in to catch feelings, but somewhere along the way, that all changed. I continued doing it because I craved him. He's become a sort of addiction that I'm not sure how I am going to live without.

I should feel bad that Julian is likely still wondering where I am, but I don't. When Kyler told me that he waited an entire week before looking for me, resentment ate at me, and I had a realization. Life with him was never the life I was meant to have. I loved the idea of him, more than anything, a normal life with a nice guy. My father would eat him alive.

It was a nice bubble to live in, but once I'm free from this place, I'll move on like I've done so many times before. I just have to find a way to contact Avery to see if she still wants to join me.

Today is a gym day, and Barrett walks into the room, gloves already on. I look over at him, grinning. Today's the day I am going to get a cheap shot on him. I just know it. He's obviously better than me, but I've made some good progress, and I plan on using my assets to distract him. I'm bored, so why not spice things up.

"Want to make a wager today?" I ask him, and he looks up at me questioningly. Shit, he knows I'm up to something.

"What sort of wager?" he asks cautiously.

"How about this? If I can get one good shot on you that you don't expect, then I win, but if you can block me, then you win."

He grins, stepping so close to me that he is able to run his nose along my neck. "Oh, princess, this sounds fun. What do I get when I win?"

"You doubt me that much?" I ask, with a renewed sense of determination burning in me at the chance to prove him wrong.

His mouth comes up next to my ear, and he whispers, "When I win, I want you to beg for it."

My cheeks flush, and shivers run down my entire body. What have I gotten myself into? I should've seen this coming. Of course, this is what he wants. He's been teasing me since the day we met. Every time I sleep in bed with him, he runs his hands all over me, working me up, but he never finishes the job. I've come close to caving a few times, but I've been too stubborn to admit he's right. I want to beg him. I want him to wreck me like I know only he is capable of.

I nod at him. "If you win, I'll beg." The look on his face is a mixture of shock and excitement. I just gave him all the fuel he needed. "If I win, I want a date."

"A date?" he questions.

"Yes, a date. Somewhere outside of these damn walls that I've been staring at. I want to go out and have a nice meal somewhere. It can be just the two of us or all four of us if that makes you feel better. I don't care." I see the way his mind is processing the information, gears turning as I try my best to keep my face as innocent-looking as possible. This could be my chance to get away from them before they find out the truth about Maxton.

"Fine, but I'm only agreeing because I know you have zero chance of winning." A smug smile crosses his face.

I take my stance, waiting for him to move first. My body relaxes as I bounce a few times, bending at the knee. I bring my arms up and tuck my chin down to peer over my gloves. He takes a similar position, and we begin our little dance around each other. He doesn't make the first move, so I do. I just need one good hit.

I begin my basic footwork. Step left, drag, step right, drag, pivot, jab, jab, jab, pivot. Every move I make, he blocks with ease. I let out a breath and try to slide to my right, hoping to catch him off guard, but that doesn't work either. I swing my right arm in an attempt to upper-cut him, and he slides back and to the side, making my swing completely useless. He lightly jabs me in the chest, pushing me back, and then wraps his arms around me and spins me around so that my back is pinned to his stomach.

He leans down and whispers in my ear, "You're going to look so good on your knees begging me to fuck you princess."

I push off of him and sneer. My mind processes his every step while I try to formulate my next move, but I don't get the chance. His words were enough to rattle me, and seconds later, I am flat on my back with him over top of me. He won, and he knows it. I only have myself to blame for this.

Chapter 21
Barrett

I've been anticipating hearing her sweet mouth begging for me for weeks. Those perfect pouty lips are just waiting to be wrapped around my cock. After we finished our match, I told her to run upstairs, shower, and be waiting for me in my bed naked. I went straight to the downstairs bathroom to wash up before meeting her there. I want her to sweat it out a little bit.

She was trying to pull a fast one on me with her innocent 'let's go on a date' but I wasn't fooled. Before heading up to see if she can follow directions, I swing by the kitchen to grab some water. If everything goes the way I have planned in my head, she'll need to hydrate afterward. When I walk in, she's wandering around doing exactly the opposite of what I told her to do.

"Princess, are you being a bad girl? You're supposed to be naked and spread for me, ready to beg." From what I can tell, she isn't wearing much, but it's more than she is supposed to have on.

"Oops," she says while biting her lips and swaying side to side playfully. She thinks this act is going to work on me. I'm not Kyler.

"Callie, take your clothes off and sit on the bed now." She giggles and continues to stand there watching me. I walk over to my nightstand, place the water down, and grab a pair of leather cuffs out of the drawer.

"Time's up," I tell her before reaching forward to grab her panties and rip them right down the middle. She gasps, holding onto my shoulders to keep her balance while I pull the shredded clothing off of her.

I grab her wrists, walking her backward a few steps to the bed before securing the cuffs around them in front of her body. Gently, I push her backward until she lands on her back on the bed. "Scoot, princess."

She scoots back until her whole body is perfectly positioned in the middle. I crawl on top of her, grabbing her arms and lifting them over her head to secure her to the small strap attached to the headboard. She isn't going anywhere now.

I can feel the rise and fall of her chest as her breathing increases. The fear and uncertainty in her eyes are enough to set me off right now. She wants me to use her body and call her a dirty slut; I just know it. I pepper a few kisses along her jawline before sliding off her and admiring the view. She tries to pull her hands down but quickly realizes she isn't going anywhere, and her eyes widen further.

"You look like the perfect little whore, tied up and ready for me to use." My words shock her, but I can smell her arousal.

"Pick a safe word, Callie, because that's the only way I plan on stopping before getting my fill of you."

Her cheeks flush the most gorgeous shade of pink as she quietly says, "Um, pickle?"

This fucking girl. "Pickle?" I say, and she giggles. It's such a sweet sound to hear.

I reach out and grab her ankles, pulling her until she is fully stretched across the length of the bed. In this position, her arms are extended straight above with no slack. From the end of the bed, I reach down to grab the strap to connect her right ankle before tightening it, keeping her leg at an angle. I do the same with her left ankle, and once she is fully secured, I step back and take a moment to admire the sight in front of me. Her beautiful fucking body spread out for me and completely at my mercy. The slack in the bindings is enough to allow her knees to bend slightly but not enough to close her legs, exactly how I want her.

She's still wearing too much clothing, though. That will need to be remedied. I climb back on top of her, my hips straddling her waist. I grab her shirt, ripping it right down the center, and let it fall to the side.

"Did you really need to rip it?" she asks.

"If you keep talking, I'll have to find a better use for that mouth. I think those lips would look gorgeous wrapped around a gag with drool dripping from your chin. What do you think?" Her eyes go wide, and she snaps her mouth shut.

"That's my good little slut," I tell her.

Reaching down, I grab my knife to further test her limits, seeing if she will let me be my full deviant self today. I take the blade and run the tip up the outside of her leg, pushing down just enough that she feels the pressure but not hard enough to break skin. Her breathing quickens, but she stays quiet.

"How do you feel about a little bit of pain?" I ask, but she doesn't tell me no. Interesting. I continue to trail the knife up her waist and over her collarbone, her eyes following my every move. Making my way back down her chest, I slide the knife between her breasts and under the center of her bra, careful not to cut her. She isn't ready for that yet. We need to build a little more trust before we get there.

She inhales sharply and nervously breathes out, "Barrett?"

"Ssshhhh, relax, princess. I won't do anything you don't want me to. Remember your safe word." I pull up quickly on the knife, slicing her bra in half, and use my other hand to push it aside. "Fuck. You're a work of art. Let me show you how good pain and pleasure can feel together."

I carefully place my knife on my nightstand before leaning over her to run my tongue up her chest. I reach her nipple and take a moment to circle my tongue around it before rolling it between my teeth, adding just the right amount of pressure. She lets out a loud squeal when I bite down.

"Tell me, Callie, do you like the pain?"

"Yes," she pants when I swirl my tongue around her to soothe my bite. I move over to her other nipple, repeating the process.

"Or do you prefer the pleasure that washes over after?" I ask her this time.

"Both," she admits, and my cock twitches. Fuck, she's perfect.

Pulling back from her, I reach my hand up and wrap my fingers around her delicate throat before gently squeezing. I can feel her heartbeat intensify and her chest moving more rapidly beneath me. I squeeze tighter, but she doesn't protest.

"Snap your fingers twice if it's too much and you can't speak, understand?" She nods as my other hand trails slowly down her stomach to her clit. When I reach it, I rub small circles around her, and she lifts her hips in approval.

"You're soaked. You like being used and at my mercy, don't you?" She doesn't answer, so I pinch her clit.

"Fuck!" she yells.

"I believe I asked you if you like being used and at my mercy."

"Yes," she moans.

I can feel her climax building to the point where she's ready to combust, so I bring her directly to the edge before pinching her clit again with my fingers. She screams loudly and bucks her hips against me, finding her release. It's the most beautiful thing I've ever seen. I loosen my grip on her throat and make my way between her legs to find my reward.

"Such a messy girl." My tongue runs up and down along her sensitive pussy until she begins to ride my face. She tastes so fucking sweet. I slam two fingers into her and focus my attention back on her clit. My teeth graze the sensitive spot, nipping at her to remind her of the delicate balance between pain and pleasure.

"Fuck, Barrett. That feels so good."

"I love it when you scream my name," I tell her as my fingers continue to pump in and out of her. I curl them at just the right angle and feel her tighten.

"Barrett, please don't stop." Like I would ever stop. This is the last one she gets for free, though. She'll have to beg for the rest. Before long, she explodes around my fingers.

"You're a filthy girl, aren't you? Look at you soaking my sheets." I move off of her and make my way to another drawer to grab the cordless massage wand I bought and stashed for this exact occasion. "We're going to play a game princess. You like playing games, right?" I click the toy on and bring it to her center to see her arch her back before pulling it back up. "Want to see how long it takes a dirty little slut like you to beg me to let you come? What do you think, Callie? Do you want to play with me?" Her eyes light up with desire and determination.

"I'll play," she says with a sly grin.

I can tell she thinks she might win, the stubbornness in her shining right through. This isn't a game she's meant to win. I won't stop until I hear that sweet mouth begging me to let her come on my cock.

Quickly stripping out of the rest of my clothing, I decide to add my own little twist to it. I position myself above her head with the wand in hand. She looks up at me in understanding, eyes widening when she spots my jewelry. Five metal bars go up my length, making up my Jacob's Ladder. I guide my cock down toward her lips and lean over her body to press the wand to her pussy. When her tongue reaches out and licks my length, I lose all the control I planned on having.

"Open wide, wouldn't want to ruin those pretty teeth of yours." I slap my dick along her cheek a few times before she opens wide enough for me to shove myself into her throat, enjoying every moment of the sweet sound of her gagging around me. When I feel like she's ready, I increase my pace, carefully fucking her plump lips and pulling the wand up from her pussy every time I feel like she might be getting close.

"That's it, choke on my cock like the needy slut you are." Her throat tightens around me as she struggles to breathe, and I pay close attention to make sure she doesn't snap her fingers. She does her best to keep her throat open for me and remain calm while I slam into her. I feel her whimper, and I know she's close again, so I lift the wand from her as tears begin to fall down her face.

"You look so beautiful when you cry." She makes a muffled noise around me, so I pull out and give her a chance to speak.

"Please," she whimpers.

She begs so nicely, so I bring the wand back over her oversensitive clit. "Please what, Callie?" A moan slips from her lips in frustration as I pull it back again, denying her the pleasure that she's desperately seeking.

"Please let me come."

"Are you ready to beg me to fuck you, princess?"

"Yes. Please fuck me."

"I don't know. You don't sound desperate enough yet."

"Please, please. I need you," she lets out, the tears still streaking down her face.

Tossing the wand off the bed, I quickly unbind her legs, leaving her arms tied above her, and flip her over. I smack her ass, silently telling her to lift herself up and rub my cock along her slit to gather her arousal.

"Please, Barrett." Hearing her beg my name is the sweetest song.

"This is going to be hard and fast, understand?"

"Yes, give me all of you."

I grab onto her hips with enough force to leave bruises before slamming into her. The thought of leaving my marks on her is turning me on further. Pumping in and out of her at a relentless pace, I slam my hand down hard over her right ass cheek, and her pussy clenches around me. A red print is already appearing when I slap her again and tell her, "I want you screaming my name when you come on my cock like a good little slut." My hand rubs along her clit, and she spasms against me again. She's close.

"Barrett, yes, fuck," she yells, and I feel her explode around me. I thrust myself deeper, picking up the pace while searching for my own release.

My hand reaches down to her mouth to shove two fingers in, but before I'm able to push them in far enough, she bites down hard, and I shudder, dumping every drop of my come inside her. I feel the sides of her face tilt up and know she must be grinning, feeling proud of herself. When I pull out, she slumps down, clearly exhausted.

"You like being used, don't you, Callie? You took me so well." Shivers flow through her.

I quickly release her bindings to pick her up and head to the bathroom. Placing her in front of me in the tub, I wrap my arms around her as I let the warm water fill around us. Her eyes are heavy; with every blink, they're slower and slower to open.

"Barrett?"

"Yeah, princess?"

"I do like it when you use me," she admits.

Her confession confuses me. I grab the loofah I bought for her and dip it in the water, running it along her skin to soothe her until she falls asleep in my arms. I let her lay there for a few minutes, enjoying the vulnerability she's gifted me before pulling her out to dry her off and slipping one of my shirts over her head.

I carry her to bed and slide in next to her, making sure she's pressed right up against me. Having her warmth here like this has me feeling things I told myself I wouldn't let happen. I lean down and gently kiss her forehead before drifting off to sleep.

Chapter 22
Sebastian

Enough is enough. I've given her space over the last seven weeks while I waited to see if she would willingly tell Barrett or Kyler anything at all about Maxton, but she hasn't. When we sat down to discuss the next move after her panic attack, we all decided to give it time, considering there's clearly some sort of deep-rooted trauma around whatever she knows. The problem is I'm tired of waiting.

My brothers and I decided to cut all contact with Gabriel. Callie knows something, and I'm tired of that son of a bitch dragging us along with false pretenses. I hope he's terrified about what we plan to do to retaliate against him for going back on his agreement.

It's time for her to fess up about what she knows. I've stood on the sidelines quietly, watching Kyler and Barrett get more involved with her. It's gotten to the point now where any time she's brought up, the two of them team up against me in her favor. We're done with all that. Today, she will sit down and tell me exactly what I want to know.

I've been avoiding her whenever she's around because I know she thinks I look familiar. I saw the way the thought crossed her mind that night over dinner. Before long, she'll realize I'm the guy from the bar, but it doesn't matter anymore. The guys have gotten close enough to her that there should be plenty of motivation for her to talk. She splits her time pretty evenly between Barrett and Kyler now, but today's a pool day, so I make my way through the backyard with one goal in mind.

I catch sight of her laughing and splashing around in the pool, and fuck, she's gorgeous. Her brown hair is slicked back, sticking to her skin just below her shoulder blades from diving underwater. Hazel eyes look up at me with confusion when I get closer to the pool instead of keeping a distance. I see Kyler lounging on one of the chairs along the side of the pool, so I step over to him to let him know I'm taking Callie for a quick chat. He laughs and waves me away, wishing me luck.

I clear my throat, finding myself a little nervous. "Callie, would you mind joining me for a drink in the pool house? There is something I need to talk to you about."

Her eyes flash with fear, and I feel compelled to reassure her. "I'm not putting you back in the cell, and it's nothing bad. I just want to talk to you for a few minutes. Once we finish, you're free to continue swimming with your golden retriever." Kyler rolls his eyes at my dig and flips me off, but he doesn't deny it.

She pulls herself out of the pool and my heart skips a beat when I catch sight of the swimsuit she is wearing. It flaunts every curve of her body. Her perky tits, perfect hourglass waist, and thighs that I would love to have wrapped around me. I get slightly annoyed when she grabs the towel to cover herself.

"Would you like a drink?" I gesture a hand toward the bar.

"Gin and tonic, please," she replies with a smile.

Grabbing what I need, I quickly mix up drinks for the two of us and take the seat across from her.

"I was hoping we could finally sit down and have a conversation about my brother." Her body tenses, and she takes in a sharp breath.

"I know you've been reluctant to talk about what you know about Maxton, but it's been weeks. We've given you ample time to process this request, and I've been patient. That time is up, and I need you to give me answers."

Her gaze narrows. "Why should I tell you? What's stopping you from tossing me to the side as soon as you have the information you want from me? What's stopping you from killing me once I'm no longer useful or sending me back to my father?"

"If I was going to kill you, I would have already. It's fairly obvious at this point that at least one of my brothers, if not both, have grown some sort of emotional attachment to you. While I personally do not give a fuck about what happens to you, I don't intend on hurting them." She thinks about what I said for a few minutes as I study her face.

"You're not going to kill me?" she questions.

"No, I'm not going to kill you. I just said that." Fuck, why do I have to keep repeating myself?

"Will you let me go home?" she asks, and the emotion in that one question pulls at something deep within me.

"That's not up for discussion right now," I state firmly.

"So let me get this straight. You expect me to tell you everything I know with no incentive. You say you aren't going to kill me, but you also won't let me leave either."

"I never said that."

She scoffs. "You said that it wasn't up for discussion, meaning it's not happening right now, regardless of what I tell you. So please tell me what sort of motivation there is for me to actually tell you anything at all because from where I'm sitting, there's none."

She takes the opportunity to down the rest of her drink. Damn, this girl is smart. The way she's able to read me isn't something I'm used to, especially from a woman. I don't think women are weak, but generally, in our line of work, the women we come across are more fragile. Callie is nowhere near fragile, and she has the brains to go along with it. I can almost understand why my brothers have grown to like her so much.

My curiosity gets the best of me. "Okay, I'll entertain an incentive for you. What would you like besides going home at this point in time?"

"A phone call," she states plainly.

"No." I shut that shit down immediately.

"One phone call to a friend so that she knows I'm safe. The three of you can sit right next to me the entire time to ensure that I don't say anything that would tell her where I am or about you in any way. I know Barrett's a skilled hacker. There's no reason why he can't give me an untraceable phone."

I consider her request because, in the long run, she's right. Barrett can make sure nobody is able to trace the call, and if the girl does end up saying something that she shouldn't, it gives me every reason I need to end this whole charade so that we can move on with our lives. It's really a win for me all around.

"One two-minute phone call, and we're in the room with you."

"Five minutes," she counters.

"Three minutes and not a second more."

She takes a moment to consider my offer. "Fine, three minutes, and I will try my best to answer any questions you might have about Maxton."

I get up to refill our drinks quickly before finally getting the answers I've been searching for. "Let's start with the easiest question. Did you know him?"

She lets out a sigh. "Yes, I knew him very well." I catch her looking down at her hands, fidgeting her fingers.

"I see. Well, it might be more beneficial for the both of us if you were able to just tell me everything you know about him. That way, I don't have to sit here and ask you so many pointless back-and-forth questions with short answers." She looks up at me with caution in her eyes but then nods. I could tell this wasn't going to be an easy story for her to tell, but I don't care. I need to know where he is and how to get in touch with him.

"Well," she begins, "I knew Maxton most of my life from the parties our families would go to together. He was always around, but I never paid much attention to him until we got a little older. When we were teenagers, we got really close since he lived in the same compound I lived in. Outside of him, there was only one other girl my age, Lacey, who lived at the compound, so the three of us spent a lot of time together. Lacey's parents sent her to boarding school when she was 15, and then it was just me and Maxton." I can see the tears welling up in her eyes before she continues with a shaky voice.

"Maxton and I started dating when we were 16, and we spent two years together before I, uh, left home."

I let out an audible gasp, taking in the bits of information she just spilled, and she pauses to look up at me. They dated for two years. Anger floods through me as I continue to process her words. She's been here for almost two months now, and all this time, she has known intimate details about him and refused to tell us. The very idea of that has me wanting to end this conversation right now and throw her back into the cell below us. I reign in my emotions and nod at her to continue.

"Maxton and I were together as much as we could be. We used to sneak out at night and spend the evenings in the field behind our houses, talking about what our life would be like outside of Rogue. Since you worked with my father, I'm assuming you have some basic knowledge of Rogue and what it is." I nod.

Rogue, I'm not impressed by it one bit. It's just another stupid society of men run by men who think they're better than everyone else. They aren't unique in any way. Even the name is stupid. Who the hell calls their society Rogue, real original.

"Most people love the lifestyle, but Maxton and I, well, we never wanted it to be our life regardless of whether or not I was supposed to rule. He was the kindest, most selfless person I've ever met in my entire life, and to this day, I can't even begin to explain the love I had for him. He was my everything. He was tall and lanky with wavy blonde hair and the most beautiful blue eyes." She looks off to the side before continuing. "Kyler has blue eyes, but the color of Maxton's was like the depths of the ocean. I used to get lost staring into them. He was my first everything: kiss, love, heartbreak. I lost my virginity to him. I truly loved him more than anything in the entire world. We made plans to leave. My father told me that he wanted me to marry some stranger when I turned 18 and that I had to break things off with Maxton. I couldn't let him go, and everything that happened is all my fault. I should've just let him go. I should've listened to my father. Things would be so different if I had just listened to him." The tears in her eyes now fully stream down her face as she cries. Snot drips down her nose, and her chest heaves as she takes short, quick breaths in between her sobs.

"Callie, what do you mean when you say he was? What's all your fault?"

"My father. He wouldn't accept me staying with him. I tried to tell him that I loved Maxton, that he was my entire world, but he didn't care. He's heartless and cruel, but I'm sure you picked up on that. Maxton and I tried to leave. We had everything set up: our supplies, a plan with my mother to have her help us get out, and he had a car waiting outside the woods on the outskirts of the compound. My father found out about our plans, and he came after us. I begged him not to hurt Maxton. I told him that I would do whatever he wanted. I would marry the stranger he wanted me to marry. I would come back with him. I would be his chess piece that he was free to move about at his whim, but that wasn't good enough anymore. Nothing was ever good enough for him." She started sobbing hysterically.

At this point, Kyler notices and comes running in to console her. There is panic in her eyes as if whatever she is about to say next will ruin her. "What the fuck did you do to her, man? She's shaking." He pulls her out of the chair and onto his lap on the small couch, holding her tight until she regains her composure. To my surprise she continues with her story.

"Someone overheard our plans to escape, and he found us. My father was hidden in the trees, waiting for us when we tried to leave. He appeared out of nowhere just as we were about to make it to the car. It was almost like some sick joke that he wanted us to believe we almost made it out. We were so close, but he stopped us. He had Maxton at gunpoint, and my mother tried to talk sense into him, but he shot her in the chest right in front of me. We tried to run to the car, but we only made it a few steps before I heard the second gunshot and felt his fingers slip out of mine. He's dead, and it's all because of me." She leans into Kyler for support.

"I think that's enough for today, man," Kyler says to me.

Callie's voice, barely a whisper now, fills the room. "No, he needs to know the rest. I didn't know what to do besides continue running because I knew that is what he would have wanted. After I got to the car, I got out of there as fast as I could and never looked back. I've been on the run from them ever since. We were supposed to run together, but I've been running by myself, living with the pain of losing my everything. My father's gotten close to finding me a few times. That's why I had a panic attack the other day when you brought up his name. I was terrified I was going to end up back there. I thought he hired you to take me back to him. I can't go back there. It can't all have been for nothing."

Her words have my heart turning to ice, and I walk over to her. She flinches as I point my finger directly in her face. "So let me get this straight. You expect me to believe that you loved Maxton, and yet you didn't even stop to make sure he was actually dead. You didn't try to pull him with you or get him into the car so that you could get him help. You just left him there and kept running like a selfish little bitch." Anger is exhuming from my body.

"Fuck you, you don't know a damn thing about what happened that night. I watched the blood gushing out of him when I turned to look back. You don't get to tell me I didn't love him. It took months for me to be able to function again after that day. I've grieved him every single day since. You have no fucking clue what I think or feel," she yells.

I toss back the rest of the whisky in my glass and throw it against the wall behind her and Kyler. She leans down and covers her head at the sound.

"You're a selfish, lying bitch," I scream.

"Why would I lie about this?" Her face is beat red from wiping her eyes and blowing her nose. It's quite the act, I'll give her that, but I don't believe it.

I can't believe that after all this time, the last link to my fucking family is dead. I can't believe that Gabriel knew he killed my brother all along and let us do that job for him. She has to be lying because if all of this is true, then I've been made to look like a fucking fool, and that is unacceptable.

Coldly, I look at her. "You're lying to protect yourself, and I'm not going to listen to this shit anymore."

I lean down and grab her by the arm, pulling her off of Kyler's lap and along with me to the storage closet and right down the stairs. She tries to pull away so I toss her over my shoulder and continue descending to the bottom floor. Kyler is hot on my heels, telling me to think this through before making my next decision, but I don't need to think about anything. I'm done dealing with her and her bullshit. She can rot down here for all I fucking care.

I scan myself into the floor, walk right into the room that still has all the things we had down here for her and toss her on the bed. She tries to scramble to her knees to get up in time to stop me before I leave the room, but she doesn't make it, and I slam the door right in her face, engaging the lock so that she can't get out. She moves herself over to the window and starts pounding on it.

"FUCK YOU SEBASTIAN! I know you can see and hear me! I'm not fucking lying, you piece of shit. You asked me for the truth, and I gave you the fucking truth. You wanted to know what happened to Maxton, and I told you everything. We had a deal, and you owe me that goddamned phone call."

Kyler raises a brow at me in question, but I just shake my head and motion for him to follow me. We need to find Barrett. The three of us need to have a serious conversation.

"Fuck you all," she screams, and it's the last thing I hear her yell before we leave.

Chapter 23
Julian

I walk into his office at his request and see him sitting there going over some paperwork while sipping on a glass of whisky. He must have heard me walk in because without even looking up at me, he says, "Where the fuck is she?"

"I'm working on it," I say as I walk over and sit in one of the chairs across from him, propping my right ankle up on my left knee and making myself comfortable.

This office has become like a second home to me. Gabriel has always been a man I look up to and respect. He's ruthless and rules with an iron fist. I admire that. My father was weak. He let people push him around and tell him what to do, but Gabriel has never been like that. If I'm being honest, I'm glad my father's dead. He never deserved to be second-in-command here.

When I made my way back to Rogue a little over six years ago, Gabriel took me under his wing and offered me his daughter. Sweet Callie. She's a little younger than I planned on my wife being, but nobody in their right mind would say no to marrying the future leader of our Society. The power that comes from being tied directly to their family line alone makes it worth it.

She had a boyfriend at the time and tried to escape, but Gabriel took care of the boyfriend, and I tracked her down. It took longer than expected, but it was always inevitable that I would find her.

For a while, I thought she went and offed herself because we couldn't find a trace of her, but she stayed in small towns, worked under the table, and knew that we would be looking for her. She fucked up when she moved to Braxton Falls, though. The town has connections to our little community. It wouldn't surprise me if she had no idea about those connections.

I slipped myself right into her life. God, it was so easy. I just had to flash her a nice little smile and pretend to be her saving grace. *Here's a few dollars to pay for your groceries. You're so beautiful. Let me take you out for coffee, pretty please.* Sweet Julian. The man who would do anything for anyone. The pathetic loser who works so hard to make sure they have the perfect life, so loving and tender. The exact opposite of who I really am.

The fact that she fell for my act for so long is honestly pathetic. She's a means to power for me, and that's it. I don't give a fuck about her or her feelings. She does have some nice ass pussy, though. Restraining myself from fucking her until she bleeds has had its challenges. I know she leaves unsatisfied sometimes, but I don't care. My dick gets wet, and the idea of her having no idea who I really am when she fucks me is enough to get me off time and time again.

My goals with her have always been to marry her and knock her up as fast as possible to secure my bloodline within the

Society. You'd think she would be more cautious about who she lets in her life, considering who she's hiding from. Her friend, Avery, saw right through my Julian act. She was able to see the black in my soul that sweet, naive Callie never could. If things continued to get worse with Avery, I would've had to handle the girl. None of that matters anymore because the game is over once I have Callie back in my grasp.

She kept secrets from me, well, Julian, but it didn't matter because I was always part of that secret. I didn't need her to tell me about Rogue or her father because I am Rogue, and I have been right at her father's side since he promised her to me all those years ago.

Her father agreed to let me play my little mind game with her after I tracked her down because I assured him it would result in what we both wanted. Fuck, it was going to be so satisfying. She marries sweet Julian and finds out she's carrying his son. What a nice little love story. Julian puts her in the car and drives her right to her father's doorstep. The look of terror on her face when she realized who I really was would have been so fucking satisfying. It would have completely destroyed her. I would have been able to jerk off to that image for the rest of my life.

Everything was right on track. I played the sweet boyfriend for a whole fucking year. Pretending to be a nice guy was exhausting, but I did find my own way to let out my frustrations with the occasional whore during my "business trips". Trips that were all me coming back to Rogue so that I could complete the rituals to take over as Gabriel's second-in-command.

It was all going perfectly. Callie was going to marry me. She had my ring on her finger until I fucked up and left the damn flight confirmation on my desk. I let her get the better of me that day, and my sights were swayed by the promise of a good fuck. She threw her little fit and managed to disappear from my grasp again. Gabriel wants her back here as soon as she is found, and I agree. The things I plan on doing to her once I have her back. Fuck.

MY bloodline will rule this Society. I will make it happen. I will ruin her and love every second of it.

"You need to work faster. I will not have all my future plans blown up in smoke because you wanted to play a little game of house with my daughter's naive mind," Gabriel tells me while eyeing me up and down with disdain.

I find the need to defend myself. "It was working though, wasn't it?"

"I don't give a fuck if it was working or not. We agreed that she would be back here. I kept my distance because you assured me you had it handled. If I knew you would go and fuck it up, I would have brought her ass right back to the compound a year ago myself," he spits.

"She would have slipped into the wind again, and you know that. How many other times did she get away from you? Who knows how long we would've wasted trying to find her again. It was sheer luck that she ended up in that town of all places," I say through gritted teeth, holding my ground. He won't belittle me.

"I don't know anything! If I did it my way, she would've been locked safely here until we were ready to move forward, but you had to go and play your stupid games. You let her out of your sight. This one is on you!" He slams his glass down on his desk and walks over to the window to look out.

I sigh. "This was the best way, and you know it! She heard too many rumors about me. She never would have willingly married me, much less let me fuck her to ensure your lineage continues. Playing the part of Julian to get her back can still work if I find her."

"If you find her? Oh, you will find her! I don't care what resources or strings you need to pull. Just do it. You will bring her back here where she belongs. The Julian bit ends now. We're doing this my way. Also, try not to let the whole fucking community know we're looking for her while you're at it. They still think I approve of her little vacation."

"I have Soren sifting through all the footage. I'll find her."

"Are we still thinking she ran on her own, or do you think someone else is involved?" Gabriel turns to look at me.

"Her friend Avery has been very persistent that she wouldn't leave town without her. Someone has her. There's no way she'd be able to avoid cameras for this long. She's good at being invisible, but she's always messed up somewhere along the way."

"Barrett," he says under his breath.

"Who the fuck is Barrett? What aren't you telling me?" I say.

"Fuck, I don't know why I didn't consider them sooner. The Monroe brothers. I hired them to kill your father," he says.

"Why would the hitmen you used to kill my father take Callie?" I ask.

"Because at this moment in time, they did the job for free," he confesses as he runs a hand through his hair.

"You didn't pay them?" I can't believe he would risk something like that. He should know those kinds of men are ruthless. He shakes his head no and sighs, which pisses me off. "So, it's your fault all the progress I made in the last year blew up in our faces? You blamed me for losing her, but it was really all because of you."

He steps toward me, pointing his finger in my face. "Listen here, boy, you may have some power now, but you will not disrespect me in my own home. Don't forget I put you where you are right now. I gave you that power. I run this place, and I can have you removed just as easily as your father was."

Fucking prick. He ruined everything, and now I have to figure out a way to pick up the pieces and put them all back together.

Once he gifted me his daughter on a silver platter, he was always a means to an end. I planned on marrying her, having our children, and then offing the bastard. We will have the bloodline secured, and I'll convince the council to let me run Rogue in the interim while my son grows up.

"Tell Soren to look into the Monroe brothers. One of them is a very experienced hacker, so you may need to motivate Soren to be better," he utters while walking back to his desk.

"On it." I pull up my phone and shoot him a quick text to look into the men, adding that if he doesn't find a way to locate them, then his wife may have a surprise visit from someone on the guard.

"I'm willing to bet they're keeping her close, so if we find them, we find her. It won't be easy to get her from them. We'll need to strike when they aren't expecting it."

"Soren is the best around. He'll get the job done," I reassure him.

"For your sake, you better hope he does because without her back in our hands, neither one of us will get what we want. Find her, Damien." His eyes narrow before he focuses back on his paperwork.

Oh, I'll find her, and when I do, she will pay for making me look like a fool in front of her father.

Chapter 24
Callie

That dumb mother fucker. I should've known not to trust him. He threw me back in this damn cell, and for what? I told him exactly what he wanted to know. How the hell is it my problem that it's not the outcome he expected?

He made me sit there and relive every single excruciating moment of Maxton's death. I thought he was at least an honorable man and expected him to follow through on his side of the bargain. Go figure, I was stupid and trusted someone I shouldn't again.

I really need to call Avery and let her know I'm ok. I do the only thing I can even think to do at this moment and start pacing in circles around the small room. FUCK! Being back in this cell is the last place I want to be. Who knows how long I'll be down here this time or if they'll even let me out.

He thinks I was lying about Maxton, which makes no sense. Why would I say he was dead? If he was alive, I'd be with him right now and not trapped in this shit hole. I never would've had a run-in with them at all because we would've been off somewhere, living our lives under the new identities like we planned outside of Rogue.

The weight of everything crashing around me is almost too much to bear, so I walk over to the bed, curl myself up into the smallest ball possible, and just let myself feel all the things.

I hate being weak, but I decided to grant myself tonight to be upset, and that's it. I need to get it together, put on my big girl panties, and reset my priorities. No matter what I do or say, they will always treat me like a disposable transaction.

Thoughts of Maxton are fresh in my mind as I remember the feeling when his hand slipped from mine. I remember the gut-wrenching pain of driving away from him and never being able to go back. I'll never be able to go to his gravesite and visit him. My mother lying on the ground in front of me flashes before my eyes again, too. She's covered in blood all because she tried to talk some sense into my father.

He didn't care when he realized he shot her. He used her the same way these guys are using me. At this moment, I feel small. I feel helpless. I feel numb, and I cry until I lose track of time and finally fall asleep.

I'm woken up by movement at the end of the bed, and I smell him before he speaks. "Wanderer, are you ok?"

"You should go back upstairs. I'm done entertaining whatever bullshit was going on between us. That ended the moment you let your piece of shit brother throw me back into this room and did nothing to stop him," I spit out.

He stands up and walks toward the top of the bed to look down at me. I can't see his face because the lights are out, but his voice is firm and secure.

"You're cute when you're mad. Are you done with your little temper tantrum?" I can tell he's grinning, and it pisses me off more.

"I'm serious, Kyler. I did everything he asked. I told him what he wanted to know about Maxton, and I got treated like I'm less than human. He literally threw me back in a cage."

He sighs and reaches a hand down, running it along my cheek and stopping at my chin. "He was just upset and needed some time to cool off. Let me make it up to you." His finger moves down my neck and trails along my collarbone. I push his hand off of me.

"You can't seriously think I am going to fuck you. I just told you I'm pissed off at you and that asshole for putting me back down here."

"You're just here for the night until he calms down. We've already discussed it at length while you were sleeping. Barrett and I both agree you were telling the truth regardless of what Seb thinks. He shouldn't have reacted the way he did."

"You think," I interrupt.

Kyler leans in to kiss my forehead. "I'd rather not leave you down here alone, so if you'll have me, I'd like to stay with you. Sex isn't necessary. I won't turn you down if you ask, though." He chuckles like it's a funny joke to try and lift the mood.

"Oh, how kind of you all to have a discussion and agree I'm not a liar. I just relived the worst day of my life to give him exactly what he asked me for and then laid down here and cried myself to sleep, Kyler. My entire life people have been lying to me and breaking my trust. I didn't think I needed to add you to that category, too."

"Callie, I'm not the saint you've concocted in your head. There are things that myself and my brothers do that you may not agree with, but at the end of the day, the three of us protect each other over everything. Right now, you're still an outsider."

"If I'm an outsider, then just let me leave. You have the information you want. You won't have anyone to protect yourselves from if I'm not here."

"We aren't ready for you to leave yet. I'm not ready for you to go, and if I am being honest, I don't know if I will ever be ready to let you go. I've grown a little attached to you, and the truth is, you want to stay, too. That's why you're pushing back so hard because it scares you how much you want to stay."

I don't answer him because he's not wrong. I do want to stay with them, and I have no idea why.

He gently touches my face again before speaking. "How about this: I stay with you tonight, we wake up in the morning, and we take on the day from there?"

I'm still pissed and emotional about everything that happened, but I'd rather not be in this room alone again. Quietly, I move over as far as I can in this little bed and give him the green light to join me.

"You sleeping here tonight doesn't change anything. We're not having sex, and if you try to so much as poke me with that thing, I'll shove you off this tiny ass bed so fast you won't even realize it until your body thumps to the floor," I tell him with a stern voice. He laughs and pulls me into him, peppering the back of my neck with kisses.

"Whatever you say, wanderer, now get some sleep."

It's so hard to stay mad at him when he's so cuddly. He really is a sweet psycho that I can't get enough of.

Chapter 25
Kyler

The bed is so small I can feel every single movement she makes, mostly because she's been rubbing her ass on my cock for the last twenty minutes now. She let out a softer side of herself yesterday that I know she doesn't let most people see. It must've been so hard for her to openly talk about everything and have Seb react like he did. I think back to what happened after Seb threw his temper tantrum and locked Callie back in this cell.

I followed him back up to the bar and sent Barrett an emergency text telling him to meet us at the pool house immediately. When he walked in, I knew he could sense the hostility in the air.

"What's going on?" Barrett asked curiously.

"Callie is back downstairs," I told him coldly while jerking my head toward Seb's direction.

Seb scoffed and continued to knock back drink after drink.

Barrett looked back and forth between us, waiting for someone to explain what happened. "Does someone want to enlighten me on why she's back down there? I thought we agreed it wasn't necessary. She's been cooperating with us. What changed?"

"She lied," Sebastian hissed.

"She didn't fucking lie, Seb. She just didn't tell you what you wanted to hear." He was really starting to piss me off with this dumb narrative of her lying. He knows she has no reason to lie to him. She looked completely heartbroken telling that story. We've all been through loss, and Seb should've recognized the vacant look in her eyes when she spoke of Maxton. It's not something that can be faked.

Seb wasn't going to speak up, so I quickly gave Barrett the short version of the events. *"Callie let us know that she knew Maxton very well. She grew up with him. He was her boyfriend for a period of time, and Gabriel shot him in front of her right after he shot her mother. She said that he fell to the ground and bled out as she ran to her car to escape her father's rule because he wanted her to marry some other man. At least, that's the short version. I can catch you up on the longer version a little later."*

"Well fuck," Barrett said while letting out a breath and walking over to the bar to grab his own glass. *"So, is Maxton dead, or is there a chance he is still alive?"* he asked.

"According to her, she is very convinced he is dead," I said.

Seb picked that specific time to chime in and yell. *"That fucking bitch said she loved him. Do you believe that? She claimed she loved him, but she ran away and left him there to die. I guess it doesn't matter anyway. I should have never let myself have hope that I would find the last bit of family I had left."*

I lost my shit on him when he said that. *"I'm going to forgive what you just said because I know you're upset, but you're being a disrespectful piece of shit right now. WE ARE YOUR FAMILY.*

We've been your family, and the fact that you'd even say something like that is fucked up, man."

He ran his hand through his hair, clearly frustrated, before looking at Barrett and me. "Fuck, this whole thing, I just..." He turned and walked a few steps toward the window before saying, "I'm sorry. I don't know where my head is right now. It's all too much. I thought we'd be able to reach out to him. Fucking Gabriel made me believe there was a chance."

There it was. The real reason everyone should be pissed right now. Callie's father hired us to take out a member of his own society with the promise of a payment that he never intended to follow through on. He was supposed to give us Maxton's most recent whereabouts, contact information, and everything he knew about him since Seb was technically a member of the society through his father's bloodline. The smug bastard hired us knowing that he killed him and had zero intention of following through on his end of the bargain.

What was he planning on doing when we figured it all out? He had to have some sort of backup plan to handle us. He knows our reputation and what happens to people who fuck with us.

"She needs to be part of this conversation. Callie's not our enemy. Regardless of how upset you are, she's just another one of Gabriel's victims." I had to convince Seb I was right.

He looked down at his empty glass, contemplating what I had said when Barrett chimed in. "I agree with Kyler. She's coming back up. We aren't leaving her down there."

That was all he needed to agree with us, but he wasn't quite ready to see her yet. "Fine, but she stays down there for the night. I just need a beat to process everything. Go down there with her if you have to, but I need her out of the house. If I accidentally run into her, I may do or say something you two disagree with," Seb said, clearly annoyed that Barrett and I both took her side on this one.

I had to volunteer before Barrett could because we both know he isn't who she needs. "I'll go down, stay with her, and calm her down a bit since I'm sure there's no way she's happy with you right now."

Bringing myself back to the moment and Callie's constant moving, I feel her push her ass onto me again. She thinks I'm still sleeping, but I've been up since the first time she pressed herself against me. Her back arches just a little again, and I resist the urge to grab her by the hip to let her know I am awake. I want to see what her next move is or how far she may be willing to go without me initiating things.

I purposely turn my head a little so that my breath hits her neck right under her ear, and I see the goosebumps form on her skin. She rubs herself on me a few more times before getting frustrated and letting out a sigh.

I take her frustration as my opportunity to whisper in her ear, "If you want me, all you have to do is ask, wanderer." My hand trails across her hip to her front, where I toy with the top of her panties.

"Kyler, please," she begs.

"Please, what?" I ask, even though I know full well what she wants from me.

"Please touch me," she breathes out.

I dip my hand down into her panties and slide a finger down her pussy. "You're soaked for me, sweet girl."

Her entire body goes rigid. She pushes herself off of me, leaving me more confused than I've been since she showed up in our lives.

"What just happened?" I ask her.

"I changed my mind. P-Pl-ease don't touch me," she stutters out before climbing off the bed and dressing herself.

"Callie, What the fuck just happened?"

"Nothing happened. I just don't want to fuck you and your fucking brothers anymore. I told you last night I'm pissed off. You threw me back down here even though I gave you the information you wanted. Maybe I just remembered how much of a liar each and every single one of you are, and I don't want you touching me."

"That's not why, and you know it. If you were still upset about that, you wouldn't have let me sleep in this bed with you, and you wouldn't have been rubbing yourself on me all morning."

She turns her body and completely closes herself off to me. I'm not sure what the fuck I just did, but apparently, I triggered this response somehow. I want to respect her boundaries, so I tell her I'm heading up to the main floor, but I'll leave the door open for her to join me whenever she's ready.

It takes her about twenty minutes before she finally emerges in front of me. She still doesn't want to talk, but I lead her into the house and to the lounge room where the guys are waiting for us. As soon as we walk in, the room has enough tension to cut with a knife. It's awkward as fuck, and nobody wants to break the silence. Surprisingly, Seb decides to be the first one to speak.

"My brother here seems to think that you were telling the truth about Maxton. I'm not as convinced, but one thing we all agree on is that you're a pretty little pawn in your father's world."

Here we go.

Chapter 26
Callie

As soon as he called me "sweet girl," it was like reality hit me right in the face. That's what Julian called me when we were together. What the hell am I doing here, letting these men use me like this? I came here against my will but have been giving myself to them, indulging in the pleasure. How the hell do I even know it's safe to trust them? They could be working for my father for all I know and lying to me just to keep me from trying to get away.

My stupid infatuation with Julian was the whole reason for all of this. I let myself be weak and allowed them to take me. I know now that I was only in love with the idea of him and the life we could've had together. I would've been free and happy, maybe some kids running around for a little bit at least. I never really loved him, and I still can't believe I was gone for an entire week before he started looking for me, whether we broke up or not.

Wait, is that actually true? Did Kyler lie about that? I don't know what is up or down anymore. I'm struggling so much with the idea of having feelings for these men. I'm drawn to not only one but two of them. It makes no sense.

Before going upstairs, Kyler told me they wanted to talk to me. We'll see how this conversation goes, considering the last time I talked with one of those assholes, it landed me back in this dank-ass room.

I guess I have to hear them out and find out what they're planning. I know one way or another, it involves me and my father. Before we get to this little talk, I want answers and proof. Barrett is some security buff, so there's no reason he won't be able to prove to me that Kyler wasn't lying about Julian waiting to look for me. If he was telling the truth, I'll do my best to work with them to take down my father. If I find out they lied, I'll make it my personal mission to destroy them.

After taking a few deep breaths, I walk upstairs to the pool house to meet Kyler. He leads me to the lounge, where we are now all sitting in the most awkward silence I've ever been a part of in my life. I take this time to shoot Sebastian a nice scowl so that he understands my disdain for him. He surprises me by being the first one to break the silence.

"My brother here seems to think that you were telling the truth about Maxton. I'm not as convinced, but we all agree that you're a pretty little pawn in your father's world." He takes a drink from his cup and looks at me, waiting for my response.

"Like I've already said, I'm not lying, so you can fuck right off if that's what you want to believe." He raises his brow at me, but I won't back down. "Here's what's going to happen. You brought me here to talk for a reason, and before I move forward with whatever conversation you want to have, I expect proof that I can trust you," I say while glancing over to Barrett.

"What sort of proof are you looking for, princess?" Barrett asks.

"Kyler told me that Julian waited a week before trying to look for me. I want to see proof of that. If I believe you, then we can continue talking. Until then, I'm not trusting you, especially after dickface decided to make me a promise, break it, and throw me in a fucking prison cell for the night." Barrett and Kyler laugh at my statement. I'm glad these assholes think my annoyance is funny.

"Give me five minutes, and I'll be back with your proof," Barrett firmly states, walking out of the room.

We sit and wait in more silence. I've had enough of this, so I get up to make myself a drink. I won't let them see me as weak anymore. Barrett returns to the room after a few minutes with his laptop in hand. He passes it over to me and tells me to press play.

The screen lights up with a video and audio clip of Julian talking to Avery. He called her from my phone, and she answered, thinking it was me calling. He's apparently confused by this and tells her he thought I was with her. They go back and forth for a few minutes before I hear Avery call him out for waiting an entire week to look for his fiancé. He conveniently left out the fact that we broke up. I stop the recording. I don't need to hear anymore. It hurts to hear Avery's voice. She must think I abandoned her.

"How do you have this?" I ask Barrett.

"When we started watching you, I put cameras in your house. We've had access to all of you since before we took you," Barrett confesses.

"Talk about invasion of privacy." I turn my gaze to the floor, thinking about all the possible conversations or private moments they could've potentially heard or watched.

"We didn't watch when things got personal." He quickly says, as if reading my mind. "I had a program set up to monitor for certain words when the feeds were off. The goal was to try and determine your routine. We didn't need to listen to every intimate conversation you had." I nod at him. The small admission makes me feel a little less intruded upon.

Seb takes the opportunity to open his stupid mouth. "If you have the proof you need, can we get a move on with all of this? I'd rather not sit here all day if I don't have to."

"That may be the first thing you and I actually agree on. The less time I have to spend in a room with you, the better," I shoot right back at him.

"I'll get straight to the point then. We want revenge on your father, and we want to know if you'd like to be a part of it," Seb says.

Are they really asking me if I want revenge on that man? Of course, I want revenge. It's something I've dreamed about my entire life. Deciding to ask me to be a part of this proves they trust me at least a little bit, so I need to use this opportunity to my benefit if I can.

"I'm in. I know you all expect me to contribute some kind of information on my father that will help take him down, and I'm happy to provide that, but I believe there's something I'm owed first." The men all look at me with questioning looks on their faces. I look Sebastian dead in the eyes as I make my next statement. "I want the phone call I was promised."

Kyler and Barrett turn to look at him as we all wait for his response. I won't accept anything less than a phone call. I need to reach out to Avery and let her know that I am okay and that I didn't willingly leave her. She needs to know that once my father is dealt with, she and I can go somewhere together and start over without the threat of Rogue.

"You want your call, fine." He tosses me the phone from out of his pocket. "You have three minutes, and we will be right here the entire time, so make good use of it."

I quickly dial Avery's number and wait for her to answer. I memorized her number when I realized how important she'd become in my life. If something were to ever happen, I needed to make sure I had a way to get in touch with her. She picks up on the fourth ring, and my heart skips a beat at the sound of her voice.

"If you're calling to spam me, do us both a favor and just hang up now," she sings out.

"Avery?"

"Cals? Where the fuck... where are you? It's been almost two months. I've been freaking out, completely sick to my stomach worrying about you."

"Listen, I only have a few minutes to talk, so I really don't have time for all the questions, but I wanted to make sure you knew I was ok."

"Was it Rogue? Did they find you? Julian has been losing his mind, too, you know. His annoying ass keeps calling me." I can almost hear her eyes rolling.

"It wasn't Rogue, and I promise you I'm ok. I'm sorry I left without telling you, but I haven't had access to a phone until just now. There are just a few things I have to handle before I come back home, but I need you to do me a favor." The guys all seem to be visibly tense when I tell her that.

"You know I'll do anything for you. What is it?"

"I need you to tell Julian that you heard from me and that I moved on. Tell him I don't want to be with him, and I won't be reaching out to him." I just want him to leave her alone.

"Are you sure? I thought you two were in a happy, just engaged bliss, and then you just disappeared."

"He lied to me, Avery. He lied, and then he never bothered to look for me."

"I know. That piece of trash waited a whole week to tell me you were missing. I made sure he realized how big of a fuck up that was."

"I told him I was done with him when I left," I reveal.

"Shocking, the lying piece of shit didn't tell me that. I'll deal with him, don't worry, Cal."

"Thank you for always having my back. I'm not sure how much longer it'll be until I come back, but just know I'll never leave without you. I made you a promise; always remember that." I can feel the tears welling up in my eyes.

"Do you need anything else from me?" she questions.

"No, I have to go now, Ave. I love you, and I'll talk to you soon."

"I love you, Cal. Be safe."

I hang up the phone and toss it on the seat next to me. Staring at the floor to try and get my emotions under control. She knows I am safe. She knows I didn't abandon her. The tears that were welling up in my eyes recede and I look up at Seb.

"She knows about Rogue?" he asks curiously at the fact that my friend knows about the very secret society I grew up in.

"She's the closest thing to family I have left. She knows everything about me."

"Interesting." The look on Sebastian's face is not his normal look of contempt.

I glance between the three of them and quickly change the topic back to the most important matter. The real reason we're all in this situation together.

"Now, what exactly is your plan to deal with my father?

Chapter 27
Sebastian

Why does she keep impressing me? After throwing her in the cell, I thought she would completely close herself off from us. She came out stronger, and I appreciate strength. She even pushed me to make sure I followed through on my phone call promise. That gesture earned so much respect from me, even though I hated the slight satisfaction she got out of being defiant. She came here with a goal and did not stop until she achieved it. It makes more sense every day why Barrett and Kyler have fallen for her.

I won't sit here and swoon over her like they do. She's the reason my brother's dead. She may not have pulled the trigger, but let's be real: she knew that defying her father could result in unforeseen consequences. Did she expect him to let her leave? Did she really think he wouldn't find out? The man runs a whole secret society. I'm sure there are cameras everywhere. That entire compound is likely covered in them.

"We need to know what your father's weakness is," I tell her.

"Wow, Captain Obvious," she whips back.

Fuck, that mouth of hers. Maybe I should put it to better use. "Cut the smart-ass remarks, Callie. If you're going to be part of this, then contribute. If not, we can find a better use for you. What do you think your father will do when he finds out we have you?" Her entire body freezes. I know I shouldn't have threatened her with that and immediately regret it.

She lifts her chin and glares at me. "I'm going to say this one time and one time only. If you plan to continue threatening me like that, then just do it. I won't live here in a state of constant worry. I won't spend every day being afraid that if I mess up, you'll send me back to him. There needs to be some kind of trust here. After how you acted last night, you're lucky I'm even speaking to you."

She's right. I knew saying that was wrong, but for some reason, I still said it. I need to reign my shit in to make this work. I don't trust her, and I know she doesn't trust me, but we can at least pretend, right?

Barrett speaks up before I'm able to respond to her. "You want trust, princess, you've got it. I'll keep Seb in line, and I'm sure Kyler will back me on that." We all look over in Ky's direction, and he nods. Of course, they're teaming up against me to support her again.

"That's the last time any of you threaten to give me to my father like that again," she states with finality.

"Fine, you want trust, then I'll try my best. That's all I can give you for now. I won't threaten you with your father again. That was out of line." I add even though they are all irritating me at the moment.

"I can deal with that." A small grin crosses her face like she won some sort of small victory. I'd like to wipe that smile right off her face and put her on her knees. I bet if I had her crawling around calling me sir, she wouldn't be smiling like that, or maybe she would. Shaking the thoughts away I walk toward the center of the room.

"I have an idea, but I don't know if you're going to like it." They all look at me, waiting for me to finish. "For this to work, you will actually have to trust that I'm not going to fuck you over. We will only have one opportunity to get our revenge on your father. It needs to be believable."

I can see the look of concern on her face, but she slowly nods for me to continue and says, "If you have an idea, I am all ears."

"You said your father has been looking for you for several years now, right? Well, why not use that to our advantage?" Her eyes flash with concern again, but I continue on. "After you came up from the pool house and we had dinner, you were worried that we would give you over to him. I think we should call him and let him think that's exactly what we plan on doing."

"No. I'm not going back there." The words come out in a shaky breath. All the confidence she had moments ago has now vanished.

"Relax. I told you that you have to trust me. I don't have any intention of giving you over to your father. Why would I want him to get what he wants when he took from me and lied about it? I just want him to think we're going to turn you over so he'll meet us, and we can grab him to carry out our revenge."

"I have a better idea," Kyler says from the corner of the room. "Seb, you're a member of Rogue by blood through your father," he says, looking in my direction. "What if we pull the same card Gabriel pulled on Callie before she ran from him? Tell him that we have his daughter, and we'll bring her back on the condition that the two of you get married."

"You're out of your mind!" she yells from across the room. If looks could kill, I am pretty sure he would be cold on the floor right now. "It's not enough. He doesn't care about me. You would need to threaten him with something he actually fears losing."

She has a point. "So, we threaten him with going public about Rogue then," I throw out as an option. "We can convince him that Barrett hacked some kind of system that shows the full member list of Rogue. Then we tell him that we will release the list and inner workings of the Society to the public unless he agrees to let me marry Callie."

"I don't think he'll fall for it. Rogue has one of the best hackers in the world. There's no way he'll believe Barrett was able to find a full member list," Callie tells me.

"Fine, then I'll remind him that he still owes us a debt, and if he's not willing to satisfy our original payment request, then this will be the only other payment we will accept. He doesn't know about my connection to Maxton or that you already told us that he killed him. I can casually drop that if he refuses my offer, then the only other way I am willing to satisfy the debt is by killing Callie. He obviously won't let that happen, so either way, we win. He agrees to my demands, and we move forward with getting our revenge on him."

"You should know he expects my husband to be ruthless and cold so that he can control them."

I grin at the prospect of being ruthless and cold. That's something I can excel in if need be.

"I can use our connections with the criminal underground to convince him further that he could potentially gain more power by having us marry. It could be a mutually beneficial union. I would gain access to the society, and he would gain access to the Monroe brothers' namesake." Raising an eyebrow in her direction, I wait to see if she thinks this could entice her father enough to do what we want him to.

"That could work actually, but you really need to sell the fact that he would gain something from it," she says.

We discuss a few details, and I actually start feeling good about this whole plan we have concocted.

"Are we ready to make the call?" I announce. The guys nod, and I look over at Callie, who has started pacing back and forth nervously. Her father must have really made things awful for her to generate this type of reaction. "Callie? Are you ready?"

She lets out a sigh. "Ready as I'll ever be, I suppose."

I scroll down to his name and press the call button. The phone rings three times before I hear the click, and his voice comes through.

"Ah, Sebastian, it's been a while. What can I do for you?"

"Gabriel. I've given you some space to do the right thing, but it's been long enough now. I believe you owe us a payment. I don't appreciate people going back on their word."

I hear a light chuckle from him. "Hmmm. Your mistake was not requesting the payment in advance. I think with the Monroe brothers' reputation, you should always collect first."

He doesn't know that we already have all the information we were looking for. Callie told us Maxton died at the hands of her father. I don't need to hear it from him. When he and I talk about Maxton, it will be the last conversation he ever has.

"Oh, Gabe, you should know that my brothers and I always come out on top. We don't let people take advantage of us, especially nobodies like you." Callie elbows me at that statement. I know the goal is to stroke his ego but fuck that.

"Are you threatening me?" he spits.

"No, I'm not threatening you. I'm simply stating facts. You refused to pay us, so I took matters into my own hands. Say hello to your father, Callie." I hold the phone out, placing it on speaker, but she refuses to speak. I see the fear and panic in her eyes. She is paralyzed. Barrett walks over to her and slaps her hard across the cheek.

"What the fuck was that!" she yells.

"Ah, there she is. She just needed a little motivation," I tell her with a wink.

Out of the corner of my eye, I see her punch him hard in the stomach, and he smiles. It's taking everything in me to not laugh.

"So, you have my daughter," Gabriel replies, doing his best to keep his tone flat, even though I know this must have him fuming.

"Indeed, it seems I do. You know, my brothers say she tastes amazing. I haven't been lucky enough to have a try myself yet."

"She always knew how to spread her legs," he snaps back.

Her body tenses, and I see tears begin to well up in her eyes. That didn't go over like I thought it would. Hearing him speak about her like that pisses me off. He doesn't get to talk to her like that anymore.

"I have a bit of a proposition for you if you are willing to hear me out," I say, trying to make it sound like something he would want.

"Whatever this proposition is, it better result in you bringing my whore of a daughter back to me." Okay, now I'm pissed off. How dare he talk about her like that!

"I'm going to tell you exactly what's going to happen from here on out. Your daughter is MINE. She is mine to use, mine to fuck, mine to control, and do whatever I goddamn please. You owe me a payment, and I'm cashing in. I know who my father was, and by blood, I am a member of Rogue. I want in, and I want a seat on the council. You remember that vacant seat you hired me to kill for? I want it. I will marry your daughter, and she will continue to be mine. Your other option is for me to send her back to you in pieces."

"You have my attention, Sebastian. What exactly do I get out of this?" he questions.

Of course, he wants something. Callie said he doesn't care about her. I didn't believe her, but this fucking guy is a real piece of shit.

"You get yourself a nice opening into our world. My brothers and I have made a name for ourselves. Not to mention, your daughter has been hiding from you for years now, right? I imagine your people are probably wondering where she went. Here's a nice, pretty bow to explain it all. She went out on her own and fell in love. You were going to marry her off anyway. At least this way, you gain some power from our world at the same time."

"You expect me to believe that after all this, all you want is a marriage to my daughter?"

"I don't want your daughter Gabriel. She is just a nice piece of ass that will sweeten the deal. I want my place in Rogue. I want the power your world can offer me."

I'm trying so hard to sell this to him, but he is being more cautious than we expected him to be, so it's time to put the nail in the coffin.

"I suggest you take my offer because, like I said, the only other option is her death. She's the last of your line, correct? Your little heir that you plan on using to breed and continue your family line? Tell me, Gabriel, who takes over once I rip out her pretty little throat and use it as a straw?"

"Fine. We can meet later this week to further these discussions. I will be in contact to set up a time and location."

I can't believe this is working. He might actually take this bait.

"I'm so glad that we're able to come to an agreement. I look forward to hearing from you." With that, I hang up and look around the room at everyone. That seems like it went pretty well.

Callie speaks up first. "He's lying. He's not interested in making this deal with you. I guarantee he knows that you know he killed Maxton, and you just told him exactly where I am. He has all the power and information yet again." Kyler walks over to her to rub her back and calm her down.

Barrett speaks up to console her. "Princess, he won't find us. I have this whole house on lockdown. There's no way he is getting to you."

"What's done is done. Now, we wait and see what he does in response. He'll either reach back out, or we will sit down and discuss further options," I tell her, but the look in her eyes has me questioning my decisions yet again. I don't like what this girl is doing to us.

Chapter 28
Callie

The days are all beginning to blur together now. It's been nearly a month since we spoke to my father and almost three months of being here with the guys. This place is starting to feel more like home every day. Kyler and Barrett still take turns spending time with me, but it's less out of necessity and more because they want to be around me. Some days, I go down to the pool, and others are spent in the gym. Occasionally, we take a lazy day and watch movies. Snuggling up on the couch, sandwiched between the two of them, makes me feel safer than I've ever felt in my life.

I've gotten pretty good at kickboxing. I'll never be a world champion, but I have enough skill now that I should be able to defend myself if I need to. Barrett is an amazing teacher. He's so patient and loves showing off the things he's good at.

Lately, he's started letting me sit in the security room with him while the guys are away on jobs. Seeing him at work in his element is extremely impressive. He has it all down to a perfect science: which cameras to pull up, the buttons he needs to erase things, the keystrokes needed to hack into just about anything.

I knew he was skilled, but being up close to witness it shines a whole new light on his true talent.

I've been going crazy being cooped up here. Having free roam of the house has been way nicer than the cell under the pool house, but I need to see something besides the boundaries of this property. Not being able to go beyond the gate is the only thing that reminds me I'm still here as their captive, although the lines are definitely blurred. I want to be here now. I don't even recognize the person I've become since they took me. I feel lighter, softer.

I've called Avery a few more times. She's a little pissed at me because I won't give her specifics on where I am, and I always keep the calls less than five minutes, but she'll just have to get over it. I can't put her in any more danger than I already have.

She's been telling me about her newest love interest or interests rather. Her free spirit won't allow her to be tied down to one person, so she found two people to obsess over. According to her, the only thing better than one person giving her orgasms is two. I can't exactly tell her she's wrong.

Julian didn't take the news of our breakup being final. When Avery told him I wasn't taking him back, he refused to let me go. He's been harassing her nonstop about how to get in touch with me, to the point where he showed up unannounced at her work. He's acting like a total psycho. I wish he would just leave her alone and move on.

The guys and I have been discussing what to do since my father hasn't reached out. We're all torn on what the right choice is, but the clock is ticking, and we need to decide something soon.

I've learned so much about the Monroe brothers over the last few weeks. Kyler has opened up to me the most, telling me about what it was like for him in foster care and a few stories about Ms. Monroe. Those boys really gave her a rough time, from what they've told me, but I think she really loved them like they were her own. Kyler speaks of her with nothing but respect.

I wish I was able to meet her. I wonder if she would approve of me. Would she approve of me being with both Kyler and Barrett? Ky is my sweet psycho, and Barrett is my escape from the pain. Can I really claim them as mine, though?

Barrett hasn't let me in as much as Ky has. He lets little pieces slip out here and there, and that's enough for me. When he's ready to tell me his story, he will, and I have a feeling it will break my heart. Under all his layers is just a sweet soul trying to escape the damage inflicted on him.

He's helped me process the pain I've been carrying with me all these years and given me a way to reform it. There's power in pain, and fully embracing it is the best way to ensure you keep all of your power. I hope he opens up more to me soon because I am silently begging for him to let me in. I trust that he will.

Oddly enough, I trust all of them, even Sebastian's brute-ass self. He values family over everything and will never do anything to hurt his brothers. I've become important to them, so in a roundabout way, I know he will also protect me.

I find myself lost in thought about them as I wander around the house, bored out of my mind. There are still a few rooms that I haven't seen, like the office downstairs. Sometimes, they all mysteriously disappear for short periods of time.

Last week, Kyler convinced me to take a bath, and as soon as I was in the tub, I heard their attempt to quietly huddle into that stupid office without me noticing. They have things they need to discuss that don't involve me, and that's fine- for now. Kyler missed out on some quality bath time, though.

I make my way to his room and get comfortable, thinking about how much I wish he joined me in the tub that day. He would've run his hands all over my body and called me his good girl.

Even the thought of it has me all worked up, so I quickly strip and position myself on his bed, picturing what he would do to me if he was here. Trailing my fingers down my body, I tease myself before bringing my hands up to my chest and squeezing. My fingers trail down my stomach, dipping lower. Just as I find myself wishing he was here with me now, he appears in the doorway.

Chapter 29
Kyler

Seb and I have been going back and forth about our job tomorrow for the last twenty minutes because he's more stressed out than usual. If he would stop being such an asshole to Callie, I'm sure she would help him destress. Chuckling to myself at that suggestion, I try again to convince him to just take her with us on this job.

"Let's just take her and see what happens."

I know she's been itching to get out of the house, and this is the perfect job to include her in. Normally, Barrett can do his job remotely, but this one requires him to be on-site just to be extra cautious.

We were hired to take out Ronnie Masters, some sort of up-and-coming rock star who's made a few enemies. The guy apparently has a huge coke addiction and likes to get high and touch women without their consent. The last girl he forced himself on has important parents who hired us to take care of him. They want their daughter to be able to feel safe in the world without having to come out and publicly announce she was assaulted.

This is the exact kind of person we love to kill. Even a criminal like me knows that when a woman says no, you respect it unless you have a safe word, and her saying no is part of the scene. This bastard deserves to die.

One concern with this hit is the number of bodyguards he has. We have to get him away from them to take him out. We only need a few private moments with him. I'd love to see him suffer, but a quick junkie overdose is what we chose for him. It shouldn't raise any suspicion, considering everyone knows he's an addict.

"If we don't take her, the only other option is to leave her here by herself. Do you really want to leave her here alone?" I see him processing what I said like he is sifting through every possible outcome in his mind. Seb has always been the more cautious of the three of us.

"Fine, but she better not fuck anything up. This is a high-profile job, and we need to be careful," he tells me before storming out of the room like a child.

I can't wait to go tell my girl about our field trip tomorrow. I run up the stairs to find her, and when I do, I am so thankful I ran. She is completely naked, on my bed, and touching herself. How the hell did I get so lucky? A soft moan comes from her lips, and her back arches slightly, her fingers trail along her clit. Wasting no time, I make my way to the bed.

"Wanderer, if you needed a release, all you had to do was ask. You don't ever have to handle this sort of situation on your own."

"Well, what are you waiting for?" She pants before letting her legs fall to the side so I can take her all in.

I lean down and whisper in her ear, "Touch yourself like you were when I walked in."

She slides her fingers back down to move small circles around her clit. I watch her as I quickly strip out of all my clothes and fist my cock in my hand at the sight. Her eyes stay locked with mine as she brings herself right to the edge.

"Stop," I tell her, and reluctantly, she does.

"You listen so well for me." I slowly climb on top of her, and she grips my length, gently leading me to her core. I inch myself forward to let her rub my cock in her arousal before pushing myself into her. The feel of her pussy stretching around me might be my favorite feeling in the world. She lets out a satisfied moan as I fully seat myself inside her, giving her a moment to adjust to my size.

"More," she whispers. I pump in and out of her at a steady pace, slowly building up the fiery sensation between our bodies.

"You feel so fucking good, wanderer."

"Yes, Ky, please give me more."

My pace quickens, and I reach out to grab her hand and lead it to her center. With her hand placed below mine, I guide her fingers along her clit.

"Look at you taking me so well." My other hand comes down to gently roll her nipple between my fingers, and I feel her pulse around me. She's so responsive.

"That's it, come on my cock." My balls tighten, and I'm ready to explode, but I won't let myself finish until she does. From what Barrett's told me, I know she likes a little pain, so I pinch harder on her nipple, and her body reacts just how I want it to.

"Don't stop, Ky! I'm going to.. Fuck, I'm.." She doesn't have to finish her sentence because I feel her clamp down on me, her pussy strangling my dick. After a few more thrusts, her body begins to relax, and I fill her up with my release, making sure she gets every last drop of me.

"I don't think I'll ever get enough of you, wanderer." I flop down beside her on the bed, grinning. "That wasn't my intention coming up here, but I'm never going to complain about being inside you."

I tell her the good news about tomorrow's job and that she's going with us this time. She straddles me, kissing me deeply in approval.

"Thank you so much for making this happen. I can't believe you got him to agree to this!"

"Come on, wanderer, let's go downstairs so we can go over tomorrow's plans and make sure you're ready." After getting dressed, we walk hand in hand back downstairs to the office she has never been in.

Chapter 30
Callie

We make our way outside to Sebastian's car, and I immediately run to make sure I get the passenger seat. The boys can indulge in each other's company together in the back. This is my first time off the property in three months, and I want to make sure I enjoy every bit of it. Sitting with either of them would only result in someone's hand in someone's pants. We have plenty of time for that while we are at the house.

Sebastian pulls onto the road, and a flood of anxiety I wasn't expecting rushes through me. I see him peek over in my direction like he can sense it.

"Everything will be fine as long as we stick to the plan," he reassures me, but that's not why I'm nervous. Leaving the property has me wondering what happens to whatever sort of relationship this has turned into once my father is dealt with.

We've been living in our fantasy world of me still being their captive, but would they let me leave now if I asked? Do I even want to leave? I make a mental note to talk with them about how they see this moving forward. I can't allow myself to keep getting closer to them until I have some answers.

It's a long drive going to wherever this job is, so I took it upon myself to be their personal DJ. I scroll from tranquil country music, before heading to rock and roll, and then I circle back to some hip-hop. Kyler and Barrett are having a blast singing along and dancing in the back seat. 500 Miles by The Proclaimers comes on next, and we all scream with excitement. Seb is being his usual grumpy self and just rolls his eyes at us.

This feels right. They feel like family. Eventually, we turn down a few more back roads and stumble upon our destination, a small festival in the middle of nowhere. I look around to see thousands of people hovering around pop-up tents with a large stage off to the side and a giant building in the center of it all.

From what Barrett said, the idea of this festival is to remove yourself from society so that you can immerse yourself in nature, music, and people of the same mindset. It's a whole weekend event with different musicians set to perform at different times of each day. We aren't here for the music, the party, or the festival. We have a job to complete, and the less attention we draw to ourselves, the better.

We make our way to the giant building with the private event Ronnie had set up for after his show and wait for our moment to shine. You can tell he's already hopped up on something by the way he's bouncing from person to person. His eyes are shifty, and the man can't seem to stop moving. His skin has a light sheen of sweat to it, and I notice his hand slightly twitching at his side. This will just make our job easier. We just need to wait until he excuses himself to get his next fix. From the looks of that twitch, it should be soon.

The plan is for Kyler and I to casually follow him, pretending to be lovers looking for a quiet corner to have some fun in. Seb paid some girl $500 in cash earlier to make a big enough distraction on the main floor to draw all the bodyguards there. He'll be hanging back to make sure she follows through. If she doesn't, he will have to do it himself.

The idea of being involved in their hit has my heart racing. They're giving me an opportunity to prove myself and putting their reputation on the line for me. It feels a bit like I'm being accepted into the family they made for themselves.

It's amazing how many people are here obsessing over such a shitty human like Ronnie. The world is so quick to idolize somebody when they gain even a little bit of popularity, regardless of their morals. It makes me sick. From what the guys told me, this creep assaults women. You'd think other women would steer clear of him, but as I look out into the room, they're all throwing themselves at him.

Drinks are being served, and the music is bumping loudly when I find myself getting bored. The guys made it clear they don't drink on jobs, but they never said anything about dancing to pass the time. Without saying anything to them, I get up and make my way to the dance floor to sway my hips to the music. Kyler watches me with amusement as I take a rare moment and let myself feel free.

A few songs have passed by the time I spin back around to where the guys are sitting and lock eyes with Seb. He looks angry and I see his jaw tic just before I feel warmth from behind me. Looking down, a hand is placed on my left hip to aid me in swaying to the beat with him.

"You might be the most gorgeous woman I have ever seen," a strange voice says.

My eyes widen briefly with panic when I realize the guy groping me from behind is actually the guy we're trying to kill. I went off script and made myself desirable to someone other than Kyler. I should've had him out here dancing with me if we were going to sell the whole lovers in the corner act. I center my thoughts without overreacting. This can still be salvaged. I can get the bag of laced drugs from Seb and handle it on my own.

The music changes to a slower upbeat song, and I feel Ronnie behind me rubbing his tiny dick on me. He's hard, and it's enough to make me want to throw up. Seb and Kyler haven't taken their eyes off of us. I assume wherever Barrett is posted, he's watching on the cameras too.

Ronnie leans down into my ear and whispers, "Do you want to take this somewhere a little more private?" I glance over my shoulder, keeping up the flirtatious act.

"With you, absolutely. Just let me snag my phone from my brother real quick." His hand leaves my waist, and I walk seductively back over to Ky and Seb, trying not to cause a scene.

"He wants me to go with him. Give me the bag, and I'll handle the job." Seb goes to open his mouth, and I quickly cut him off. "We don't have time to argue. I have the in, give it to me. Now."

Without further hesitation, he reaches into his pocket and slips me the bag. "Don't fuck this up, and Callie, for fucks sake, do not touch what's in that bag. It will kill you."

I nod and slip it into the pocket of my jeans, slowly spinning back around to where Ronnie's waiting for me with his arm extended. After wrapping my arm around his, we walk to the back of the building, through a door, and down a long hall. When we make it to the end of the hallway, there's a door on the left that opens up into a huge room full of lounge furniture, a pool table, a bar, and enough things to keep the party going for a while. He walks over to the bar and tells me that he's going to grab something to make the night a little more fun, and I use this as my opportunity.

"I have a better idea," I say as I grab the baggie from my pocket and dangle in the air in front of him. His face breaks out into a huge grin.

"You little minx. You've been holding out on me."

"Maybe, but I'm not now." Shyly, I bite my lip to appear more seductive. I just need this dumb fuck to take the drugs so I can get the hell out of here.

He gestures over to one of the bar stools. "Join mc."

I walk over and stand next to the barstool to watch as he pulls out the baggie, lines the coke on the top of the bar, and sections two portions out. He thinks I'm going to do a line with him.

"Ladies first." He winks, but I need to think quickly because there is no way I'm touching that shit. I lean forward and touch his arm instead.

"Normally, I'd agree, but it's such an honor to be here with you. I'd love to see what you think first. That stuff is supposed to be the best of the best. I got it especially for you." I do my best to bat my eyes and play the innocent Barbie he wants me to be, all while stroking his ego. This is too easy.

"Fuck yes, gorgeous and smart. I hit the jackpot tonight." He leans down and sniffs the powder up in a quick action, letting out a loud groan. "That is some prime product. Where did you ge- Whe- Fu-." Blood starts to pour out of his nose, and his face slams down onto the bar as whatever is in the bag takes action.

I grab the towel off of the bar to snag up the baggie that has my fingerprints on it, being careful not to touch what's inside, and use my shirt to open the door back into the hallway. When we walked in, I was careful not to touch anything, so there shouldn't be any trace of me ever being in this room. I quickly make my way back down the hallway and out the door we came in through, depositing myself back into the main room.

I glance around quickly to see if anyone noticed me, but nobody's looking in my direction, so I head back to where the guys are sitting. Seb is on the phone and is clearly pissed off. It sounds like he's talking to Barrett. He turns his head, sees me, grabs me by the arm, and pulls me out of the event's building.

"Careful, I still have this." I hold up the bag of drugs wrapped up in the towel. He snatches it from my hand and shoves me forward.

"Give me that and get in the fucking car."

Barrett pulls the car to where we are standing and looks just as upset as Seb. Kyler ignores me and slips in the front seat, leaving me in the back with dickface. As soon as we are moving, Seb lays into me.

"What the fuck were you thinking going off script like that? We have plans in place for a reason." Sebastian scolds me.

"It's fine. The job is done. He's dead. I don't see what the big deal is." I shrug.

Sebastian grabs my chin hard, forcing me to look at him. "Someone got a jump on Barrett because he was so preoccupied with watching you shake your ass on the dancefloor. He wasn't watching his camera pointed at the car, and someone knocked him out. It was sheer fucking luck that Ky was coming out there to see if he could find out where Ronnie took YOU. If he hadn't come out when he did, Barrett could be dead."

A mixture of shame and guilt washes over me as I take in his words. I almost got them killed because I was bored. How could I be so stupid? I fucked this up so bad.

"I didn't know. I'm so sorry." Tears well up in my eyes when I think about how I could have potentially lost another person who has become such an important fixture of my life.

"It's okay, princess; don't sweat it," Barrett tells me with a wink from the front seat. "If I die because I was looking at your fine ass, I'd be ok with that," he says, clearly trying to lighten the mood, but it only makes me feel worse.

The remainder of the car ride back to the house is nothing but complete silence. I don't blame them for being upset. When we pull up to the gate, Barrett scans us in, and everyone quietly goes their separate ways. I can't deal with any of this right now, so I decide to go take a shower and wash the stench of Ronnie off of me before trying to smooth things over with them.

Chapter 31
Callie

After I get out of the shower, I walk down the hall to Barrett's room without clothes on and a mission on my mind. I nearly got him killed, but I intend to do everything in my power to make up for it.

When I walk in the doorway, I freeze. All three of them are in the room wearing nothing but boxers, and their gaze lands straight on me. I catch Sebastian looking at my body up and down, and I flush at the thought of him seeing all of me like this. What the hell is going on?

Kyler speaks up before I have time to fully process the moment. "Oh wanderer, you don't realize what you just walked into. You have one chance to walk away. If you choose to stay, we won't be taking it easy on you. That stunt you pulled earlier deserves punishment."

I look over at Barrett, and the grin on his face should scare me, but it has my pussy twitching with need. My body yearns to atone for my earlier mistake in whatever way they deem necessary.

"I'm staying," I breathe out in a barely audible tone.

"Speak up, Callie," Barrett throws back at me.

"I'm staying. Do what you need to do to make it right."

"Good. Now get your pretty little ass on the bed- now." Barrett pats the bed next to where he is sitting.

"No, make her crawl," Seb says from the corner. My eyes instantly widen at his words. I didn't realize he was staying.

"Would you like that, princess? A filthy slut like you desperate for some cock and crawling around for the three of us?" Barrett asks, and fuck, if it doesn't immediately have my pussy dripping for them. I can't form words, so I nod my head.

"Be our good little whore and crawl like Seb told you to." I want to protest Barrett's request, but I don't have control of my own body.

I lower myself to my hands and knees and make my way toward where he and Kyler are sitting on the edge of the bed. The feeling of the carpet beneath my knees and knowing all three of them have their eyes fixed on my naked body has me blazing with desire.

"That's our good girl," I hear Kyler say, and it sends chills right through me.

I stop when I'm between the two of them, unsure of who to go to, so I sit back on my knees, place my hands on my thighs, and peer up. Barrett widens his legs, cueing me to move in that direction, so I do.

He reaches down and takes my chin between his fingers, lifting my head up to look at him. "You could've ruined everything today, you know that, right?"

I nod. I messed up. I shouldn't have gotten up to dance.

Barrett's hand caresses my face in an eerily reassuring way. "Since it was all three of us that you disobeyed, I think it's only fitting that you receive a punishment from each of us. What do you think, boys?"

"I think that's more than fair," Kyler speaks up first.

"I don't know if she can handle my punishment," Seb says, and I snap my head in his direction.

"I think I've proven that I can handle more than you think," I retort. He's still an annoying asshole, but I can let that slide just this once, right?

"Hmmm, maybe, but I still don't think you're quite ready." His head tilts to the side. "Last chance."

"My safe word is pickle," I state, not backing down.

He stands up, and out of nowhere, Barrett lifts me up onto his lap so that my bare back is touching his stomach. He places one leg over each of his knees, fully spreading me out, and then leans back flat on the bed. This position has me more vulnerable than I think I want to be. When I try to sit up, one of Barrett's hands latch around my neck. The other wraps around my waist to hold me in place. His grip is firm but not tight enough to where I can't breathe.

Sebastian makes his way between my legs and leans down. "Look how wet you are. We haven't even touched you yet. Tell me, Callie, are you that much of a desperate little slut?"

All I can focus on is his words and what they're doing to me. I am a desperate, needy slut for all of them. My body craves this submission.

"You're already making a mess of yourself." His hand trails down, and I feel his fingers trace the outside of my pussy, spreading my arousal around before slamming two fingers into me.

"Fuck," I yell as I bring my hands to Barrett's arms and dig my nails into his skin hard enough to make him bleed. I can feel him getting hard under me. He loves the pain.

Seb moves his fingers in and out of me at a quick pace, building me up before curling his fingers into me like he knows exactly how to make my body respond to him. Just as I'm on the precipice of exploding, he rips his fingers out and slaps my pussy hard. I squeal, and he shoves the fingers he just had inside me into my mouth.

"Taste yourself and tell me how sweet you are." I swirl my tongue around his fingers and look directly into his eyes in time to see them darken with approval. He pulls his fingers out and spits in my mouth before placing his hand back down to cover it.

"Swallow like the good girl Ky claims you are." Shock flows through me, but I don't hesitate to obey. His hand leaves my face, and he slaps my pussy again. It has me moaning and arching my back, wanting more.

"She likes the pain, doesn't she?" He's talking to Barrett this time.

I can feel Barrett nod. "Oh, she's a needy slut for it." I feel a sharp pinch on my clit and look down to see Seb pinching the most sensitive part of me between his fingers. It sends a shooting sensation of ecstasy through my entire body.

"Seb, please," I beg him.

"You call me Sir when I have my hands on you, Callie." He slaps my pussy for a third time. This time was much harder than the previous two.

"Fine, Sir, will you make me come? It's too much." I plead with him, and he chuckles. He fucking chuckles, then steps back to admire his work before sitting back down in that damn chair.

Barrett leans the two of us back up into a sitting position, my legs still perched onto his and my pussy still fully on display, and I hear Seb say, "Girls who are being punished don't get pleasure from me, Callie. You're lucky I took it easy on you."

Barrett uses my momentary distraction to flip me around and place me ass up on his lap, my head resting on Kyler's knee beside him. I look up in confusion when Barrett says, "My turn. Don't worry. I'll take it easy on you this time, too. How about we count? What do you say?"

Before I have a chance to reply and ask what he is talking about, a hand hits my left ass cheek, and fuck, it stings like a bitch. He slaps again, only this time harder in the same place.

"Count, Callie. The ones you don't count are all freebies for me." He slaps a third time. Why am I not counting? Another slap. I let him get three freebies before I could make myself speak.

"One," I say and add, "But what are we counting to?" My words come out in a breathless moan as another slap comes down hard. This time, he rubs his hand on my sensitive skin afterward. "Two." This is a whole new sensation, and I'm unsure about it. Two more slaps come rapidly. "Three, four," I cry out.

"How about we do ten since you're finally listening so well." Slap. Slap. Slap. Rub.

"Five, six, seven. Fuck." My pussy is throbbing from his mixture of pleasure and pain. Sebastian already left me panting and needy, but this is another level. Slap. "Eight," I hear myself say. Tears have started to stream down my face, and I'm not really sure why. Slap. Slap. "Nine, Ten," I say as he rubs my cheeks.

"Your ass turns the perfect shade of red for me," Barrett says. His cock is so hard I can feel it pushing up into my pelvis, but he doesn't try to fuck me. He just keeps rubbing and massaging my sore cheeks. The mixture of sensations is too much.

"Please, Barrett." I don't even know what I am asking for at this point, but I need some sort of release. I need more.

His only response is to pull me up and sit me on his lap. I wince at the pain, my ass still tender from his punishment, and his eyes widen a bit, fire and desire coursing through them. He reaches up and grabs a handful of my hair to pull my head to him, and his mouth devours me in an all-consuming kiss. A moan leaves my mouth as my lips part.

I reach my hand up to wipe the tears from my face, but he pulls it away and then licks up the length of my cheek. "Your tears taste like heaven, Callie."

I hear Kyler speak up next to us. "It's my turn, wanderer. I loved watching you redden from the punishment Barrett and Seb gave you, but I prefer to punish you in a different way." He looks so mischievous right now. "I'm going to punish you with pleasure."

My brows raise in confusion. That doesn't sound like a punishment at all. If he wants to take it easy on me, I'm definitely not going to argue.

"You've been such a good fucking girl for them, haven't you? You took everything they gave you so well." He stands up and reaches his hand out to me, bringing me to a standing position in front of him. I nod, waiting for his next move. He gently leads me to the bed and sits me down, pushing my back toward the mattress.

"Lie back and let me get to work. You're so pretty when you let me use you." He kneels in front of me and flips my legs onto his shoulders, wrapping an arm around each one and pulling me to the edge of the bed. I don't have a chance to even react to the feeling of his breath on my pussy before he dives right in. Within seconds, I'm falling right over the edge of the orgasm both Seb and Barrett denied me. I feel the bed shift beside us and notice Barrett slipping out of the room.

Kyler pulls me back to my current reality when he says, "That's my good girl. Now another." He dives right back in and licks me from top to bottom. "You taste so good."

His mouth suctions to my clit, and I'm thrown over the edge again and again, my body starting to become oversensitive from the amount of pleasure he's given me. He pushes one finger into me and curls it slightly, finding that spot that nearly has me tipping over the edge again. I didn't even think my body could react like this. His tongue laps at me, determined to bring me right back to the cliff I just fell off of. I feel so overwhelmed, and my body is trembling at this point. He pulls back, giving me a small moment of relief before deciding he isn't finished with me yet.

"Ky, I can't, it's too much." My legs shake around his face.

"You can take it. Give me one more." He pushes two fingers into me as his tongue focuses back on my clit. The sensation drives me absolutely wild. I can feel every nerve-ending tingling in my body coursing with heat. Another moan leaves me, and before I realize what's happening, I feel a warm gush coming out of me as I reach another climax.

"Fuck, Callie, did you just squirt?" he asks before pulling me up to a seated position.

"I... I.. that's never happened before. I don't.." He interrupts me by grabbing the back of my neck and pulling me into a kiss.

He pulls back and whispers in my ear, "You're perfect for us. Our perfect fucking girl." Taking away every shred of embarrassment I may have felt just seconds ago. My body is weak, and I don't know how much more of this I can take.

Thankfully, it seems like the punishments are over because he lifts me up to carry me to the bathroom. I notice the tub is full of water and Barrett is standing in the corner waiting for Ky to put me in. That must be where he went when I felt the bed shift. This man came in to run me a warm bath.

Kyler places me in the tub and runs the washcloth along my body. The warm water instantly relaxes my muscles and makes my eyes heavy. "No sleeping just yet, wanderer. Let us finish taking care of you, and then we'll get in bed."

My eyes close disobediently, and I feel hands on me, pulling me out of the water and drying me off. I feel a shirt slip over my head, and a hand rubbing some kind of cream on my backside. It's cool and feels nice.

Barrett lifts me bridal style to carry me back to the bedroom, and I snuggle into him. He smells so good. He puts me down on the fluffy mattress and pulls the covers over me as I drift off into unconsciousness, completely blissed out.

A few hours later, I wake up and look around the room to see where I ended up. It looks dark outside, but I'm in Kyler's bed with him sleeping on one side of me and Barrett on the other. This is exactly where I want to be, so I snuggle back into them and go back to sleep.

Chapter 32
Barrett

Waking up next to Callie has become something I look forward to. Her beautiful brown hair is spread across the pillows, and the sound of her breathing soothes something in me. She's the first bit of brightness I've had in my life in a long time.

I've discovered that just like my brothers and I, she has pieces of herself that she only lets out when she feels comfortable around you. A beautiful puzzle that has become my own secret mission to complete.

When she's not with me, I watch her. She is like an addiction that I can't get enough of. When we brought her here, it was under extraordinary circumstances. None of us could have imagined her becoming so willingly intertwined with us, and now that she has, none of us want to let her go.

Despite how much Seb tries to push her away, even he will admit she's ours. The bed shifts beside me, and those beautiful hazel eyes pop open to meet mine. A smile crosses her face, and she leans into me. I think she's happy here with us. I think she would want to stay if we gave her the choice.

Bending down, I kiss the top of her head. "Morning, princess."

She looks around, not seeing anyone else in the room, and looks up to me in question.

"They went to do another job. Don't worry. They'll be back in a few hours. We didn't want to wake you after last night."

"That was... umm... unexpected." She looks nervous.

"Do you want to talk about it?" I ask her.

"We don't have to. I have no complaints if that's what you're worried about," she says.

"Good. You know your safe word applies to all of us, even in situations outside of the bedroom. I want you to feel at peace here." Those words are the truest words I've ever spoken. Her happiness has become something I've come to want over my own. It's an odd feeling for someone like me.

"Barrett?" Her eyes look a bit sad as she brings her hand to caress the side of my cheek.

"What do you need, princess?"

"If I wanted to leave, would you guys let me?"

I know this is something that she's been thinking about, but I don't know what the right answer is. Would we let her leave? I want to say yes if that's what she truly wanted, but the monster in me says hell no, she's not going anywhere. I try my best to give her the most truthful answer I can.

"I don't know. We've gotten past the point where you're a prisoner here if that's what you're wondering. You've become so much more to us. We want you to stay at least until your father is taken care of, but once he's dead, that would fully be your choice whether to stay or leave. If it's up to me, I want you to stay." I hate the vulnerable feeling of that admission as I wait for her response. Her eyes flicker back and forth between mine, almost as if she is making sure I'm sincere. Another smile crosses her face and she leans up to kiss me softly on the lips. It's as if what I said to her was exactly what she needed to hear.

"Tell me something about you that I don't know," she says to me, and I know what she wants. She wants to see me, all of me.

I knew this time would come. There are very few people in this world who fully know me. To be exact, there are two of them, and they both live in this house. I take a deep breath, hoping this doesn't change her view of me. "My mom and stepdad died in a fire when I was young. It was the reason I ended up in foster care."

She looks at me, waiting to see if I'm going to continue before saying anything. I roll onto my back to look up at the ceiling.

"I was eight when my mom got married to my stepdad. He was the first real father figure I had in my life because my mom never knew who my real father was. She was a bit promiscuous when she ended up pregnant with me. Everything was normal for the first few months, and we felt like a real family. My mom started working late shifts and leaving me at home with Stan, my stepfather." I look over at her to see she is listening intently, and she brings her arm up to rest it on my chest as a sign of support.

"It started slowly. He would come into my room and make me change in front of him. A few weeks later, he was helping me change, and there would be a stray touch here and there. A few weeks after that, he got the courage to take things further. He claimed he wanted to teach me about being a man and how our bodies worked. I was a kid. I didn't know it was wrong, so when I brought it up over dinner one night, my mom lost it on me. She told me that I shouldn't tell lies and that it was dangerous to talk about adults like that. She was never really a good mom to me like Ky and Seb had. She focused on the men coming in and out of our lives and always chose them over me."

"Barrett, I'm so sorry your mom didn't hear you." Her hand reaches up to caress my face and I place mine over hers.

"That night after dinner was the worst of them all. The things he did to me, I wanted to die. He was angry that I told my mom about what we did in our private time, and he wanted to make sure I knew the consequences if I ever told anyone again." I can tell my admission is breaking her heart. I don't want people to pity me. My life hasn't always been the best, but it was all part of the path that led me here with Seb and Ky, and I wouldn't change a single thing.

"He used me and left me there, crying and feeling ashamed for hours. When I had the courage to pick myself off the bed, there was blood everywhere. My little body was broken, Callie. Before I even realized what I was doing, I had gone into the kitchen, grabbed the matchbook from the drawer, and walked into their bedroom. I stood there, at the base of their bed, for a few minutes watching them sleep, feeling completely disgusted at my mother for taking Stan's side and at Stan for using my body like that. I lit a match and tossed it right on their bed."

She lets out an audible gasp, but I continue. "I'm not sure why my mother didn't wake up when the flames started to cover the mattress. Sometimes she took sleeping pills, and maybe that was one of those nights. Stan drank heavily, so he was likely blacked out from the alcohol, but neither one of them woke up. When the smoke got too heavy for me to breathe, I ran out of the house and stood on the street as I watched it burn to the ground. It was the middle of the night, so it took a while for someone to notice and call the police. I kept waiting for either of them to run out of the house, but they never did. Stan was a smoker, so the fire chief ruled the blaze accidental. They claimed he must've fallen asleep holding a cigarette since the fire started in bed. I didn't have any other living family. They took me right into state custody. I never told anyone it was really me who lit that fire until I met Sebastian and Kyler, and now you."

"Can I ask you a question?" I hear her say.

I nod, anxious to know what she thinks of this confession.

"Is that why you have panic attacks?" I can see the pained look in her eyes now that she knows the full truth of my upbringing.

"It is, well, was. I took back control of my narrative to keep them at bay. I've found a way to guide that pain into a different sensation. For a long time, I let what he did to me define me, but a therapist along the way recommended I try to channel my pain into something I love instead. I'm sure she meant maybe painting or art, but I chose sex. It's my own personal way of taking back control of my past."

She nods in understanding. This woman pushes me to want to be a better person every day. When we first brought her here, I never would've imagined being here at this moment telling her my darkest secret, but I want her to know me more than I've wanted anything before.

"Barrett," she whispers. I turn to face her, placing my hand on her hip and looking her in the eyes.

"Yeah, princess?"

"Thank you for telling me that. I'm so sorry that happened to you."

"I'm not. Everyone endures pain at some point in their lives, but my pain made me who I am today. It brought me to my brothers, and it brought me to you."

A tear slips and rolls down her cheek, and she turns away from me like she's conflicted about being so vulnerable around me. I bring my hand up to swipe her face dry and then lift a finger to my mouth.

"Your tears are mine, Callie. You don't ever need to be afraid of having emotions around me."

"I feel things with you that I shouldn't be feeling Barrett. I don't know how to describe what is happening in the mess that is my brain."

She's struggling, and it's a familiar feeling. I have so many new emotions since being around her. I've never been the kind of person to openly share my life with others, but she brings that out of me. I want to find a way to reassure her that whatever she is feeling isn't wrong, so I do it the only way I can. I confess it all. I lay everything on the line and take the risk because, for the first time in a long time, there's something I'm afraid of losing.

"Callie, I need to tell you something else."

"You can tell me anything."

I steady myself and look deep into her eyes. "Having you here has changed something in me. I want to be around you all the time. I want to see your hazel eyes looking up at me when you wake up and before you go to sleep. I want to push you to your limits so I can see you thrive from the challenge. I want to see your best and worst. I don't know what love feels like, but if that's what love is, then I need you to know that I'm in love with you."

I let the power of the words flow through me. I've never known a woman's love. My mother only loved herself and her boyfriends. I never let myself get close enough to another woman to even have this be a possibility. She tries to respond to me, but I bring my finger up to her lips, shushing her.

"I don't want you saying anything yet. Take some time to really understand what I'm telling you. This isn't something I say lightly. You have my love if you want it. I'm yours. All of me." She nods, and I lean in to give her a reassuring kiss.

When I pull back, my finger trails across her jawline, running my thumb along her bottom lip. Her mouth parts slightly, allowing me to push my thumb in, and I feel her tongue around me. "Suck." She obeys so well, licking and sucking on my thumb until I pull it from her with a popping noise. "Strip and get on your knees in front of the bed." She moves quickly, like she needs this moment between us just as much as I do. I undress and position myself seated on the bed in front of her, my cock straining for her lips to be wrapped around it.

"Open your mouth and take it deep for me, Callie." She leans forward, licking my length, swirling her tongue around each one of the piercings that line my shaft before moving to the tip and gently nipping at it. Her lips part, and she takes me in, bobbing up and down. My cock feels so tight in her throat. I groan in approval before burying my fingers in her hair and taking control. The thrusts become harder and faster as she gags around me with drool rolling down her chin.

"Yes, that's it. Swallow my cock like a good little slut." She whimpers, sending vibrations through me. I can feel my balls begin to tighten, so I use one hand to pull her head back and bring the other to my cock, stroking myself a few more times before painting her face with my come. She looks up at me, panting, her eyes blazing with a fiery need.

"You look so pretty when you're messy. I love seeing my come dripping from your chin." My dirty girl grins before sliding her thumb across her chin and sticking it in her mouth to lick my release off of it. I groan in approval.

This girl is perfect for me. "Up on the bed and lay on your back," I tell her. "I fully intend on fucking you like my dirty whore over and over again, but first things first." I reach over to grab my knife. I bared my soul to her. Now, let's see how much she's really willing to take. "Do you trust me?"

"Yes," she breathes out.

"Remember your safe word, princess."

I slide the tip of the knife over her collarbone and run it down her torso, swirling around her stomach as it moves up and down. I carefully move the cold tip lower before placing it on her clit. She lets out a breathless moan, her entire body freezing up, not knowing what to expect next.

"Should I fuck you with it? Would a dirty slut like you like that?"

Her entire face flushes a deep crimson, but she doesn't deny she wants it. "Yes."

"Beg."

"Fuck me with your knife, Barrett, please," she tells me, and who am I to deny her.

"You sound so sweet when you beg. I love it." I flip the knife around in my hand, taking hold of the blade before spreading the base around her soaking entrance. Slowly, I slide it in, locking eyes with her, a small growl escaping my chest as I begin to move it in and out. I bring up my other hand to put pressure on her clit, and she lifts her hips, causing the sharp edge to slice into my palm. "Stay still," I tell her before picking up the pace.

"You're taking it so well."

She moans, legs beginning to shake as I see the familiar look of pleasure wash over her face. She's so beautiful when she falls apart. Pulling the knife from her, I toss it on the floor and line myself up at her entrance.

"You're bleeding," she tells me in a slightly panicked voice, but I don't care. She tries to sit up, and I push her back down.

"I would let every last drop of blood drain from my body if it meant seeing the look of pleasure on your face again."

I throw both of her legs over my shoulders, lifting her back off the mattress, and slam into her. Thrusting in and out until I feel her strangle my cock with her pussy. It's not enough. I'll never get enough of her. I pull out and flip her over onto her stomach, running my fingers along the curves of her skin.

Smack. I crash my hand along the base of her ass, and she raises up to me, groaning in pleasure. Kneeling behind her, my fingers find her hips, and I seat myself back inside her where I belong. She is so wet and messy. Slowly my thumb rubs around the wetness before dipping into her ass.

"Barrett, fuck!"

"You want me to use both of your holes, princess?" I circle my thumb inside her, slowly stretching her out.

"All of me." That is all she has the energy to say before she clamps down on my cock again. I feel the warmth of her release on my cock, and I lose any restraint I thought I had. The next thing I know, I'm filling up her sweet pussy with my come.

Pulling out of her and lying down, I bring her close to me so I can hold her for just a few minutes while we both come down from the high. She relaxes in my arms and lets the exhaustion take her over, pulling her back to sleep. I carefully get up to clean the cut on my hand, bandage it, and grab a warm washcloth for her.

Afterward, I curl back in bed next to her and whisper, "I love you," before drifting off to unconscious happiness, enjoying the moment with her. The start of our day can wait a few more hours.

Chapter 33
Damien (Julian)

My phone vibrates inside my pocket. Looking down, I see Soren calling, and it better be with good news this time. Not bothering to endure the pleasantries, I jump right to the point, "Tell me you've got something."

"Oh, I've got something. I know exactly where they are and exactly how to get her out. You were right. All we had to do was wait for them to fuck up."

Yes! This is what I've been waiting for.

"Perfect. I'm booking a flight and will be back at the compound in a few hours. I want you to meet me there to discuss all the details and specs in person. The sooner we get this done and over with, the better." I hang up and immediately dial Gabriel to let him know we found his precious little girl.

"You better be calling for a reason, Damien. It's been three months, and my daughter is still not back here where she belongs."

"I was calling to tell you we found her. Soren and I are meeting at the compound later tonight if you'd like to join us and find out further details. If all goes well, she should be back with us within the next 48 hours."

"I don't want the details. This is your mess to clean up. Do what you need to do, Damien, just get her back here."

"Of course, sir. I'll let you know as soon as I have her, and we are en route to you."

"Damien?"

"Yes, sir?"

"Don't fuck this up again. This is your last opportunity." My last opportunity. I want to tell him to eat shit, but that isn't going to give me the power that I need, so I'll play his fucking lacky just a little longer.

"Understood." I hang up and pocket my phone, driving straight home to pack a quick bag and get to the airport. There are always flights to Nashville every few hours.

When I pull up to the airport, the worker at the flight desk advises me that the next flight is flying out in two hours. That's perfect. I shoot a quick text to Soren, letting him know what time to meet me at the compound to put together our plan, and he confirms almost instantly. Now I wait.

If I had known before she went missing that playing the Julian role would lead to this much of a mess, I would never have gone through with it. I would've grabbed her as soon as I found her and taken her back to the house, maybe chained her to my bed until she learned her lesson for running from her fate. How fucking stupid on my part.

Giving her the idea of freedom was only ever supposed to be a game, but I let it go on for too long. I got caught up in being her little saving grace and the idea of her entire soul being crushed when she found out the truth. Getting her back is going to be worth it. With any luck, she still doesn't realize who I really am.

After a few hours of plotting and planning how I intend to make her pay for every minute she's been away from me, I pull into the compound and meet Soren in the main building. We go into a small conference room and get to work on the plan to go get my future wife and bring her back where she belongs.

Soren immediately jumps in, starting the conversation. "Just like we suspected your wife to be has been shacked up with the Monroe brothers. I didn't know for sure until recently because it was always just them every time they left the house. They fucked up and took her out in public this week. My software flagged her face, and I was able to have a member of the guard get what I needed so we can infiltrate their house. You said you wanted to make sure you're the one to bring her back to Gabriel, right?" I nod at him in approval, completely in awe that, for once, someone was able to listen and do their job correctly.

"The house is on complete lockdown with no way to get through the gate. Whoever set up their security is almost as good as I am, but I'm better," Soren tells me, but I don't care about any of that.

"Get to the point," I cut back at him.

"I was able to get the access I needed, and we have the full capability of coming and going right through their front gate without them ever knowing anything is out of order. If we're smart about it, we should go in the middle of the night with a small team when they're asleep to ensure they don't see us coming."

The idea of busting into their house and grabbing her out of her sleep sends a thrill right to my bones.

"They won't get their usual alerts when someone breaches their gate because I was able to override it. As long as we don't wake them when we pull up, we should be able to completely surprise them. Get in, take her, and get out. Whatever we do outside of that while we're there is up to your discretion."

I consider both options but decide to tell him it's best to not make enemies. "We don't need to make any more enemies than we have to. If we can get in and get her, that is all I am worried about. The Monroe brothers are Gabriel's problem. If anyone gets in the way of the goal, we use whatever force necessary to get her out of there."

We go over a few more details of our plan, like what time and how many men we'll be taking with us, before deciding we have all of our bases covered and call it a night. Tomorrow night we will go get her, and my little bitch will be exactly where she is supposed to be. Her father can get off my back and life will go back to normal.

I still can't believe she's been with those fucking brothers this whole time. I'm sure they've been keeping her in a cage somewhere or using her like a dirty whore. After doing whatever Gabriel plans with her the first few nights, the first thing we will take care of is getting her a doctor's visit setup. I have to make sure all is well with my property after all.

From there, I'll move forward with the wedding, and all the other plans for her will fall into place. I'm sure she'll fight us throughout the process, and God, I hope she does. She let me into her mind while I was playing the part of Julian, and I know she has at least one weakness- Avery. I will use that cunt against her if I have to. I never liked her to begin with. She always knew something about me wasn't right.

Even if Callie had listened to her, it wouldn't have made a difference. I just wouldn't have had the chance to play my game with her mind. She was always destined to end up back in my grasp.

Callie will marry me, and she will make me a father. I don't give a fuck what happens to her after that. I'll have the next in line to raise at my side. Once my son is secured, I'll kill her and her father if I must.

It's ironic really. Her father put all these plans in place to make sure that he had an heir to take over once he dies, but what the dumb fuck didn't realize is that by giving himself an heir, he's signing his death warrant.

"Let's go get my fiancé," I tell Soren.

Chapter 34
Callie

The guys are all busy doing their own things this afternoon, so I take this as the perfect opportunity to have a bit of a me day. It's raining outside, and I'm not really in the mood to work out, so I head over to their lounge room to scour the bookshelf that they added for me.

After the first few weeks of being here, they realized the books they had tossed on the floor in the cell wouldn't be enough. I find peace in escaping to a new world, so Kyler surprised me with a shelf full of at least 100 books ranging from thrillers to downright pure smut. The variety has been nice.

Today, I picked up a romance novel. After the night I had with Barrett, you could say that love is in the air, even if I'm not ready to say it back to him yet. I make myself comfortable on the couch and dive right in.

A few hours pass by the time I near the end of the book, I and wish I had read more about this one before picking it up. The female main character's love interest just died in a car accident, and now I'm sitting here bawling my eyes out.

Love and loss. Painful thoughts shoot through me as I recall the night I lost Maxton. The ache of wanting someone so much but never being able to feel them or hold them again.

I try to practice the exercises Barrett taught me and bring my mind to better thoughts to keep myself from spiraling into another panic attack. I land on the day Maxton and I went to the drive-in movies with our moms. We drove separately so my father didn't ask questions about why we were going with them. My mother was always supportive of my relationship with Maxton.

When we got to the movies, we parked our car next to theirs and laid out the blanket and pillows on the ground in front of the car. My mom snuck over to his mom's blanket and left us on our own. I wish I could thank her for giving me those moments with him. I can't remember what the movie we watched was called, but it was an older movie that had us laughing the entire time. Toward the end of the movie, Maxton shifted his body closer to mine and grabbed my hand so that I'd look at him before he leaned in to kiss me. I was so worried about our moms seeing us that I didn't enjoy the moment. I regret that now. Kyler walks in just as I get to the part of the memory where Maxton kisses me. He takes in my appearance slowly and sits next to me on the couch.

"What's on your mind, wanderer?"

"Oh, it's nothing, just lost in thought."

"It's not nothing. The look on your face isn't one that I've seen on you before, and I want to know what's causing it."

"I'm sorry. I was just thinking about Maxton and some of the things we used to do together."

"Do you want to talk about it?"

"You would want me to talk to you about him?" I ask hesitantly.

"Of course I do. He was important to you, and he was Seb's brother."

I nod and proceed to tell him about our drive-in date with our moms. He sits there listening as I move on to the next story about the day we all went to the park and then the memory of our first baseball game, the trips to the supermarket, and the day we snuck off into the woods to swim in the nearby lake. Sharing these happy moments with him has lifted the pain off of my heart in a way I can't describe. I feel relieved. I look down at Ky, thankful for the space he's given me to share these things with him.

"Thank you for listening. You don't realize how much it means to me."

"Thank you for sharing. I want to know everything about you, Callie. I care about you more than you realize. Everything with you started out as an obsession, watching you and learning as much as I could, but it's developed into so much more now. I want you to know that you can talk to me about anything whenever you want. I'm always here to listen."

My thoughts whirl around my head. Last night, Barrett confessed his feelings to me, and I have the sudden urge to do the same to Kyler. He puts the air in my lungs and makes me feel whole. He never judges me and is always the first one to offer support.

"Kyler, I.." He brings his hand up to my face to stop the words from coming out of my mouth, shaking his head like he knows what I am about to say. He doesn't want them said like this, not after we just talked about Maxton. He wants his own moment, and I understand, so I lean in and kiss him.

Our kiss deepens before he moves to my neck to kiss and suck all the way up to my ear. "Do you want to be my good girl tonight?"

Hell yes! I want to be his good girl every night. I nod, and he stands up, reaching out to grab my hand. Slowly, he strips the two of us of all of our clothes before he motions for me to sit back down on the couch. As soon as I sit, he drops to his knees in front of me and runs his hands up and down my thighs. "You're so fucking beautiful."

He leans in, pushing my knees out as far as they go before his tongue trails along my opening. I lean back to give him better access while his tongue moves in and out of me at a slow pace. Wetness drips down from me, and he brings his hand up to catch some of it before swirling around my back entrance. I immediately tense up, and he pulls back.

"You said you wanted to be my good girl, right?" he asks, and I nod. "Then you can take it." Slowly he pushes one finger into my ass as he leans back down to continue feasting on my pussy. He moves his finger in unison with the flicks of his tongue, and my body feels like it's on fire. He pushes a second finger in, and

I see stars coming so hard on his face that I'm surprised he can still breathe.

"That's my girl. I'm so proud of you." He stands up in front of me, pulling me up and positioning my body so that I'm bent over on the side of the couch. Anyone could walk in and see us, and it turns me on even more. Slowly, he pushes into me, hitting a deeper spot than ever before. "You're always so fucking tight."

His hand reaches up to the back of my neck, and he pushes my head down as he thrusts into me from behind. I grip the cushions of the couch as electricity builds in me. He thrusts harder, and my body tightens. I hear footsteps, and my head jerks up. Barrett is standing there watching as Kyler continues to move in and out of me, my body getting closer and closer to the point of no return.

He takes another step further before locking eyes with me. "I could keep watching, or I could join. The choice is yours, princess." Kyler slows while he waits for my response, saying nothing to contradict Barrett's question.

Both of them? I never considered the possibility of both of them together, and it thrills me! Without saying words, I reach my hand out toward him, signaling for him to join us. He looks at Ky in a silent conversation, and Ky nods before pulling out of me and sitting on the couch in front of me, just out of reach. I try to stand and join him, but he shakes his head. "Stay."

I feel a warm hand slide along my ass moments later. Barrett has rid himself of his clothing and stepped in Kyler's place behind me. His hand smacks so hard against my ass it makes my toes curl.

"Does Ky know how dirty you like it, princess?" Another smack lands on the other cheek, and I peer up at Kyler. Another smack.

"Tell him. Tell him you like it when I use you like a filthy whore." Another smack.

"I love it!" I gasp when he pushes two fingers into my pussy, moving them in and out at a slow pace.

"He already got you nice and worked up, didn't he?" Barrett groans.

Kyler's gaze goes to Barrett briefly before he slides closer to me at the end of the couch, placing his cock directly in front of my face. I'm panting with the need to finish when Barrett pulls his fingers back out of me, leaving me right on the edge again.

"Be a good little slut and make my brother come with that beautiful mouth." Another smack hits my ass, and I lick my lips leaning forward to take Kyler in. He reaches his hand up to grab my hair and pushes my head down to the hilt. I try my best to keep my breathing under control so I don't gag on his length before he pulls my head back up to allow me air. He keeps a slow pace, moving my head up and down as I swirl my tongue around him at every opportunity I'm afforded.

Behind me, Barrett pushes two fingers back into my pussy briefly before pulling them out and circling them around my ass. He gives me no notice before pushing them into my tight hole. I moan around Kyler's cock at the feeling of him stretching me. A few minutes later, he adds a third finger, and it's almost too much. The burning pain from being so full pushes me up to the edge that I'm dying to fall over.

Kyler must sense my hesitation and briefly pulls me off of his cock to look down at me and rub my head in a reassuring gesture. "You can take him. Let him in."

I relax by letting them use my body however they need. Barrett's fingers disappear from my ass, and I feel the cool tip of metal tracing my pussy before pushing in. His piercings rub along my walls, igniting the fire from within. My face is pressed back down to Kyler's base, and he thrusts inside of me. Another smack hits my ass, and the pain radiates along my skin. My pussy clenches at the feeling.

"You don't come until Kyler does," Barrett tells me, pulling his cock from my pussy and rubbing it along my backside.

Kyler picks up his pace, pumping in and out of my mouth, grunting every time I gag around him. I feel Barrett begin to slowly push his cock into my ass, and I scream around Kyler in response. He prepped me well enough that it hurt the perfect amount when he eased his way into me.

Once the tip of him fully breaches me, the rest guides in with ease. I feel every piercing sliding in one by one. "So fucking tight. You like it when we use all of your holes, don't you?" He mutters before bringing his other hand down to my pussy and pushing two fingers in. I feel so fucking full. My pussy spasms around him as he pumps into me.

Trying to bring my focus to Kyler, I do everything I can to aid him to his point of no return. Just when I feel like I can't take it anymore, I feel a warm spurt release into my mouth, and he groans in pleasure. "Swallow, wanderer."

I lick him clean, taking in every last drop when Barrett says, "Our perfect little whore." I can barely keep it together while he slams into both of my entrances. "Now, princess. Come for me like a good slut."

My eyes roll to the back of my head, and a tornado of sensations shoots through me. Shocks radiate to my fingertips, and I pulse around his fingers. I've never experienced an orgasm that intense in my entire life. Barrett thrusts harder, pulling his hand from me and gripping my hips until he finds his own completion and fills my ass with his warm come.

He pulls out of me and lifts me up in his embrace. "You did so good for us tonight, Callie." I hum at his approval, and he leans in to kiss me before leaving me with Kyler.

Kyler carries me back upstairs to clean me up before putting me in his bed and pulling me into him. What a perfect way to end the night. I find comfort in his arms and drift off to a blissful sleep with him holding me tightly like he never wants to let go.

Chapter 35
Callie

There's some sort of commotion going on in the hallway that wakes us up. Thinking it's just Sebastian and Barrett messing around, I roll out from under the covers and hop out of bed to throw some clothes on. What the hell are they doing up this late, and why are they being so loud? Kyler turns on his lamp and sits up, swinging his legs over the edge of the bed. The noises get louder, and we start to hear muffled whispers.

I pause just a few steps away from the door, and out of nowhere, there is a loud banging sound. I freeze in place. Is that? No, there's no way I'm hearing gunshots. Why would there be gunshots? Barrett has this whole place locked down like a fortress. How would anyone even be able to get in? We didn't hear any alerts, and an alert would have been sent to Ky's phone if someone got in.

Acting on instinct, Kyler stands up, grabs his gun from beside his bed, and motions for me to step to the corner of the room. I nod. We don't know who this is, but he isn't taking any chances. The gesture of protection from him doesn't go unnoticed. I feel so safe with him, and if he wants me in the corner, that's exactly where I'll be.

He goes to make his way to the door to see what's happening in the hallway but only makes it a few feet before the door swings open in front of him. I hear another loud bang and look over at Kyler to see him take two steps backward toward the wall behind him. The gun falls from his hand when he grabs his stomach to look down at the blood flowing from between his fingers before glancing back up at me. We lock eyes while his legs begin to wobble beneath him. There's so much pain in his face when he realizes he isn't going to be able to protect me from whoever this is. He sways to the right, knocking over the lamp on his nightstand while trying to grab onto anything he can to keep himself upright.

My eyes begin to well up as I let out a gut-wrenching scream. Flashbacks from Maxton and my mother dying in front of me begin playing in my mind. This isn't happening again. How is this happening again? Not Kyler, no! It's like watching a reel in my mind on repeat, reliving the same traumatic event from years ago that is now meshed with another. For the second time in my life, a man I love just fell to the ground and is surrounded by his own blood. I love him. I can't lose him. I haven't even had a chance to tell him that I love him.

He moves his eyes away from mine for just a moment to look over at the doorway, and I see his jaw tic. I can't take my eyes off him. I need to do something to save him. I see the moment those gorgeous blues start to lose their special glimmer, and panic begins to set in. I'm not sure what to do or how to help him, so I stand there frozen in my own combination of fear and trauma, not even realizing that the entire time, I haven't stopped screaming. Pressure. My brain finally clicks in. I need to find something to put pressure on the wound.

I look around frantically for something to use, and a familiar voice calls out my name from the doorway, momentarily pulling me out of my state of shock. "Callie! Callie!" I turn my head and see Julian standing there, his gun still pointing in Kyler's direction. "Callie, we have to go!" he yells. I shake my head. I can't leave. He needs me. Why does Julian have a gun? Wait, Julian is here? He shot Kyler. My mind is spinning a million miles an hour.

"Callie!" he says again.

"I.. I.." I just keep shaking my head back and forth as I look between Julian and Kyler. With every glance in Kyler's direction, I see his breathing becoming more and more labored, the light in his eyes dimming even further.

Julian makes my decision for me when he grabs onto my hand and pulls me out of Kyler's room and down the stairs. We make it to the entryway just before the front door when my mind whips back to Kyler upstairs. I picture him lying there like Maxton was, helpless and in pain, and I rip my hand from Julian's grasp. He looks down at me with confusion.

"You shot him! We have to go back and help him. I need to make sure he's ok," I yell through the tears streaming down my face.

"Callie, they kidnapped you. We're not going to help him. I hope the bastard is dead," he spits before grabbing onto my arm again and pulling me out the front door.

We make our way down the stairs of the house, gunshots still echoing in the distance. I try to pull free from him again, and Julian sways, smashing into the planter on the steps. I watch as it crashes off the side of the porch, dirt splashing out on the ground around it. Everything is a mess, like the broken pieces of the planter. My mind reels, trying to process what is currently happening. Julian. Kyler. Julian. Barrett. Seb. Kyler. Is he ok? Are any of them still alive? How did Julian even get into their house?

Julian drags me toward the black SUV idling in the driveway, gripping me tighter every time I try to get away from him. Grabbing the handle on the back door, he rips it open and shoves me in before crawling onto the seat next to me. I see him nod at whoever is in the front, signaling for them to drive. The mystery man slams on the gas pedal, making the tires squeal on the Range Rover. In a matter of seconds, we are down the long driveway, driving right through the open gate onto the road.

My heart is racing. I try to get a grip on everything that just happened. I look down at my hands and notice they're shaking. Julian found me. Kyler was shot. Julian said they kidnapped me. They kept me there against my will. I wanted to be there. Am I in shock?

One second, I was sleeping with Kyler's big muscular arm wrapped around me, and the next, I was watching a bullet go through him as he fell to the ground with blood pouring out of him. Kyler, Maxton, Mom. I feel my heart beating in my chest, the panic rising in my throat. Breathing starts to become harder and harder. I have to take short, quick breaths just to get some sort of oxygen in my lungs. Everything starts to blur, and I feel the corners of my vision starting to fade as Julian reaches over to grab my hand. It's not the comfort I need to pull me out of this episode. Everything around me begins to spin, and I can feel my heart racing and my body beginning to sweat.

Use your tools. I hear Barrett's voice in my head and try my best to calm myself, trying to take longer, deeper breaths between the shorter, quick ones. I focus on happy memories. Barrett, he loves me. After a few minutes, I'm able to regulate my breathing and center my thoughts- for now. Julian notices that I've calmed down and decides to open his stupid mouth.

"Did they hurt you? Fuck, Callie, I was so worried I was never going to find you."

"Whaa – What? Why would they hurt me?" He doesn't understand everything that happened between the guys and me. How could he know they would never hurt me?

"Sweet girl, they took you away from me for too long. I'll make sure nobody ever takes you from me again."

The mystery man driving our car takes us closer to the city. All this time, I was never that far from Braxton Falls. We went in the opposite direction when we left for that job. When we come up to the exit that will take us to Julian's house, the man keeps going straight onto the highway.

"Julian, I don't understand. How did you even find me? Things between us ended. I didn't want to be rescued."

"I would search to the ends of the earth for you, Callie. You're mine, and it will stay that way, just as you were always meant to be."

Hearing him say that only causes more confusion. Why is he talking like that? The man I knew would never treat me like I was some kind of possession. Julian is kind and gentle. He's not the possessive, controlling type.

"How did you find me?" I ask again, but I'm met with nothing but silence. "Where are we going? You're scaring me, and I don't want to be in this car with you right now."

He clenches his jaw, and I get the impression there's something he doesn't want to tell me. That doesn't make sense, though. What would be so bad about what he had to do to find me that he couldn't tell me? I have no idea what the hell is going on. Why he can't just answer some simple fucking questions so that I can have some sort of resolve about this whole situation.

"Just go to sleep, sweet girl. We can't go back to Braxton Falls. They'll look for us there, and I need to keep you safe. We can talk about everything after you sleep. The only thing that's important is that you are back where you belong."

I don't even know how to react to what he is saying right now. Back where I belong? There he goes again, talking like a completely different person. My mind tracks back to the guys. I don't need to be kept safe from them. They would never hurt me. Well, Barrett might, but only if I begged him to.

Julian seems to think I was only there because they took me, but I wanted to be there with them. I still want to be with them now. If we look at all the facts, Julian is also kidnapping me right now. He forced me into the car and refuses to tell me where we're going. I told Avery to make sure he knew I didn't love him and I didn't want to be with him, but he went out of his way to make sure he found me. He never stopped looking for me for months. Should I give him a chance to explain himself?

The Julian sitting next to me almost seems like a different person than the one I spent an entire year with before Sebastian, Kyler, and Barrett. Something is off, but I can't place it. My mind continues to race, bouncing back and forth between Julian and the guys until my eyes begin to feel heavy from the massive adrenaline drop I just experienced, and I drift off into a deep sleep.

When I finally wake up, we're still driving. The sun is out now, and I have no clue how much time has passed. Judging by the clock on the car radio, it looks like it's been about eight hours. Julian sits next to me, not yet realizing I'm awake. He looks stressed, like he hasn't slept at all. He's on his phone with his fingers rapidly typing. There's a look of hostility to him that I've never seen.

A few moments pass before he looks over at me and smiles, wiping his face clean of his previous demeanor. It seems fake. "Good morning, my sweet girl. How did you sleep?"

"Um, fine," I reply. "I must have been exhausted from everything that happened because I haven't slept that hard in a long time." I take a moment to look out the window, trees flying by all around us. The road we are on looks like some small-town back road that hardly ever sees travel.

"Julian, what's going on? Why are we still driving?" For some reason, when he said we couldn't go home, I assumed we would drive outside of town and grab a hotel for the night. Us still being in the car driving for eight-plus hours doesn't seem right. I get that weird feeling again. The one where you instantly know to be anxious about a situation but can't explain why.

Julian reaches out to run his hand along my face, his thumb trailing along my bottom lip, and he looks at me with a strange sort of renewed determination in his eyes. It takes everything in me to not cringe and pull back from his touch. I don't belong to him anymore.

"We're going to stay with a friend. Are you hungry? We can stop somewhere and grab you something to eat."

At the mention of food, my stomach growls. The last bit of food I ate was dinner last night with Kyler. He made me the most amazing chicken parm I've ever had in my entire life. Oh my god, Kyler? My heart aches again at the thought of him. Flashbacks of him lying there next to the wall, surrounded by his crimson liquid, have the tears welling up in my eyes. I force them away.

"I'm a little hungry," I admit.

"A little? The girl I know never goes more than a few hours without at least some kind of snack. Usually, you can't even make it through the night without sneaking down to the pantry to sneak a granola bar or some ice cream."

Staring down at my hands, I fiddle my thumbs together to try and keep myself grounded. I'm not the same girl he knew before. I can't stop thinking about the guys and whether or not they're ok.

"Callie, I know you must be confused right now. I have no idea what they put you through, but I promise you will never have to worry about them getting to you again. Please stay in the moment with me. I missed you so much. I thought I'd never see you again." I look over at him, and he sighs. He really has no idea what's going on inside my head.

"That night when you left the house, I should've come after you. I thought you went to stay with Avery, but when I called her and realized you weren't with her, it scared the shit out of me." Shaking his head, he grabs my chin and forces my gaze to his. "I thought I lost you forever."

He did lose me forever. Being in his presence has some lingering feelings popping up, but my heart belongs to the guys now. I only loved the idea of Julian, I remind myself. Something was always missing between him and me. The Monroe brothers were missing. I fell for them while I was with them. Seb might be an asshole, but he is the way he is because he wants to protect his family. Things between the two of us aren't perfect, but I respect him. Kyler and Barrett made me fall for them fully, and I regret not telling them sooner.

After a few moments, Julian calls out to the mystery driver, who I completely forgot was there. Who even is he? Just more questions I need to figure out.

"Paul, can you stop at the next restaurant we drive past? My sweet girl needs to eat."

"Of course, sir," Paul replies.

Him calling me sweet girl is getting super fucking annoying. He spends the next 15 minutes catching me up on everything that's happened over the last few months. While it's nice to hear about Braxton Falls, it's almost like he's steering the conversation away from any real question I have on purpose. He tells me that Avery has been going out of her mind since I went missing. That's not true. I've talked to her a bunch of times. He's exactly who I thought he was- a liar.

Once we get to this restaurant to eat, I'm going to signal to one of the waitresses that I'm in trouble. If I tell Julian that I don't want to go with him on whatever road trip he is taking us on, there's a chance he might lash out. He's been acting like a complete psycho since he shot Kyler and took me from their house. I'm getting away from him and back to the guys so that I can find out what is going on. I have to hope that they're all still alive and ok.

We pull up to a small rundown restaurant off the beaten path. Walking in, I notice the sign that says to seat yourself, so I walk over to the booth in the corner by the emergency exit and slide in. Aside from us, there's only one other couple in the place. It's not ideal if Julian does make a commotion, but with the kickboxing skills Barrett taught me, I should manage just fine. I still wish there were more people here.

The server walks over to us, hands us our menus, and tells us about the specials of the day. I try making eye contact with her, but she doesn't look at me at all. Her gaze is focused on staring at fucking Julian.

Eating is the last thing on my mind right now, but Julian is insisting I eat something. I order a sweet tea, burger, and fries just to pacify him before excusing myself to the bathroom. I just need a minute to myself before I attempt this conversation.

When I walk into the bathroom, I look around, trying to find a backup plan. If the conversation between Julian and I goes awry, maybe I can sneak back in here and out a window. I'm disappointed when all I see is walls. Windows would make things way too easy. The emergency exit next to our table will need to suffice for plan B. I think I can outrun him. I can at least get a far enough head start that I can hide and wait him out.

After washing my hands, I head back to the table to see our drinks have already arrived. I sit myself down and drink half of it in one gulp, not realizing how dehydrated I let myself get. Almost immediately after drinking the brown liquid, I realize something isn't right. My head feels light, the room starts to spin, and before I know it, everything is consumed in darkness.

Chapter 36
Kyler

Someone's in the house. I nod over to Callie for her to stay where she is. I don't want whoever this is to see her. Hopefully, she can tuck into the corner and hide once I get out into the hallway and figure out what's going on.

I grab my gun and go to walk out the door, but before I have time to react, the bedroom door whips open, and I hear a loud bang. I feel a sharp pain in my stomach and look down to see blood oozing out. Immediately my hand goes to cover it but fuck, it's coming out so fast. Everything starts to spin, and I feel a little dizzy. I have to keep myself focused. Callie is still in trouble. Whoever this is could hurt her. My legs begin to feel wobbly as I grab onto the nightstand to try and keep myself upright, but my mind starts to blur.

I look over to Callie and see her pale face full of shock and horror. She lets out a gut-wrenching scream. "Kyler!"

I can't respond to her. I'm right here, wanderer. Everything's going to be okay. I try to say the words, but they don't come out. My vision begins fading in and out. I just need to make sure she's safe, but I don't know what to do. She hasn't stopped screaming for me.

I look back over at the door and see a man standing there. I can't make out who he is, but thankfully, he keeps his gun aimed in my direction and not hers. I'll gladly take another bullet to ensure she is safe.

He yells out for her and grabs her by the arm, pulling her toward him. Hey, you fucking asshole! Don't touch my girl! I'll fucking kill you! Get your hands off of her!! The words swirl around in my head, but I'm not able to make them come out of my mouth. I feel a shooting pain coming from my abdomen and so much blood. It's all around me. I look up to try to find her again, but I can't see her anymore. I hear her yelling for me in the distance. "Kyler! Kyler!" She won't stop screaming my name. Finally, everything around me fully fades, and the darkness consumes me.

I come to a few minutes later, but I can't move. I see flecks of light coming and going, but I have no idea what is going on. The world around me has a quiet haze to it. From a distance, I hear voices, but nothing sounds like words. Where's my girl? I need to make sure she's okay. Fuck, why can't I open my eyes? Why can't I see her? She was just right here with me. The confusion swirls around me, and I remember someone shot me and took her. I swear if whoever took her hurts her, I'll hunt them down and kill them. Everything goes black again.

Chapter 37
Sebastian

The shooting finally stopped, and everyone who found their way into our house is either dead or has retreated. I search through the top floor one last time, room by room, to assess the damage and ensure nobody is left alive. The first person I spot is Barrett. His head pops out of his room into the hallway at the same time mine does. Good, he's okay.

He and I clear our rooms, shutting the doors behind us to ensure if there is someone left in here, they can't easily run into them and hide. Barrett pops into the bathroom to clear it, and I head to Kyler's room. We keep the door for the fourth bedroom on the floor locked because we didn't want Callie to know it's actually a spare bedroom, so that room doesn't need to be cleared.

My whole world stops when I breach the doorway of Kyler's room. The scene in front of me is terrifying. Kyler is lying on the floor not far from the bed in a pool of his own blood, and Callie is gone. I'm not even worried about clearing the rest of the house now. If someone is in here, they can come to me. I'll kill every last one of the bastards.

"Barrett! Get in here now!" I yell out as I run over to Ky to check his pulse. Fuck, it's weak, but for now, it's still there. I grab the top sheet from the bed and push it into his stomach to try and stop some of the bleeding. Barrett runs in and sees Kyler on the ground and rushes over to us.

"His pulse is weak, but it's there. Bring the car to the front door and call Dr. X to tell him we're on our way. We pay him extra to be on call for emergencies like this, so he better be ready." Barrett nods and is out the door in a matter of seconds. X is our own personal doctor we have on retainer. When you work in a field like we do, there's always the risk of injury. It never hurts to be prepared.

"Ky, can you hear me? I need to get you up." He doesn't respond to me. A minute later, Barrett runs back into the room telling me that the car is out front and X is waiting for us.

"Help me get him up. He isn't responding." I tie the sheet around his waist while grabbing the top half of his body to lift him. Barrett grabs the bottom, and somehow, we rush down the stairs without dropping him and slide him into the car. Barrett climbs up front and floors it down the driveway. Ky's going to be pissed when he finds the blood in his car.

This is such a mess. I was supposed to keep them all safe, but I failed, and now Kyler's fighting for his life, and Callie's gone. As much as I hate to admit it, she grew on me in the time that she was here. She found her place here with us, and while I may not feel as deeply for her as Barrett and Kyler do, she still belongs with us. We don't respond well to people who take what's ours.

Today, our girl was taken from us, and we will get her back. I just need to figure out how this happened.

"How the hell did they get past the gate!" I yell to Barrett in the front seat. He pulls up his phone and starts scrolling through things while driving.

"I don't know, Seb. Everything looks fine. I didn't see any alarms go off, and everything was showing that it was all still engaged. It's like they cloned the system and made it think nothing was happening. The hacking it would take to do something like this is serious."

"So you think it was Rogue?"

"Who else would it have been? Rogue is the only one with the motivation to attack us like this and take Callie. They obviously have the means to have someone with this skill set on their books."

Fuck! Fuck! We lock eyes in the rearview mirror, and he mutters the words I've been thinking but am not able to voice out loud.

"We need to get her back," Barrett states plainly.

I nod and bring my focus back down to Kyler, making sure to keep as much pressure on the wound as possible. The bleeding seems to have slowed down, but I'm not sure if that's because what I'm doing is working or if he's just lost so much blood that there isn't as much pumping through his veins anymore. The drive is short and quick. We reach Dr. X's house, and the next few hours all blur together as he gets to work trying to save my brother's life.

Chapter 38
Barrett

Seb and I are both on edge. It was supposed to be my responsibility to make sure that the house was protected, but I dropped the ball. Kyler's lying in a hospital bed, fighting for his life, and the girl we love is missing! Moreover, there's nothing I can do to help Kyler right now. It's up to him to fight and come back to us. The only thing I can do is try to find Callie.

We're fairly certain it was her father who sent someone to collect her, but what we don't know is if he took her back to the compound or if he is holding her somewhere else. It would be better for us if he was holding her somewhere else, considering there are three of us, well, two currently, and who knows how many members of their guard. If he had taken her to the compound, I'm sure he would have called in all bodies to protect them from our retaliation. He's smart.

I run through every possibility of how they could've bypassed my security system. They shouldn't have been able to. Everything's fully functional, there were no outages, and none of us misplaced our phones. If a phone was lost, that would have been a huge in for their hacker. It's easy to clone a phone. It only takes a matter of minutes if you have the right tools and know what you're doing.

Realization sets in, and the pieces all connect together. They've most likely been trailing us since we called Gabriel and told him that we had Callie. If they have a hacker on their team, it wouldn't be hard to run our faces through recognition software and receive an alert as soon as we were out and about. That was the first job we took her on, and they must have been waiting for confirmation that we had her. They wanted a way to track her back to our house. I have our phones blocked, so our location can't be tracked from them, but if the guy is as good as me, then maybe he could turn the block off with the right access.

The day we worked that hit on Ronnie Masters, someone got the best of me and knocked me out for a few minutes. We assumed it was one of Ronnie's bodyguards that we didn't account for, but what if it was a member of Rogue's guard or even their hacker? I slam my fist into the table, and Seb looks over at me curiously.

"I know how they got into the house," I tell him.

He listens as I go over my theory of a Rogue member being the one who knocked me out at the festival and then took my phone, which gave them access to clone the security software. It was a massive oversight on my part. I should've set up an additional security measure. It was stupid to assume nobody could get their hands on my phone. Fucking rookie mistake. I tell him that none of the alarms went off because they overrode them on the cloned phone to think that they weren't being activated. I would have to go home and run a quick system check to confirm if my suspicions are correct, but this is the only possible explanation that makes sense.

"We need to get that fixed, Barrett. If what you're saying is true, as of now, they can still get into the house."

"I'll update everything as soon as we're back. I fucked up, Seb. I'm so sorry."

"This isn't on you, Barrett. I never should have let her come on that job with us."

Both of us feel some sort of guilt around the entire situation, but in reality, there's only one person who is to blame, and I cannot wait until the day I get to peel that bastard's skin off. He will die a painful, miserable death. I'll make sure of it.

Chapter 39
Callie

As I regain consciousness, I try to blink my eyes, but they're still heavy, and everything is hazy. Where am I, and why the fuck do I keep finding myself in situations like this?

The last thing I remember was sitting at the restaurant with Julian. I was about to talk to him about leaving and how he found me. I blink a few more times, trying to shake off the fuzzy film surrounding my vision. Things start to become clearer, and everything looks familiar.

To my left, there's a small dresser with framed photos. One of my mom and I from when I was seven. We had just gotten done dancing at one of Rogue's Balls, and she pulled me in for a picture. The smile on her face is pure joy. I fucking miss her so much. There's another of her and I next to it, but this one is a few years later. I think I was 14. The third frame I look at almost rips my heart out of my chest. It's a picture of me and Maxton when we were 17. It was just before all the madness when we were simply lovestruck teenagers. To my right, I see Mr. Fluffogas, the ratty old stuffed elephant I used to sleep with every night as a kid.

Realization sets in, and I know exactly where I am. I shoot upright in the bed and try to jump out of it, but I'm instantly pulled backward. There's a sharp sting in my wrist that's cuffed to the corner of the bed. I never thought I'd be here again. No, no, no, no, this isn't happening! I feel the panic start to rise in my chest, my breathing becoming more rapid, and my eyes widen with fear as I frantically look around the room. Everything is the same. It's exactly how I left it over six years ago when I ran away from this fucking place!

My mind is racing. How did I get here? Where is Julian? Did they hurt him too? My father probably killed him just like he killed Maxton and my mother. I didn't want to be with him, but he didn't deserve to die.

The door creaks open, and I see the rotten bastard standing there with the same smug smile on his face that he had when I was a kid.

"Ah, my daughter, you're awake. Good."

I narrow my eyes at him, refusing to let him see any of the weakness or fear I may be feeling. The truth is I'm terrified. After all this time, I have no idea what to expect. Taking a few steps toward me, he chuckles.

"I hope you don't mind the minor adjustments I made to your bed. I must say, I'm proud of you for managing to evade me for so long. Make no mistake, you were always going to end up back here. As Rogue's leader, it's my responsibility to ensure the future leader fulfills her duties to the society."

Of course, all he cares about is this stupid fucking society. He doesn't want to know where I've been or what sort of struggles I've encountered. He fishes a small key out of his front pocket and walks over to uncuff me from the bed. I rub my wrist, easing the pain from when I pulled at it.

"Get yourself together and meet me in my office. You have five minutes. If you're not there willingly, I'll send someone up here to drag you down. Your fiancé will be meeting with us momentarily to discuss your upcoming nuptials. I believe six and a half years is enough time for you to roam about and have your fun. You and Damien will finally be wed, and there's a lot of planning that needs to be done. This will be the biggest celebration Rogue has seen in years, after all."

He walks out the door, leaving it open behind him, expecting me to follow along like a lost puppy. Once I hear him reach the bottom of the steps, I let my mask fall, and the emotions flow out of me. The weight of everything that happened over the last 24 hours sinks in. Kyler is likely dead. I am back in my father's grasp and about to be forced to marry a stranger. It's Déjà vu. It was all for nothing.

I can't afford to let anyone see me like this, so I walk into the ensuite bathroom and splash my face with cool water, washing away any evidence of the tears I just shed. Straightening my shoulders and lifting my head high, I take one more deep breath before walking out of the room and down the oak staircase to my father's office. I stop at the landing for a brief moment. Once

I'm sure I have myself put together and the mask is fully in place, I turn toward the first door on the right.

The door is ajar as I walk up to it. Everything looks just as it did before. My father is sitting at his desk, writing something in an old-looking notebook. I saw him use it a few times when I was younger, but he never let me see what was inside. I got curious one night and came in here to peek at it before realizing he kept it locked in the small safe hidden behind the bookshelf. He sees me standing there, closes the notebook, and motions for me to come in and take a seat. I walk over to the winged back, faux leather, dark walnut-colored chairs across from his desk.

"Thank you for being prompt with your presence, Callie. It's nice to know you still have the ability to follow directions."

I don't bother responding to him because I know he doesn't give a shit about what I have to say anyway. I just sit there, continuing to scowl at him.

"It really is a shame we lost all those years together," he says. "I was so sure that you were close to completing your training. You were shaping up to be the perfect leader for Rogue. It seems we'll have to start training again to ensure you're up to the standard of the position." I just stare at him, refusing to give him any sort of emotion besides disgust. After a few moments, there is a light tap on the door frame that leads into his office.

"Yes, yes, come in." Keeping my eyes on my father, I hear footsteps shuffling into the room before stopping in front of the chair next to mine. Slowly, I peel my eyes off my father and look over at the man standing next to me. What the hell?

Chapter 40
Callie

"Julian?" I whisper, jumping out of the chair and flinging myself into his arms. For a moment, I feel a small sense of safety and security. My father didn't kill him, and he found me again. He's going to get me out of here.

Realization begins to sink in, and something about this isn't right. Why would Julian be in my father's office, in my childhood home, in the middle of Rogue's compound? My father killed Maxton for threatening his precious kingdom. There's no reason for me to believe he wouldn't do the same to Julian. I push off him, frantically moving backward, tripping over myself, and falling onto the floor next to the chair I was just sitting in. My heart is pounding, and I don't know what to do besides look back and forth between my father and Julian.

My father sighs and looks over to Julian, motioning at the chair beside me. "Damien, thank you for joining us. Please excuse my daughter's rash behavior and take a seat. We have things to discuss."

"My pleasure, sir."

Damien? Why is my father calling him Damien? Thoughts rush through my mind at a million miles an hour. Oh my god, there's no way.

"Callie, get off the floor and sit down. Now." My father snarls.

I look over, glaring at him as I rise to my feet and step back over to my chair, flopping down in it. Upon sitting, Julian or Damien, whoever he is, reaches over and grabs my hand, interlocking his fingers with mine. I try to pull away from him, but his grip tightens forcefully. His hold is tight enough now that I know there will be bruises there tomorrow.

Letting it go, I look back over at my father with a newfound fierceness in my tone. "Would someone like to clue me in on exactly what the fuck is going on?"

Ignoring my question, my father looks over at Damien. "We're here to discuss the upcoming wedding and what will be required of you both before the event occurs. I'll be quick as our dinner reservation is rapidly approaching, and you know how I feel about tardiness."

My father looks back at me. "This is Damien, your fiancé." My face drops. I'm exactly where I was all those years ago, and this time, there's no escape.

"The two of you will be wed in three months. I know that's not a ton of time to plan a grand event, but given Callie's track record, I'd like to have this done as soon as possible." Glancing back in Damien's direction, he continues, "Since you're now my second-in-command, I'd like the event to be bigger than we originally planned years ago. I trust you can manage making the tweaks and confirm the more finite details. Being that we cannot trust my daughter to leave this compound, I'll have a stylist come to us with a variety of dresses she can choose from and have fitted."

Like I give a fuck about a dress. There is no way this wedding is happening if I have any say in the matter.

My father continues rambling on. "This will be the biggest event the majority of our community will attend in their lifetime, outside of the next leader being initiated, so we must live up to the expectations of grandeur. I want invitations finalized and sent out by the end of the week." Damien nods at his request.

"Callie, you will be present and smiling throughout the next few months. The society will have questions upon seeing you've returned to the compound. When you left, the people were informed you requested some time away to live freely before stepping into a more formal role within the community. They are under the impression that you've been living in unison with Damien at the international chapter, and they will continue to believe that. If, for any reason, you make it seem like the two of you are anything less than a happy-in-love couple, you will be confined to your room until you say I do. Being that you spent a year together with him under the guise of Julian, this shouldn't be an issue for you. Draw inspiration from your previous time together if you must."

He pushes his chair out from behind him and proceeds to stand up. Glancing once more at me and then Damien, he says blandly, "Now that everyone understands the expectations required of them, I'll give you two some time alone to get reacquainted before dinner. Damien, please bring Callie to the dining hall at 7pm." My father then walks out of the room, closing the door behind him.

I look over at Julian, I mean Damien, and stare at him blankly. He releases my hand and stands up to walk over to me. Everything my father said hits me all at once. He's my father's second? When did this even take place?

Anytime there's a change in the council, several rituals must take place for the initiation of a new council member. I was never privy to what exactly they involved because only members being sworn in have knowledge of the tasks. If it was known ahead of time what the tasks were, a person could prepare, and you can't have a true test of loyalty if it's something you can prepare for.

"Where is it?" I ask him. I've been so careful, and I've never seen the raven brand anywhere on his body.

"Where is what?"

"Your brand. Where is your fucking brand?" I demand.

He slowly removes the watch from his left wrist and reveals a small raven brand. An evil grin crosses his face when he sees my shock. He's enjoying every single moment of my torture and pain.

His fucking watch. I flash back through all of my time spent with him, trying to remember if I ever saw him without his watch on, but I don't think I did. This entire time, the face of his watch was hiding my biggest fear.

"How long?" I spit. "How long have you been my father's little pet?"

"I'm sure you remember my father, Barry, who was your father's second-in-command. He had a misfortunate incident that ended his life a little over four months ago, and I was lucky enough to take his place. The initiation process began not long after."

Four months ago, that was right before I was taken by the guys. Right around the time Julian started having all these business meetings that he had to leave town for. All the pieces start to fall into place, and everything makes so much more sense. This whole time, Julian was Damien. He wasn't going to business meetings. He was coming to Rogue so he could be initiated as a council member. The plane tickets to Nashville, the possessive way he was acting after he took me from the guys' house, the army of men he showed up with. They were the guard. It was Rogue all along. The pieces all connect simultaneously. This bastard has been part of Rogue all along.

Complete disbelief shakes through my entire body. I spent a year with this man and let my guard down. We were intimate, and I trusted him, but all along, he was my father's little minion. Thinking about how long he lied has me fuming. He pretended to be a completely different man. I don't even know the person standing in front of me.

Realizing that I've zoned out for the entire speech he's been reciting for the last few minutes, he walks toward me and grips my chin forcing me to look up at him.

"If you think I'll willingly marry you, you're out of your fucking mind. I ran so that I wouldn't be shackled to you. What makes you think I'll just bow down and do it now? You're nothing to me," I spit at him.

Letting go of my chin, he bends down and places his arms on the armrests of my chair, boxing me in. "You will not speak to me in that manner. You are to be my wife and the future leader of Rogue. It's time you begin to act like it. I will no longer accept any disrespect from you. I'll be forced to punish you if you continue to be disrespectful," he says angrily. His tone was so familiar to my father when he would lecture me as a child.

"Punished? So, you're telling me being forced to marry a lying piece of shit like you isn't punishment enough?!" I yell.

"You need to learn your place, Callie. You may be Gabriel's daughter, but I will not tell you again." His gaze appears so intense that any other girl would be instantly thrown into submission.

"Fuck you, Damien," I yell.

He rips me out of the chair and slams me against the wall with so much force a photo frame falls to the ground, and glass shatters around us.

"Do I need to force you to your knees and shove my cock so far down your throat that you remember exactly who I am to you?" he states.

"Don't fucking touch me. You're nothing to me, and I'll never be yours." My lip curls up in disgust.

"Sweet girl, since the day your father advised you of our marriage all those years ago, you were mine. When we were living together in Braxton Falls, and you were begging me to fuck you, you were mine. When I had you pinned to the bed licking that sweet pussy, making you come all over my face time and time again, you were mine. I was gentle with you before, but now that you're where you belong, I no longer have to be. I can use you however I please, and there isn't a damn thing you can do about it because Daddy isn't going to save you."

Fuck, Avery was right all along. She always saw the inner darkness in him that I refused to accept. I should have believed her.

He leans in and whispers in my ear, so close that I can feel his breath on my neck, making me want to gag. "You have always been mine, and I will force that attitude of yours right into submission if I must. Now, be a good girl, go to your room, and change. We have an important dinner to get to. Your father has requested we be punctual. There's someone who's been waiting to see you. I believe you remember the way?" His smug smile adds flames to the burning fire inside me.

When he finally leans back to give me the space I desperately need, I bite my tongue, and slip out of the old office, walking right up the stairs to what used to be my childhood bedroom. Slamming the door behind me, I walk over to sit on the bed so that I can process what in the actual fuck just happened.

Julian was a completely made-up person. How is it that I never saw right through his disguise? He made me believe he was a kind, giving person who didn't have a mean bone in his body, but in reality, he's the complete opposite. Thinking of everything he and I did together is enough to make me sick to my stomach. When we were intimate, it always seemed like he was holding back, and now I understand why. He was pretending to be an entirely different person the whole time. He was holding back. I never would have imagined the person he was in those situations was who he really is. It makes me feel so violated.

The person I was when I was with him in Braxton Falls was a weak version of myself. I should've known better than to trust anyone. The only person still alive who's never deliberately broken my trust is Avery, and I hope for her sake that she stays as far away from this place as possible.

Fuck Damien. He thinks he knows me so well. He's a fool. That man has never seen the woman who spent her entire life adapting to shitty situations just to survive- the real me. The person he knew was the fragile girl I turned into when I got comfortable living in my fantasy world. Julian or Damien, whatever he is calling himself these days, thinks he can control and manipulate me, but that's not fucking happening anymore. I am nobody's possession, and he is about to find out exactly who the real Callie Ashford is.

Deciding it's time to regain some control of this little charade, I get up and walk into my bathroom to shower and get ready for dinner. The performance of a lifetime is about to begin. The only person I can count on is myself, and it's all about survival now.

I haven't decided what I plan on doing yet, but getting rid of my father is the best possible outcome, considering he's calling all the shots right now. If I find a way to take him out, I would become the leader of Rogue and would be able to name my own second-in-command.

Damien will be a non-issue at that point. I could place the blame on him, kill my father, and say Damien did it in order to rise to power. That just might work. I would just need the approval of the council to take him out. If they truly believe he betrayed the community and conspired to murder the leader, shit, they would vote with me in a heartbeat.

Vengeance is a bitch, and so am I. My father's biggest mistake was letting everyone believe I was away with his permission. He should've taken Sebastian's deal. Nobody knows Callie never wanted to be the leader. Nobody knows Callie was tricked by Damien. Being stuck here might not be so bad after all.

I quickly strip out of my clothes and catch a glimpse of the mark Barrett left on my upper right thigh. It hurts to think about them and not know what happened. After everything, it's ironic that I was safest when I was with them. The trio of men who kidnapped me and made me fall for them. Deciding to let myself have a small moment of vulnerability, I remember the night he marked me as his forever while I shower the weight of the day off of me.

I was riding on top of him in a rare moment where I had some control. He grabbed my hips and pulled me into him, slamming me down hard. His mouth roamed down my neck, sucking and leaving a trail of bruises in its path. "Fuck princess, make yourself come like the good little slut I know you are."

I let the water from the shower surround me with warmth. I push two fingers into myself, remembering his words and how much they turned me on. I mimic his movements, moving my fingers in and out of my pussy while bringing my other hand down to rub my clit.

My mind slips back to the memory when he reached beside him, pulling out his knife. "Do you want me to mark you princess? Do you want to bleed for me while you ride my cock?" I wasn't sure at the time if I wanted that until he told me, "Stop thinking, Callie. Let yourself get lost in the pleasure." Immediately, I felt safe and wanted to give in to all that he was offering me.

"Do it," I told him. "Make me yours." He brought his knife down to my thigh before glancing up at me one more time. I nodded in approval.

He made one straight line and took a minute to watch the blood slowly trickle from the cut. The sharp sting from the cut immediately filled my senses. I could feel his cock twitching inside of me at the sight, and it made my pussy clench. He continued making two almost full circles along the line. His initial. He was marking me with his initial.

The pain was almost too much for me to bear, and I was close to telling him to stop when he brought his other hand to my clit, reminding me of the way pain and pleasure can coexist. I rode him faster, feeling the heat build in my core. Just before I was about to explode, his hand slammed down on the fresh cuts, the pain pushing me right over the edge into pure bliss. "Mine," he whispered before releasing inside of me a few seconds later.

I shuddered back to reality, letting out a small moan as the memory has me coming on my own fingers. I wish it was him instead. He would be so proud of me for channeling my anxious energy into a sexual act.

After finishing in the shower, I step out to dry myself off, and a few tears slip from my eyes. I need to get through tonight, and then I'll find my way back to them. I put my stone face back on and head back into my room to dress for dinner.

Chapter 41
Callie

Damien throws the door open and eyes me up and down. I chose a simple black dress that falls to the knee, with a high neckline and black flats to match. After getting dressed, I made my way to the bed to sit and wait, assuming someone would come for me. I was right.

"It's a little disappointing that you actually listened to directions so well. I was looking forward to forcing you into submission." He walks over and grabs my hand, sliding a familiar ring back onto my finger.

"Thought you might want this back," he says with a wink before pulling me up toward the door.

What I used to see as a beautiful representation of the love between Julian and me has been replaced with complete disgust. This ring represents the entire lie he spun for an entire year. It represents all the trust I mistakenly gave him. He grips my arm roughly and pulls me up toward the door.

When I kill him, I'll make sure it's slow so he feels every bit of pain I know I will endure in the coming weeks. If he's as brutal as they warned me about all those years ago, I'm sure he's only gotten worse.

He was able to play the part of Mr. Nice Guy so well it's almost sadistic. He fully tricked me, but this time, I need to be smarter. I'll need to give them the impression that I'm the well-behaved placeholder they want.

I know he'll want to use my body whether I want him to or not, and I'm terrified, but I still have some time to put together a plan before that happens. He will want to make sure the guys didn't impregnate me before he tries to. There's at least some reprieve in that.

Before we make it out of my bedroom, he slams the door in front of us and pushes my back up against it. I try to push him away, but he grabs both of my arms and lifts them over my head. Leaning down, he whispers in my ear, "If you embarrass me tonight, you will regret it. Everything you do from here on out is a direct representation of me. Do your best to remember that. I will not allow my wife to be disobedient." He brings a hand down to grope my breasts before saying, "It's a shame you covered these up. You have great tits." It takes everything in me to not revolt from his touch with the amount of disgust I feel toward him. He pushes off of me, pulls the door open, and drags me down the stairs.

We cross the compound and end up at the main building in the center that houses the dining hall. This room is used for a variety of events within the community. Tonight, it's set up with a singular round table in the middle with four seats and a small cart off to the side holding various bottles of liquor. Damien pulls out my seat at the table, pretending to be a gentleman.

Fuck him. I move over one and sit in the seat next to the one he pulled out. His jaw flexes as he sits down in the chair next to me that he pulled out. I know I'm going to pay for that decision later, but at this moment, I don't care.

My father chuckles at my little outburst. "Callie, I've invited someone to join us in a little bit, who I am sure you're going to love to see." The possibilities race through my mind at who he could have invited here. Did they take Avery? Is it one of the guys?

I trace my finger along the infinity symbol tattooed on my wrist, like Kyler used to, trying to soothe myself. I need to find a way to get in touch with the guys and find out if they're okay. I can't live without knowing whether or not Kyler is dead. I didn't even see Seb or Barrett before Damien pulled me out of the house and shoved me in his fucking car. Every single choice I make going forward regarding Damien and my father depends on whether or not they're alive.

I can't bear to think of the way Kyler looked at me after he was shot. He was so desperate to protect me, even in the one moment where he should've been worried about himself. My heart aches at the memory, wishing I was there to know how everything played out. I feel the tears begin to well up, and I have to shake the thoughts from my mind. I need to be strong to get through whatever my father and Damien have in store for me.

Damien reaches under the table and grips my thigh tightly, just above my knee. "Sweet girl, your father was speaking to you, and it's rude to ignore him."

"Don't mind her, Damien. It's better for the both of us the longer she keeps that useless mouth of hers shut," my father tells him. I have the urge to tell him to go fuck himself right here and now, but something catches my eye from the corner of the room.

A figure emerges from one of the doorways opposite of where we came in. My mind is frozen in shock as it tries to catch up with the sight currently in front of me. A woman I never thought I'd see again stands there looking frail and defeated in the perfect black cocktail dress and matching shoes. Her eyes are downcast, hands perfectly clasped in front of her body as she waits to be told what to do next.

My father trails my line of sight, and a wicked grin crosses his face. "Get in here and sit down, Natasha," he yells toward her.

Her body jolts slightly at the volume of his request, but she complies and walks over to the table to pull out the chair next to my father and sits down. She lets out a few shaky breaths before her eyes finally roam upwards and lock with mine.

"Mom?" I whisper.

To be continued....

Acknowledgements

Thank you to all the readers who took a chance on my book. This little dream wouldn't be possible without all of you!

Hubby, thank you for being so supportive of this journey. It hasn't always been easy. Some days you listen to me complain for hours on end but you always make sure to let me know that you're right by my side to support my author dream. You push me to be the best I can be, and I can't thank you enough for that. I love you so much!

Amanda, from the first draft to the final edits, you helped with every step of the way. Thank you so much.

To my author friends, I love and appreciate you! Being part of such an amazing group of people has been so rewarding and you all hold a special place in my heart! We are our own little family.

To my beta readers, Sarah, Lo, Kayla, Amanda J, Britt, Hayley, Sam, Kait, and everyone who helped behind the scenes, I can't thank you all enough! You're all amazing. This book wouldn't be possible without any of you.

To my darling editor Taylor, I simply adore you! Thank you times a million for taking on the mess that was this book and helping to mold it into perfection.

About the author

K.M. Baker is a Dark Romance author who lives in a small town in Pennsylvania with her husband. She has three dogs, two German Shepherds and a Bichon Frise, who are like children to her.

Writing has always been a dream, but she never had the courage to do it until recently.

Most of her free time is spent reading all the spicy books she can get her hands on (the dirtier, the better). Outside of reading, she enjoys gardening, crafting, and taking her 1972 Sprint Mustang to car shows. Coffee, red wine, and blankets are some of her favorite things to indulge in. She is passionate about traveling and hopes to one day move and live outside the US.

Stalk Me:
Tik Tok: @K.M.Bakerauthor
Instagram: @K.M.Bakerauthor
Facebook: K.M. Baker's Bookworms
Email: KMBakerauthor@gmail.com

Books by K.M. Baker

The Darkness Duet:
Evading Darkness
Darkness Falls

Standalones:
The Afterthought
Endless

Printed in Great Britain
by Amazon